AN
INCONSIDERATE
DEATH

Recent Titles by Betty Rowlands from Severn House

A HIVE OF BEES

AN INCONSIDERATE DEATH

Betty Rowlands

This first world edition published in Great Britain 1997 by
SEVERN HOUSE PUBLISHERS LTD of
9–15 High Street, Sutton, Surrey SM1 1DF.
This first edition published in the U.S.A. 1997 by
SEVERN HOUSE PUBLISHERS INC of
595 Madison Avenue, New York, NY 10022.

Copyright © 1997 by Betty Rowlands.

MYS
R883in

British Library Cataloguing in Publication Data

Rowlands,   Betty
      An inconsiderate death
      1.   Detective and mystery stories
      I.   Title
      823.9'14 [F]

      ISBN 0-7278-5233-7

All situations in this publication are fictitious and
any resemblance to living persons is purely coincidental.

Typeset by Hewer Text Composition Services Ltd.,
Edinburgh, Scotland.
Printed and bound in Great Britain by
Hartnolls Ltd, Bodmin, Cornwall.

Prologue

It is half-past three in the afternoon and things are pretty quiet in the High Street branch of the Regional Bank. A normal Wednesday afternoon, in fact. Although most of the shops have long since abandoned the old-fashioned custom of early closing, many of the locals have not. Typically, therefore, there are few people about in the town centre at the moment. Things will probably get busier later on when classes at the technical college are over and the students begin dropping in to draw cash for their evening's entertainment. Meanwhile, a mere handful of customers – none of them in any apparent hurry – are waiting to cash cheques or pay bills.

For the moment there is only one teller on duty. A colleague has just taken delivery of cash from a security van – always a slightly anxious time but everything has gone smoothly and safely as usual. No one talks openly about the possibility of a raid, but there is a sense of relief when the time of greatest potential danger has once more passed uneventfully. Now everyone can relax. The two women glance at the clock, anticipating the afternoon cup of tea.

Suddenly the doors burst open and two men wearing black balaclava helmets and waving sawn-off shotguns rush in from the street. They seem nervous. Nervous gunmen are extra dangerous, the police tell the witnesses later, but no one thinks of that for the moment. One woman says that for a second or two there was something almost comical in the way the men swung their guns from side to side, like actors

1

in a movie. "It was like watching something on the telly," she tells reporters. "I thought for a moment, this isn't true, I can't believe it's happening."

But moments later it becomes a horrifying reality. The terrified customers are made to lie on the floor and one of the gunmen stands guard over them while the other throws a holdall over the top of the screen and yells at the two employees to fill it with money. With the barrel of the gun pressed against the glass he keeps on shouting, "Get a move on! I want all the money! More! More!" as, with hands that shake so violently they can hardly control them, the women stuff wads of notes into the bag.

"You! Lie still or you'll get it!" A gun barrel is jabbed into the neck of one of the prone customers who is feebly trying to retrieve his spectacles, which fell off as he dived to the floor. The man freezes, but not quickly enough for the second gunman, who raises a booted foot and stamps viciously on the outstretched hand. The victim lets out an anguished groan.

"Shut up!" screams the assailant. "Shut up and keep still!"

The command is ignored. Perhaps it has not even registered. Moaning faintly, the injured man reaches out, seeking with one hand to stem the blood oozing from the other. Without another word, the gunman brings the butt of his shotgun crashing down on the man's head. The blow makes a horrid, cracking sound. Transfixed with terror, the rest of the victims shut their eyes and will themselves not to scream, not to make a sound, not to move a muscle, so that they will not be attacked. All they want now is to stay alive.

They hear a hoarse cry of "Let's go!" followed by charging footsteps and the crash of the swing doors, signalling that the nightmare is over. From out in the street comes the sound of a powerful car speeding away. Someone presses an alarm switch. The shaken customers pick themselves up and begin, almost mechanically, to dust themselves down.

All, that is, except one.

*　　*　　*

The raid occurred too late to reach the evening editions, but the following day it was reported that a car believed to be the getaway vehicle had been discovered burnt out on a patch of waste ground outside the town. Two men had been arrested and a third was being sought. The injured man had been rushed to hospital but was found to be dead on arrival.

In due course, Terence Holland and Frank Pearce were tried, convicted and sentenced to terms of imprisonment. To date, none of the money has been recovered and the third man has not been traced. The case remains open.

Chapter One

Hugo Bayliss swaggered out of the men's changing room at the Bodywise Health Club in Gloucester wearing his new designer label exercise gear. He had spent several moments studying the effect in the mirror and decided he looked good. He cast an eye over the other fitness freaks, sizing up the talent. A couple of middle-aged hausfrau types were pounding away on treadmills while keeping up a breathless conversation. Nothing doing there. A few muscular young men with bull-necks, fiercely bulging muscles and legs like tree trunks were pumping iron as if their lives depended on it. They were fine specimens, but Hugo wasn't that way inclined. But in the far corner, on one of the exercise bikes, a slim woman with short dark hair and pale, sharp features was pedalling steadily and with little apparent effort in time with the pop music blasting from loudspeakers fixed on the walls.

Hugo strolled across and nodded a greeting. She turned her head and gave him a brief smile in return. She had nice eyes, white, even teeth and a firm jawline, and she was wearing close-fitting black shorts and top. Under a pretence of adjusting the load on the bike next to hers, he treated himself to a surreptitious glance at the smooth, lightly tanned leg moving rhythmically at his elbow and then, as he straightened up, a quick eyeful of firmly rounded breasts and a very satisfactory cleavage. Somewhere in her thirties, he judged. Not too old, but good and mature. Just his type.

He mounted his bike and began pedalling, looking ahead

at the screen which was showing a Michael Jackson video. Over the blare of the music, he remarked casually, "Haven't seen you here before. Just joined, have you?"

She sat upright, took her hands from the handlebars and rested them lightly on her thighs, still pedalling. He saw that she was wearing a wedding ring. That was a good sign. Hugo avoided single women, they tended to get possessive. Not that the married ones couldn't be a problem sometimes. Like Lorraine, for instance. He'd already made up his mind to ditch her. This one looked as if she could be a worthy successor.

"I joined six months ago, but I don't come at fixed times," she said. "It depends on when I happen to be free."

"Work irregular hours, do you?"

She gave a faint smile, "You could say that."

"Now, let me guess. You're a model?" She shook her head, her smile deepening. "You should be, you've got the looks." He was careful not to say figure.

She tilted her head back slightly, her mouth curving in amusement. "Thanks," she said. She jumped off the bike and went over to a rowing machine. She had her back to him as she settled into the seat. She had a delicious-looking bottom.

Hugo carried on with his workout, keeping an eye on her as she went through hers, waiting for a chance to speak to her again. It came when she seemed to have difficulty adjusting the load on one of the climbers.

"Want a hand?" he asked.

"That's kind of you. These things are always so tight," she complained. "I'm trying to set it on four."

"No problem." He altered the setting and she hopped on and began jigging up and down. He mounted the adjacent machine. After a few seconds he said, "So what is your job, then?"

"I'm a photographer."

"That's interesting. You work for the local paper?"

5

"No."

"You take portraits?"

She seemed to find the question faintly comical. "Sometimes."

Hugo thought a photo session with this woman, whose manner held a hint of secrecy which he found intriguing, might be a very good lead-in to something more interesting. Sex, for example. He persevered.

"What else?"

"It depends on what's thrown at me."

"You mean, you're freelance?" She made no reply. He had a sudden inspiration. "You go to people's houses? Do features like in *Hello*! magazine?"

She tilted her head back a second time and laughed. Her breasts rose and fell. He was aware of something stirring in his own anatomy and hoped it wouldn't show under his shorts, but she wasn't looking at him anyway. "What's so funny? Did I guess right?"

She turned to face him for a moment. "In a way, I suppose you did."

"Tell you what," he said eagerly, "I'm looking for someone to do some shots of my place. Some really good ones of the garden and the pool and conservatory and so on. The wife's always nagging me about it, but I never get around to it. Too tied up with business, I guess. What d'you say?"

She shook her head. A beep from her climber indicated that her time was up and she hopped off. "Sorry."

"Why not? I'll pay whatever you ask."

"Sorry," she repeated. "Not my line."

Sod it, he thought, *I've been too obvious, too pushy.* Aloud, he said, "Well, if you change your mind, you'll find me here most Monday mornings. What's your name, by the way?"

"Sukey," she replied.

"Sukey what?"

"Just Sukey."

6

"Unusual name. Pretty, too. Suits you." She didn't ask for his, but that didn't stop him. "Mine's Gary by the way." He never used his real name at the club. None of the instructors knew who he was, only the manager, and it was more than Dave's job was worth to talk out of turn.

"So long, Gary," said Sukey. She picked up her towel and headed for the ladies' changing room.

Hugo carried on with his workout until she emerged, clad in an emerald green tracksuit, a nylon holdall slung casually over her shoulder. Her hair was damp from the shower and clung to her head in little chocolate-brown ringlets. She looked stunning and he really fancied her. He watched out of the corner of his eye as she signed off and handed her programme to the duty instructor, who initialled it before returning it to the file. Hugo gnawed his lip in frustration. As the club's owner, he had a perfect right to check on any of the members, but young Rick had no idea who he was, and he had no intention of letting on. If only Dave had been on duty – but, what the hell, she'd be here again, he could wait.

Meanwhile, there was his current bird to settle.

There was no doubt about it, Lorraine was a really good lay and it had been great at first. He'd known she fancied him the day he went to her house to discuss the installation of the sauna and Jacuzzi she'd conned her old man into buying for her. After they'd wrapped up the details there were drinks all round and when she handed him his scotch on the rocks she'd brushed her little finger against his, so lightly that he might have imagined it if he hadn't simultaneously caught the invitation in her eye. He'd called her up the very next day, pretending that there were one or two points that hadn't been settled. Her husband was away on business, she said, but she was sure she could deal with the queries. The only query had been how quickly they could get into bed. She was that hot for him.

As time went on she became more and more demanding,

7

sulking and storming at him if he didn't come running every time she called him on the phone. He had, naturally, not told her his home number, which was ex-directory and would never be revealed by anyone in his office, but just the same he worried that Barbie might find out. Barbie knew better than to question him about things that were none of her business, but if he started getting calls from a strange woman it could get awkward. So Lorraine would have to go.

He knew it wouldn't be easy, but he did his best to sound convincing. "Darling, I'm afraid I won't be seeing you for a few months," he said when he had got his breath back. She had been unusually energetic that afternoon and he was tired after his workout. "Got to go to the States to set up a new company."

She nestled her naked body against his. *God*, he thought, *she's ready to go again. Where does she get her energy?* Instinctively, he edged away, but she followed. "Where to?" she breathed in his ear. "Why don't I come with you?"

He sighed, trying to sound genuinely sorrowful. "Not a chance, pet. I'll be taking the wife, and she won't appreciate the idea of a *ménage à trois*."

"We could have a great time." Unexpectedly, she rolled away from him, got out of bed and put on a satin dressing gown and slippers. "I've got something to show you. Here, put this on."

He got up, grabbing the towelling robe she threw at him, and followed her from the room. She led the way along the landing and opened a door at the far end. "This is Arthur's study."

It was a smallish room overlooking the garden. Bookshelves lined two walls and a mahogany desk stood in front of the window. Lorraine pushed some of the books aside to uncover a wall safe. With practised fingers she rotated the knob until the door clicked open. Inside was a heap of jewel cases. She picked one up, opened it and casually displayed a diamond necklace. "My latest present from my doting husband," she said. There was a hint of scorn in her voice and Hugo thought, poor bastard, if he only knew.

Aloud, he said, "Is that it?"

She gave a little laugh. "Of course not."

Below the jewel cases was a metal drawer. She pulled it open, rummaged under a heap of papers and took out a key. Hugo watched curiously as she dragged the swivel chair away from the desk, went down on all fours, removed a loose mat and then rolled back the piece of carpet underneath to reveal another safe set in the floorboards.

Lorraine sat back on her heels and looked up at Hugo. "There," she said simply.

He shrugged. "So your old man needs more than one safe. What am I supposed to do about it?"

"Don't you want to see what's in it?"

"If you want to show me."

She inserted the key into the lock, raised the hinged lid and laid it back on the floor. "How about that, then?"

Hugo almost rubbed his eyes. The sizeable cavity was jam-packed with bundles of sterling banknotes. The ones on the top layer were fifties. Wordlessly, he went on his knees beside Lorraine and picked up a bundle. The ones underneath it were fifties as well. "Jesus!" he exclaimed in a hoarse whisper. "Where the hell did he get this lot?"

"Haven't a clue. He never talks business with me."

"Must be some business. Any idea how much there is?"

"About a quarter of a million." Her voice was ice cool, but her eyes, as she turned to face him, were burning with excitement. She leaned towards him until her mouth brushed against his. "Think what we could do with it, just you and I!" she breathed.

He dropped the bundle he was still holding as if it had sprouted thorns. "What are you suggesting?" As if he didn't know. She'd been hinting for some time that she wanted him

9

to go away with her and he'd stonewalled. But he'd never envisaged anything like this. His eyes went back to the open safe and its contents, and the germ of a plan began to form in his head.

"We could go to South Africa, or Australia, or somewhere else far away and exciting," she was saying. "We could change our names . . . it shouldn't be too difficult . . . you must know lots of people—"

He interrupted her. "Just let me think about it, leave it with me for a day or two. You'd better put this lot back the way it was before Arthur comes home."

"Oh, he's up north somewhere, he won't be back till tomorrow." She closed the safe, locked it and put the carpet and the chair back. Then she stood up and replaced the key in the wall safe, relocked it and covered it with the books.

"How did you find it?" he asked. "Did Arthur show it to you?"

"Of course not. He doesn't trust me that far."

"Then how—?"

"I came home unexpectedly the other day and found him and the local handyman in here. Terry had cut out part of the floor and Arthur said the wood was rotten and needed replacing. I pretended to believe him and left them to get on with it, but I'd spotted the pieces that were cut out and they certainly weren't rotten. So at the first opportunity I had a look for myself. It didn't take too long to find the key – Arthur isn't a very original thinker when it comes to hiding places."

Hugo's brain was buzzing away like a dozen silicon chips. "Did this guy Terry fit the safe?" he asked.

"I'm pretty certain he did. I saw him later, taking something heavy out of his van. It was in a box with printing on the outside." She looked at him enquiringly. "Does it matter?"

"No, of course not. Just an idle question." He leaned

10

across and kissed her, his lips nibbling at hers, his tongue busy. The plan was shaping up nicely. "The sight of all that dosh has turned me on," he murmured. "Let's go back to bed."

Chapter Two

Things were comparatively quiet until towards the end of the afternoon: a break-in which was so unmistakably the work of a problem teenager recently absconded from a children's home that dusting for fingerprints was a mere formality; a couple of mugshots down at the station. Then, just as Sukey was hoping to get away on time so that she could tidy the house and start preparations for the evening meal before Fergus got home from school, she was sent to the general hospital, where a pensioner was being treated for injuries following an attempted mugging. Two teenage thugs had tried to steal her handbag, but despite being savagely punched and kicked the old woman had grimly clung on to it and the would-be muggers had run off empty-handed when a passing motorist had stopped to intervene. By the time Sukey had photographed the bruised ribs, the two black eyes and the split and swollen lips of the badly shaken victim and spent half an hour comforting her while the hard-pressed casualty staff found her a bed, it was getting on for six o'clock.

She reached the little semi in Brockworth just as Fergus was putting his bike away after his paper round. He waved her into the open garage and stood waiting while she got out of the car and dragged out the shopping she'd managed to grab before reporting for duty. He took the bag from her and then brought the up-and-over door down with a bang. Sukey winced. "Do you have to slam it like that?" she grumbled and then, seeing his slightly hurt look, clapped him gently on the shoulder and said, "Sorry son, I guess you're tired too."

"I am a bit." He had his key at the ready and opened the front door, stepping aside to let his mother enter first. She never ceased to feel pleasure at his natural courtesy. It must have been picked up subconsciously from his father. Paul had always been meticulous about helping women on with their coats, opening and closing doors for them, walking on the outside of the pavement, standing up when they entered the room and so forth. It was a pity he had shown his son the ultimate *dis*courtesy by leaving home for another woman two days after his tenth birthday. Sukey had had to abandon a promising career in the police to look after Fergus. It was only recently that she had felt able to pick up the threads of that career, this time as a civilian Scene of Crime Officer.

Fergus put the bag of shopping on the kitchen table and switched on the electric kettle. He had put out cups and saucers and the teapot and tea caddy stood ready. "Had a good day, Mum?" he asked while she unpacked groceries.

"Not bad. Had to go to casualty to take pictures of an attempted mugging. That's what made me late."

"Was it bad?"

"Not pretty, but not too serious either. Someone stopped them before they did any real damage."

"That's good." He made the tea and poured it out. Sukey cleared away the last of the groceries and they sat opposite one another at the table.

"What was your day like?" she asked.

"OK. Kevin Potter and a couple of kids in the third year were caught in the toilets with a spliff and the Head called their parents in." His tone was matter of fact; such things were too commonplace these days to arouse much excitement. "Oh, and we had a double period of chemistry and Maisie Kemp singed her hair in a Bunsen burner. Served her right really. Old Samuels is always telling the girls to tie their hair back in the lab. More tea?"

"Thanks." She held out her cup. "How old is this Potter character?"

"Nearly seventeen, I guess. He's in the year above me."

"D'you reckon he's dealing?"

"Could be."

"Has the Head told our people?" She wasn't officially police any more, but they were still her people.

"Guess so." Fergus had lost interest. He took a crumpled sheet of paper from his pocket and spread it on the table. "Mum, will you have a look at this?"

"What is it?"

"It's about a canoe trip to France in September."

Sukey picked up the paper and scanned it while sipping her tea. One week at a centre in the Dordogne. Travel, full board and hire of equipment included. There was a picture of a broad river spanned by a stone bridge with a backdrop of cliffs crowned by a medieval castle, indifferently reproduced but nonetheless alluring. Her eye homed in on the figure at the bottom of the page and she winced. "It's a bit expensive," she said doubtfully.

"I've got fifty pounds saved from my paper round," Fergus said eagerly. "And there's time to save quite a bit more . . . and you needn't give me anything much at Christmas." His eyes were bright, his young face slightly flushed with eagerness. He so badly wanted to go.

Sukey shook her head doubtfully. "I'm not sure I can manage it all. Have you asked Dad?"

"I thought I'd wait till I'd spoken to you. You would let me go . . . if we can afford it, I mean?"

"I don't see why not. But I can't promise right away. It's a lot of money."

"Yeah, I know. Could you manage half, if Dad coughed up the rest?"

Sukey did some quick sums in her head, anticipating her likely commitments. "I guess so," she said, "but don't bank on it. You know how Petal played up over last year's trip to Paris." Petal was Paul's pet name for Myrna, his second wife. Fergus had reported it with some scorn after the first weekend spent with them and he and Sukey had giggled over it together.

"Didn't get her anywhere though, did it? Dad shelled out just the same." Fergus went to the refrigerator and carefully attached the paper to the door with a magnet in the form of the Eiffel Tower, a memento of the trip. "Can we have supper in the sitting room?" he asked. "There's a European Cup match on in half an hour."

"What about your homework?"

"I haven't got much – I'll do it afterwards."

"Make sure you do." Sukey got up and went to the sink to peel potatoes. "I did a workout first thing this morning and guess what, a rather dishy man chatted me up."

"Mum! You didn't—"

"Didn't what?" She turned to face him with a teasing smile. He hesitated, looking embarrassed. She knew exactly what he was thinking. Various small indicators told her he was becoming increasingly aware of his own budding sexuality; at the same time he was disturbed by the notion that a man might find his mother desirable. It was touching, and somewhat illogical. After all, he had managed to come to terms with the knowledge that his father had taken up with another woman.

"Don't worry, he didn't ask for a date, and I wouldn't have gone anyway," she said and saw the look of relief in her son's eyes. "He did offer me a commission, though. Asked me to do some photographs of his house and garden. Said his *wife* wanted them," she added wryly.

"You didn't agree, did you?" Fergus looked anxious again. "Did you let on what your job is?"

"I said I was a photographer but I didn't tell him I was a SOCO. He looked a bit miffed when I turned him down . . . he really thought he was getting somewhere, and it was all so obvious." Sukey chuckled at the recollection. She glanced at the clock. "It's nearly time for the match. You go and switch on. I'll bring supper in when it's ready."

"Thanks, Mum." He gave her shoulders a quick squeeze and dropped a kiss on her temple, something he would only do these days when they were on their own. He was rising sixteen and growing up fast. Already he was half a head taller than she was. And so like his father to look at. With a sigh, Sukey lit the gas under the potatoes and set the chops to grill.

Hugo spent the week devising what he considered a foolproof plan to get Lorraine out of the way while he entered the house and emptied the floor safe. Every time he thought of all that loot he practically slavered. He'd made some dud bets lately and ready cash – plenty of it – was exactly what he needed to keep the bookies happy. Lorraine, of course, would be as mad as a wet hen when she realised how she'd been duped, but there was bugger all she could do about it without dropping herself right in the shit. Another thing that made the whole thing so sweet was that Hugo was pretty certain the tax man didn't know about the nest egg under the floor boards, in which case Arthur Chant wouldn't dare report its disappearance to the police. But just in case . . . before leaving the house after Lorraine had shown him the money, he had casually asked where he could contact Terry, the odd-job man, on the pretext of wanting something done at home. Terry would have had an opportunity, before installing the safe, to get a spare key cut. There was no reason to suppose he had, of course, but it mightn't be a bad idea to lay a false trail to throw suspicion elsewhere. He'd been to sus the guy out and what he'd learned had given him a shock. He'd put it down to one of life's unlucky coincidences, but it made the business more urgent. If by yet another mischance their paths should cross, things could get really nasty.

Lorraine had been like a cat on hot bricks waiting for him to make up his mind, but he'd explained there were all sorts of things he had to settle before they actually took off. You couldn't board a plane with a bag full of money these days, not when it was likely to be searched by security staff. It would take time to transfer the cash – and other assets – abroad.

Lorraine didn't know a thing about business so she'd swallowed it all without question. She wasn't over bright, really. It would be a relief to be shot of her. Then he'd be free to go after that little bird he'd met in the health club. Sukey. Odd name, but it suited her somehow, with her sharp features and aloof manner. She wouldn't be a pushover, which would make the pursuit all the more exciting. He was confident he'd score in the end.

Lorraine was to tell Arthur that she'd been invited to the wedding of an old school friend and would be away for a few days. He'd agreed without question that she could go. She was to fly to Amsterdam, check into a hotel and wait for Hugo. It might be several days, a week even, before he could meet her there. He told her he knew someone who could organise new passports for them with no questions asked and as soon as he had those, he'd book the tickets to Rio. Rio had been her choice – she thought it sounded romantic, the ideal place to begin their new life together. Poor cow. He almost laughed aloud at her naïvety as on Friday morning he headed, for the last time, for the Chants' house.

Everything went according to plan at first. Lorraine had assured him that there was no rush. Her husband had a full schedule that day and wouldn't be back till the evening. He normally left the house at nine o'clock and she would leave an hour later for the airport. At the pre-arranged time of half past ten, Hugo drove to the house in the van he'd stolen from outside Terry's place during the night and parked it round the

17

back of the house. The property stood in the middle of a large plot, surrounded by landscaped gardens and well screened by trees. Absolutely ideal. Hugo found the window; Lorraine had pointed it out to him from inside the house, but she hadn't warned him about the roses growing beneath it. He swore under his breath as a thorn found bare flesh between glove and cuff, giving him a nasty scratch. Another thorn caught the seat of Terry's overalls and he felt a sharp jab as it penetrated his rump, but he managed to clamber onto the sill, jump down into what Lorraine had described as the breakfast room and immediately set about laying the false trail. Then he went up to the study.

He was shaking slightly with excitement and his gloves made him a trifle clumsy. Lorraine had given him the combination of the wall safe, but it took him a couple of tries before he got it right and the door swung open. The jewel cases were still there, but their contents were missing. He cursed again. She was only supposed to take five grand in cash to keep her going until he joined her. Not that he had any intention of joining her, of course, but she wasn't to know that. He'd expressly told her to leave the rocks for him, saying he knew people who'd fence them in London. That was, he estimated, a cool thirty thousand down the tube. Arthur Chant must be loaded.

No use wasting time fretting about it. Hugo pulled out the drawer, found the key to the floor safe, rolled back the carpet, opened it – and found himself gazing open-mouthed into an empty cavity. "Bloody hell!" he muttered, aghast. "Bloody, fucking hell!"

He was still trying to take it in when he heard a movement beside him. He swung round in alarm, scrambled to his feet, and met Lorraine's cool gaze. She was dressed in travelling clothes, with a handbag slung over her shoulder and a bunch of keys dangling from one finger. "It's all right, darling," she said, "it's in here." She gave him one of her most ravishing smiles as she indicated the holdall she held in the other hand. "The rest of my luggage is in my car. Shall we go?"

"Go? Go where?" His brain was reeling. What the hell was she up to? "Why aren't you on the way to Heathrow?"

"The wedding was cancelled," she said, and there was a mockery in her voice and a steely glint in her eyes that he had never seen before. It was dawning on him, too late, that she wasn't as green as he'd believed.

"I thought we'd go to London together instead," she went on. "Stay in some nice, quiet hotel while you get everything organised like we agreed. I thought this," she held up the holdall, "would be safer if we were both around to look after it."

Hugo felt cornered. There was only one way out. He recalled a scene in an old black and white movie from way back. It seemed to suit the occasion very well. "I'll take care of this," he said grimly, yanking the suitcase out of her hand. "The deal's off. This is goodbye, baby."

Later that day, Terry's van was discovered abandoned in a side street a couple of miles outside the city. The police constable who came to tell him about it said some stranded reveller had probably 'borrowed' it to drive home. It happened all the time, he said. He drove Terry to the spot and asked him to identify it, which he was only too happy to do. He was even happier when it emerged that none of his tools or equipment had been nicked. It was dusted for fingerprints before the police let him have it back and they took his own prints – for elimination purposes, they explained. The prints would be destroyed in his presence once there was no further use for them.

"Ever had this done before?" the young officer joked as he inked Terry's fingers and rolled them one at a time on the paper.

"Oh sure, I'm a seasoned villain," Terry joked back.

At six o'clock that evening a distraught Arthur Chant reported finding his wife's body. She had been strangled.

Chapter Three

Sukey had been on a daytime shift all week, but on the Friday of the Lorraine Chant murder she had agreed to be on standby until ten, covering for a sick colleague. The summons came over her personal radio shortly after six, just as she was finishing her prawn stir-fry supper. Fergus was not fond of rice dishes, so on the weekends when he was with Paul she often pigged out on Chinese or Indian.

Resignedly, she swallowed the last few mouthfuls, put her plate in the sink and returned the chocolate mousse to the refrigerator. She went into the sitting room to set up the video for the repeat of an early episode of *Inspector Morse* that she had been hoping to watch later. Then she got into her working clothes, checked her gear and set off. By the time she had picked up the van from the central police station in Gloucester the homeward bound traffic had thinned out and the ring road was comparatively clear, but even so it was almost seven o'clock before she left the city behind her and headed south along the Bristol Road.

She had been given detailed directions to the Chants' house, but the village of Marsdean itself was tricky to find. The signpost on the main road was so weathered that she spotted it too late and had to drive on for nearly a mile before she found a suitable place to turn and go back. Even then she might have missed it a second time had there not been a farm shop close to the turning to serve as a landmark.

It was a mild, sunny evening in early June. The narrow lane,

21

winding gently between open fields, was bounded on either side by hedges of hawthorn, elder and ash which still showed signs of having been ruthlessly hacked down to a geometric neatness during the winter but were defiantly responding to the butchery with masses of vigorous, untidy new growth. At their feet, the brilliant green of the verges was spattered with dandelions whose sunshiny golden yellow made a perfect foil for the creamy elder blossoms overhead.

Sukey had driven almost another two miles before a carved and painted wooden sign, almost invisible in the shade of a tall holly tree, informed her that she had reached her destination. A final bend in the road revealed the village itself. It had a self-consciously picturesque appearance, with an ancient church set among clipped yew trees and weathered tombstones, trim houses surrounded by tidy gardens, and a smoothly shaven village green with a stone war memorial in the middle. A few of the houses were modern, but most were what local estate agents were fond of describing as immaculately maintained period properties, with walls of mellowed brick, tiled roofs encrusted with lichen and tiny, white-painted wooden windows. There were a few shops, one of which had a letter box let into the wall, an old-fashioned red telephone kiosk and a pub with a thatched roof and swags of wisteria flowers dangling like bunches of pale blue grapes around the door. A discreetly painted sign in a wrought-iron frame proclaimed it to be 'The Historic Priory Inn, circa 1680'.

Sukey slowed the van to a crawl and wound down the window. From behind a dense evergreen hedge came the sound of a motor mower; the sharp fragrance of cut grass drifted on the still air. When they were first married, she and Paul had a dream that one day they would live in just such a place. Paul had realised that dream . . . but he was sharing it with someone else. Not for the first time, she experienced a stab of bitterness, then reminded herself that she had a job to do and this was no time for self-pity.

The normal indicators that something unusual had occurred – knots of people standing around looking puzzled or uneasy and scrutinising every passing vehicle – were nowhere to be seen, but she sensed that more than one pair of eyes were keeping watch from behind their curtains. She drove slowly along the main street, looking out for the turning to the Chants' house. There was no one about who might have directed her, but she found it at last on the far side of the green, tucked away behind the church. A small painted board read, 'Access to The Hill only'. It occurred to Sukey as she swung the wheel and crawled along the narrow track in second gear that the inhabitants of Marsdean went to considerable lengths to guard their privacy.

There were just three houses in the secluded enclave, all set well back from the gravelled approach, which was shaped like a shepherd's crook. The Chants' property was at the apex of the curve, separated from those on either side by paddocks and, like them, screened by tall hedges and mature trees. The residents would need to be very dedicated neighbourhood watchers indeed to keep a check on each other's comings and goings. It would be interesting, thought Sukey as she parked alongside an ambulance, two police cars and a dog-handler's van already standing in the forecourt of Priory View, to learn if house-to-house enquiries revealed anything of substance.

Detective Inspector Jim Castle met her at the front door. His manner was brisk and impersonal. "You took your time," he said, glancing at his watch.

"Sorry. I didn't hang about, I just happen to live on the wrong side of town," she apologised, reflecting as she spoke that it was true in more ways than one.

"Looks as if entry was effected through a ground-floor window at the rear," he went on. "The body's upstairs. The ambulance was already here when we arrived but there was nothing the paramedics could do and we're waiting for

23

a doctor. There's been some disturbance downstairs – you could be dealing with that until he gets here."

"Right. I'll start outside so that the dog handler can get to work."

"Do that. You'll find him in the back garden."

The handler was Constable Ronnie Morris, whose German Shepherd seemed anxious to leap through a half-open window.

"This is where our man got in," said Ronnie. "Panther's picked up a trail from here to the forecourt and we reckon that's where the getaway vehicle was parked. You'll find a patch of oil on the gravel. There's another trail from there to the front door, so matey must have left that way."

"I hope Panther hasn't disturbed any evidence out here," said Sukey as she took her camera from its case.

"Course not, he knows better than that," said Ronnie with a grin and the dog, sitting on its haunches at his side, turned intelligent eyes up to him as if to endorse the remark.

"Oh yes?" Sukey was taking shots of the window, noting a smudge of white powder on the bottom of the frame. She zoomed in closer and spotted a wisp of dark green thread clinging to a broken shoot on one of the rose bushes just below the sill. "Something there for forensics to play with," she remarked as she took her samples. She peered through the window into what looked like a small breakfast room and saw more white traces on the carpet. "Matey wasn't too careful about what he trod in," she remarked over her shoulder. "Those prints might tell us something."

"Give me a shout as soon as you're through," said Ronnie.

"Sure." She went to the place he had indicated to get her shot of the patch of oil. Then she went indoors.

It was a scene she had seen scores of times, always with a sense of disgust at the wanton destructiveness with which the average burglar goes about his business. The sitting room was in a sorry state: cupboards and drawers emptied and their contents scattered in heaps on the floor, display cabinets smashed open and stripped of their contents, some shards of china and glass where the intruder must have fumbled and dropped them in his haste. Or perhaps, she thought as she moved carefully among the debris, taking her pictures, he had smashed them deliberately in a spasm of rage on realising that he had wasted his time grabbing something comparatively worthless. That they might have a sentimental value to their owner would mean nothing to him.

When she had finished in the sitting room she went upstairs, scrutinising the carpet as she went for further traces of shoeprints but found none. The sound of voices led her to what was evidently the main bedroom. Like the rest of the house, it showed every sign of having been furnished on a generous budget; there were elaborate drapes at the windows and plenty of white furniture picked out in gold. On the king-sized bed, like a dark stain against the peach-coloured satin headboard and coverlet, lay the fully-clothed body of a young woman. A grey-haired man in a sports jacket was bending over her. As Sukey entered he straightened up, turned to DI Castle who was standing beside him and said quietly, "She's dead all right. There's some quite severe bruising to the face, but the cause of death was almost certainly manual strangulation."

"Can you give an approximate time?"

"Hard to say. It's a mild evening . . . rigor's begun and she's still warm . . . anything between three and eight hours ago. It'll need a postmortem to set the time more precisely."

"Did you know her?"

"By sight, that's all."

"How long have the Chants lived here?"

The doctor pursed his lips, considering. "A couple of years, perhaps."

"But you never got to know them?"

"Hardly at all. They never socialised with anyone in the village, so far as I know."

"Well, thank you for stepping into the breach, Doctor."

"Not at all." The doctor took a last look at the dead woman, shaking his head. "Very sad," he observed. "Pretty woman . . . plenty of money, by the looks of all this." He took a final peer round the room, picked up his bag and left. Sukey stood aside to let him pass, which he did without looking at her.

"The police surgeon's out on another call," said Castle in response to her questioning glance. "That's Doctor Handley, retired, lives in the village." He turned back to the bed. "Make sure you get a good shot of those marks on the throat. There's an en suite bathroom – it doesn't appear to have been disturbed, but I want the dog to have a sniff round just in case."

"What about the other upstairs rooms?"

"All the doors were closed and there's no sign of disturbance in any of them. I reckon he came straight in here."

"OK. I'll let you know when I've done."

"Do that. I'll be downstairs."

Sukey nodded mechanically, focusing her camera. It was not her first contact with murder and she had seen bodies that were considerably messier than this one, but she never failed to experience a contraction of the stomach and a tightening of the throat at the sight of death. The sensation passed in a moment as she gave herself up to the job in hand.

Lorraine Chant lay face upwards, arms outflung, hands clenched, eyes staring blindly at the ceiling. What could be seen of her skin was blue – the classic sign of asphyxia – and her throat showed signs of bruising where brutal hands had choked the life out of her. There was a further livid mark on one cheek, as if she had been struck before being throttled. She did not seem to have put up much of a struggle; there was no sign of disorder in the room and her clothing – a dark navy blue coat and skirt and a white silk blouse, all very chic and expensive-looking – was hardly disarranged.

26

One of her shoes had fallen off and lay on the thick peach carpet. It appeared that her attacker had no time to ransack the room before – presumably – she came in and disturbed him. And once he had killed her, he hadn't bothered to search further, but had left with whatever he had picked up downstairs. Sukey had no formal training in detection, but she had seen her CID colleagues at work and her mind was clicking away as methodically as her camera.

The en suite bathroom would not have disgraced a movie mogul's penthouse, with its huge sunken tub, gold fittings and a profusion of bottles and jars of expensive toiletries on a shelf above the vanity unit. Everything was immaculate; as she dusted each item for fingerprints, Sukey found herself thinking how the dead woman would have hated this soiling by a stranger's hands of her intimate possessions.

She finished her task and went downstairs. Ronnie was waiting by the front door with Panther. "OK to go up now?" he asked.

"I guess so. Where's Inspector Castle?"

"In there, interviewing the husband." Ronnie nodded at a door leading out of the hall, which was about the size of Sukey's sitting room. He gave an appreciative glance round. "Not short of a bob or two, are they?" he commented and headed upstairs, with Panther eagerly nosing the floor as they went.

Sukey tapped on the door he had indicated; after a moment, it opened and the Inspector came out, closing it behind him. "Finished?" he asked.

"I guess so. Anything else you want me to do?"

For a moment, the official mask slipped. "Any chance you could rustle up some strong coffee? He," Castle jerked his head towards the door, "seems pretty shaken up. He's already been at the bottle by the looks of him – can't get any sense out of him so far."

"Typical," muttered Sukey under her breath as she went in search of the kitchen. "If you want some menial task performed, pick on the only woman in the team." Still, she thought, remembering her interrupted supper as she filled a kettle and hunted in cupboards for what she needed, coffee wasn't a bad idea. She could do with a cup herself.

She was returning with the tray when Ronnie came downstairs with Panther and headed for the room where the bereaved husband was being interviewed. He tapped on the door, popped his head round it and said, "Can I have a word, Guv?"

The Inspector emerged a second time, saw the coffee and gestured to Sukey to take it in before following the dog handler upstairs. "Be down in a minute," he said in a low voice. "See if you can persuade him to say something – anything. He hasn't uttered a word since we got here."

Arthur Chant was in the dining room, which was as lavishly furnished as the rest of the house. He was slumped in a chair, his face hidden in his hands, with his elbows propped on the table in the centre of which stood an elaborate silver epergne piled with highly-coloured artificial fruit. When Sukey entered he half raised his head and stared at her. He was, she judged, considerably older than his late wife. Not exactly handsome either – 'homely' was the word that came into her mind. His eyes, beneath thick eyebrows and a jutting forehead, were dull and lifeless. A plain-clothes detective, Sergeant Radcliffe, was seated at his side with an open notebook in front of him. An empty chair opposite, where the Inspector had evidently been sitting before being called away, was pushed back from the table, its padded cushion lying on the floor. Sukey guessed that it had fallen as the occupant stood up. Jim Castle was, she knew from experience, given to sudden, impatient movements which often resulted in things being overturned or displaced. She put the tray carefully on the table, picked up the cushion and replaced it.

"Are there any mats?" she asked. Chant stared silently at

her, his gaze blank. "I don't want to mark this lovely table," she explained.

He made a vague gesture at the mahogany sideboard. Sukey began searching in cupboards and eventually found a box of silver coasters. She put three on the table. "Do you take milk and sugar in your coffee?" she asked. He shook his head. "Black, then?" He nodded.

She poured coffee into a bone china mug and set it in front of him. She filled two more, gave one to Radcliffe and put the third by the empty chair. Then she sat down and put a hand on the arm of the stricken man. "Mr Chant, I'm . . . that is, we're all so very sorry about what has happened," she said gently.

For the first time, he looked straight at her. His eyes lost their dullness and became bright with tears. He swallowed, his mouth crimping in an effort to contain his distress. For the first time, he spoke. "I loved her so much," he whispered.

"Then you want us to find the man who killed her, don't you?" she said.

He made a weary gesture, almost knocking over the untouched mug of coffee. "What's the use? Nothing can bring her back," he muttered.

"No, but if he isn't caught he might do it again, to someone else's wife."

"You think so?" A slight lift of his shoulders implied, *So what is that to me?*

"It's been known," she said. She pushed the mug a little closer to him. "Drink that, it'll do you good." After a moment's hesitation he picked it up and took a mouthful. "There's a very dangerous person out there and we have to think of other potential victims," she went on. "You can take your time, but it's important that you tell the officers everything you can think of that might help."

He gave a half nod and continued drinking the coffee. When he had finished he set it down and flexed his hands, staring down at them and rubbing them softly together. They were large and

29

well kept, the skin smooth, the nails manicured. They were the hands of a wealthy man who had never known manual labour. His jacket was hand tailored, his shirt and tie were silk. He wore a Cartier watch and a heavy gold signet ring set with a diamond on his wedding finger. Everything – the house and its contents, the landscaped grounds, the owner himself – reeked of money. The place was an obvious target for thieves, but murder was something else. It was hardly surprising, Sukey thought with compassion, that the man was in shock.

He was sitting more upright now and she realised he was a bigger man than she had supposed when she first saw him, slumped forward and bowed with grief. He was beginning to lose his air of detachment, a look of concentration replacing the blankness in his eyes.

Across the table, Radcliffe gave Sukey an approving nod as if to say, *Well done, you've got through to him*, and held his pen hopefully at the ready. He leaned forward and said coaxingly, "Mr Chant, if you could begin by telling us what time you arrived home."

"It was just after six o'clock. The news was just starting."

"Would that have been on your car radio?"

"That's right."

Much as she would have liked to hear the story first hand, Sukey knew she had no business to stay in the room. She got up quietly and went out, just as DI Castle was coming back downstairs.

"Your coffee's in there," she told him. "I hope it hasn't gone cold."

"Thanks." He paused with his hand on the doorknob. "Any progress?"

"He's started to give a statement."

"Fine. I want you to go back upstairs and check the study. There's no apparent disturbance, but the dog seems pretty sure our man was in there."

"Right." Sukey returned the tray to the kitchen, swallowed

the coffee – now nearly cold – that she had poured for herself before serving the others, and went in search of Ronnie Morris. She wondered if Jim Castle had forgotten that they were supposed to have a date for lunch the following day.

Chapter Four

While Inspector Castle and his team were attempting to piece together the events of Lorraine Chant's last hours, Barbie Bayliss was at her dressing table in the master bedroom of her luxury home in the Charlton Kings area of Cheltenham. She was getting ready to go out to dinner with her husband and she was not looking forward to the evening. She hated most of Hugo's friends. In fact, apart from the material comforts and the apparently unlimited amounts of money that his business brought in, she hated a lot of things about their present life. She hated having to call herself Barbie, for a start, and she thought Hugo a cissy sort of name, but he'd insisted that when they moved into what he called a 'posh noo meelioo' they ought to have posh-sounding names. It had taken her a while to get used to it and once she'd slipped up and addressed him as Charlie in front of some business associate he'd brought home. He'd laughed it off at the time, but he'd roughed her up afterwards and she'd had to wear dark glasses for a week and pretend she'd bumped into a door. He'd threatened her with worse if she made that mistake again, but she never had.

Barbie longed for the old days when she was surrounded by people of her own type and Auntie Gwen was living just round the corner. Auntie Gwen had been like a second mum to Barbie – Brenda as she was then – after her own parents had died and she missed not being able to see her regularly. She wasn't supposed to see her at all; Hugo had forbidden her to contact anyone from the old days, or let them know where they were living. If he knew she sneaked up to London now and again to visit Auntie Gwen, he'd knock hell out of her, but she'd managed to keep it a secret so far.

She was sitting in front of the mirror in her dressing gown, putting the finishing touches to her make-up and wondering which of the three dresses she'd taken out of her wardrobe she should wear to this bloody dinner party. She wondered who else would be there. Probably not Steven Lovett, Hugo's office manager. Single men and widowers never seemed to get invited to dinner parties. Stand up drinks parties, yes. She and Steven had enjoyed quite a few chats at that sort of informal function. There had also been other occasions, during Hugo's all too seldom absences on business trips, when they'd enjoyed something more than conversation. Barbie's favourite daydream was that Steven suddenly came into unlimited wealth – won the lottery, for example – and arrived like a knight on a charger to take her away from Hugo forever. As it was, the odd stolen couple of hours was all they could manage and there were times when she wondered whether even that was worth the risk. If Hugo found out, he'd half kill her. The fact that he'd had almost as many affairs as he'd had good dinners didn't mean he'd make any allowances for his wife's occasional fling.

Barbie studied her reflection, an activity which gave her considerable satisfaction. She still looked pretty good, all things considered. She'd kept her figure – Hugo's not wanting kids had something to do with that, of course. That had upset her at first, but with hindsight she knew it was just as well. The one he had fathered, the one he'd always refused to acknowledge was his even though the mother was a sixteen-year-old virgin before he got his hands on her, had had a pretty thin time and so had young Ivy, poor cow. At least she was at peace now, and a fat lot Hugo – Charlie as he was in those days – would have cared if he'd known how she'd suffered towards the end.

Barbie put away her lipstick and picked up a comb. Her skin and hair always looked good, thanks to regular facials and visits to the hairdresser. Hugo kept her on a tight rein as far as ready cash was concerned, but he let her run up as many bills as she liked on clothes and beauty treatments and he always paid them without a quibble. "Just as long as you go on looking good for me, love," he'd say, handing her a cheque with one hand while fumbling in her knickers with the other. Never could keep his hands to himself, it was almost a reflex action. And what was the point of looking good, she thought despondently, when it was only now and again there was someone around who really appreciated you?

Behind her, the bathroom door opened and Hugo emerged swathed in a striped towelling robe and smelling of Chanel's *Pour Monsieur*. His eyes met hers in the mirror. On his freshly-shaven face was the satisfied smirk that meant he was feeling exceptionally pleased with himself. At forty-five he was still handsome and he had the kind of personality that had women flocking round him at parties and other gatherings. Barbie had watched him time and time again, lapping up the admiration, his eyes roving from one to the other, sizing them up, deciding which ones he fancied screwing. Oh yes, she thought as she dutifully responded to his smile, I know what you get up to when I'm not around. And I'll tell you something else, you lecherous pig, I don't give a toss – not a fucking toss. I just wish you'd keep it for your fancy women and leave me alone.

He came up behind her and put his hands on her shoulders, then slid them down under her armpits and over her breasts. "Got something for you," he whispered, his tongue probing her ear. "Wanna see it?"

"I've just done my hair and make-up," she protested. *Surely,* she thought, *the bloody old ram doesn't want it now. We're supposed to be leaving in fifteen minutes.*

34

"That's OK, I can wait for that till we get home. No, this is something else."

"What is it?"

"Shut your eyes and I'll give it to you." He gave her breasts a quick squeeze – a hint of what was to come later, she thought resignedly. She heard a faint click, then felt something cool against the skin of her throat. He fumbled for a moment at the back of her neck, then said, "OK, you can look now."

Barbie opened her eyes and stared in the glass at the glistening gold circlet. "Smashing, innit?" he said smugly.

"It's lovely," she said, and meant it. "Must have cost a packet."

"You betcha. There's earrings to match. You'll have to put 'em on yourself." He laid a shiny lacquered box on the dressing table. "Well, go on then, let's see how they look."

Barbie clipped the earrings into place and tilted her head to study the effect. The set looked good on her, she had to admit. She wondered how Hugo had come by it, whether it had been nicked and if so who from. As long as it wasn't from any of the women they'd be meeting tonight . . . but no, however moronic he might be in other ways, he was too shrewd to make that sort of blunder. "Thank you, dear," she said and gave him the kiss that was expected of her. "They're beautiful." She stood up and unfastened her robe. "I must get dressed now, and so must you."

"Good to you, ain't I?" he said. He put his arms round her, ran his hands down her back and gave her bottom a squeeze before releasing her.

"Yes dear, you are."

He threw off his own robe and went to a drawer to look out clean underwear. Barbie saw him steal a satisfied glance at his reflection in the wardrobe mirror. Vain old sod, she thought, although she had to admit he was a pretty fine specimen. She wondered how he'd come by the scratches on his hand and his backside. Screwing some bird with sharp nails, probably.

35

No point in asking; he'd only come out with some stupid lie. It didn't matter anyway. Once, she had thrilled to the sight of his naked body and the touch of his hands as they explored her own. Not any more.

At approximately the same time as Mr and Mrs Hugo Bayliss left to keep their dinner engagement, Terry and Rita Holland and their ten-year-old son Billy sat down to supper in the kitchen of their terraced house a short distance from the centre of Gloucester. The Friday ritual was always the same: Terry picked up fish and chips on the way home from his last job of the afternoon, Rita put it on plates in the oven to keep hot while she cut bread and butter and made tea, and Terry went with Billy into the tiny living room to watch children's television. Rita never called them until the programme was over. She wondered sometimes which of them enjoyed it the most.

He was a good dad, was Terry. Pity he'd missed so much of Billy's childhood, being inside for so long. When he came out, Rita made him promise to go straight and he'd kept his promise, doing his best to make up to her and Billy for all the lost years. He'd learned a trade in prison and was making quite a decent living doing carpentry and building jobs. It had been her idea to move away from their old haunts and make a completely fresh start, but she hadn't reckoned on coming so far afield. "Why Gloucester?" she had asked, but all he would say was, "Why not? It's a nice place", and she hadn't bothered to argue. The important thing was that the three of them were together again, and that was how she wanted things to stay. Being so far from London meant they'd completely lost contact with Terry's old cronies, and seeing what they'd led him into in the past, that was all to the good.

Today had started badly. Couldn't have been worse, in fact. Someone had nicked Terry's van during the night with all his tools and working clothes in it. At least it was all insured. Rita had insisted; it was important, she said, when it was his livelihood and he had to leave it outside in the street. She'd paid the premium out of the money she earned as a dinner lady at Billy's school and from doing odd cleaning jobs. But until the insurance company shelled out, Terry was faced with losing some of the work he had lined up so things looked like being tough for a while. Then, almost unbelievably, the van turned up after just a few hours, with all the stuff intact. Three cheers for the Old Bill, Terry had said, then added with a grin that he never thought to hear himself say that.

When she heard the signing-off tune of the kids' programme, Rita put her head round the living room door. "Supper's ready," she said and they came out to the kitchen laughing at some joke they'd heard, Billy's happy face upturned to his father's, Terry's hand on his son's shoulder. *Please God, let it stay this way,* she said silently to herself as she fetched the plates from the oven. *No more days like today, please!*

After supper, Billy went out to play with his friends. Rita washed the dishes and Terry dried them.

"Fancy coming out for a drink later?" he said. "To celebrate getting the van back," he added as she hesitated.

"If Christine will come and look after Billy." That was something she'd never do, leave Billy alone in the house.

"Oh, come on, he's nearly eleven. He'll be OK."

"We're not leaving him," she insisted.

He hung the teacloth on its hook and put an arm round her as she was rinsing away the washing-up water. "You're a good mum, Reet," he said, "and a good wife. I'll never forget the way you've stood by us . . . me and Billy. You won't ever leave me, will you?"

She dried her hands and turned to face him. "What brought this on?" she asked. "What have you been up to?"

"Nothing," he said defensively, but he could tell from the look in her eye that she didn't believe him. She had to know sooner or later anyway. He turned away to put a dish in the cupboard. He kept his back to her as he said, trying to sound casual, "I had a call from Reg Hodson while you were at work."

He didn't need to see her face to know what she was thinking. Her voice sounded harsh as she demanded, "How did Reg get hold of our number?"

"I gave it to him. I'd asked him a favour."

"What kind of favour?"

Terry went over to the window and stared out. Billy and one or two other kids were riding their bikes up and down the street. It was a quiet side turning so it was fairly safe so long as they didn't go out into the main road. Billy was pretty good about that – he'd had it hammered into him enough times.

Rita grabbed him by the arm. "You promised me you'd finished with the old mob," she said fiercely.

He swung round to face her. "There's something I forgot to tell you," he said at last. It'd been a mistake to mention Reg, or the phone call. Trouble was, she read him so well, she'd give him no peace until he told her what was on his mind. Not just on his mind . . . in his guts, eating him up, tearing him apart with the sheer bloody injustice of it all. "I saw Charlie Foss the other day."

She gaped at him, apprehension replacing the anger in her eyes. "Where, for God's sake?" Her voice was a croak; he could see her mind racing ahead, seeing nothing but trouble.

"In the car park of a place in Cheltenham where I was doing a job. He didn't see me."

"Thank God for that." Rita relaxed her grip on his arm. Then it tightened again and the anxiety returned. "Where does Reg Hodson come into it?"

"I took Charlie's car number and asked him to see if he could get a check on it, find out where he lives." Reg knew a bent policeman who did him the odd favour in exchange for a share in the profits of one or other of his petty scams. "It was a flashy great Jag," he added bitterly, "a company car."

"What company?"

Terry's gaze slid back to the window. "Never you mind. The less you know about it, the better."

Rita had gone very white and he knew exactly what she was thinking. She grabbed both his hands, forcing him to look at her. "Did you know he was living somewhere round here?" she asked. "Is that why you brought us to Gloucester, so's you could find him? You did know, didn't you?" Anger sent her voice racing up the scale and the last words were almost a scream.

He shook himself free. "What if I did?"

"How d'you find out?"

"Brenda told her Auntie Gwen before they left that they'd be living somewhere near Gloucester. She found that out because she saw something from an estate agent, something she wasn't supposed to see. Charlie hadn't told her anything and he threatened to knock the living daylights out of her if she let on to a living soul where they were."

"He'd have done it, too. Poor old Bren, I'll bet she misses her Auntie Gwen something rotten." For the moment, Rita forgot her own problems, remembering the hard time Charlie used to give his long-suffering wife. Only for a moment, though. "Terry, you're not going after Charlie, are you?" she begged.

"Why not?" She'd put him on the defensive and he didn't like it. "He owes me and he owes Frank. He's got our share from the bank job. I've done time, Frank's still banged up and that shit can swan around in a posh car and live the life of Riley."

"What are you going to do?" Her eyes were streaming. "Terry, please let it go. We're doing all right, we don't need the money."

"Don't need the money?" His eyes swept round the cramped kitchen with its shabby fittings and worn furniture. "We live in this rabbit hutch 'cos we can't afford nothing better and you reckon we're doing all right? Listen!" He grabbed her shoulders and put his face close to hers. "That job was worth at least sixty grand, and twenty of it's mine – ours. If he doesn't give it to me, I'll shop him."

"How can you? Charlie never had a record, you couldn't prove nothing, he'd only laugh at you, or pretend he'd never seen you before. He might complain to the police you'd been trying to blackmail him. Please, Tel, it's not worth it."

"Just leave it, will you." He let her go and began putting dishes away as if nothing had happened. "You'd better go and wash your face and get changed if we're going out. I'll go next door and ask Christine if she'll come and sit with Billy, if that's what you want."

With a despairing gesture, Rita left the room and went upstairs. She was half frantic, seeing everything they'd built up over the past year falling apart, knowing all too well that once Terry set his mind on something it was useless to try and talk him out of it. Until half an hour ago she really believed they'd left the old life behind them, yet all the time he'd been watching and waiting for the chance to get his hands on his share of the stolen money. There must have been signs – how could she have missed them?

If that's what I want, she thought bitterly as she splashed cold water over her face and repaired the damage to her make-up. *What do you care what I want? And I thought everything was all right, I thought we were happy.*

Chapter Five

Jim Castle called Sukey on Saturday morning to say that he had checked with the lab and the prints would be ready that afternoon and would it be all right if he dropped by around five so that she could talk him through them? The sub-text of all this read: Sorry, can't make it for lunch but look forward to seeing you later. The fact that he made no overt reference to their date caused her no surprise. This was official business and there were sure to be other people around. From the outset, they had agreed to keep their friendship entirely separate from their working relationship, and if anyone suspected an attraction between Detective Inspector Castle and one of the SOCOs, they never gave the slightest hint of it. To their colleagues, she was simply a member of the team, which sometimes meant that if he was in an impatient mood she was as likely as anyone else to get bawled out.

She took the change in their arrangements philosophically. It wasn't the first time the job had interfered with their plans, and it wouldn't be the last. It was the uncertainties of police life that had caused Jim's marriage to founder. She often wondered how it would have been if she had married him herself. She was pretty sure he would have asked her, given half a chance. They had first met when he was a young constable doing his two years on the beat and she a new recruit. They had dated a few times and he looked like getting serious, but then she had met Paul and fallen for him in a big way. Their marriage too had failed, but it had nothing to do with irregular hours

41

and everything to do with Myrna's glamorous lifestyle and money.

Sukey finished her breakfast and went upstairs to change the bed linen. She came down, loaded the washing machine and got out the vacuum cleaner. As she went methodically about her routine household tasks, she reflected on the twist of fate that had brought her and Jim together again. A few months after she picked up the threads of her old job with the police, this time in a civilian capacity, Jim – by then a detective inspector – had rejoined the Gloucestershire Force after serving for several years in London. He had lost no time in asking her out, saying that life had given them a second chance and they would be daft not to take it. He was an impetuous type, so different from Paul with his calculating accountant's brain. Sukey herself had reacted more cautiously. She enjoyed Jim's company; he was considerate and dependable – everything, in fact, that Paul was not – and, but for Fergus, she would have accepted without hesitation. But she had resolved, after Paul walked out, never to start a serious relationship with anyone else until Fergus was mature enough to cope with it.

She found herself looking forward to the evening visit with mixed feelings. Fergus knew about Jim; the two had actually met at a friendly football match between the police and a local youth club and they seemed to take to one another, but Sukey had been careful to introduce him very casually as an old friend from her rookie days. This evening was different. She would be on call until ten, so going out for a meal wouldn't be on the cards, but Jim might offer to fetch a takeaway and with Fergus at Paul's house until Sunday afternoon it would be difficult to refuse . . . and then what? She knew what he wanted, and to be honest, that was what she wanted as well – wasn't it?

An insistent whirring clatter from the washing machine reminded her that the cycle was nearly over. Pushing the unsettling thoughts away, she went out into the back garden to set up the rotary dryer. The fine weather looked set to last for the weekend. She pegged the laundry out, made a cup of coffee and sat down in the kitchen to write out a grocery list while she drank it. Life had to go on.

It was nearly half-past seven when Jim's car drew up outside Sukey's house. That he was still, mentally at any rate, on duty was immediately apparent. He strode into the kitchen ahead of her, sat down, took a large envelope from his briefcase and spread the contents on the table. She pulled up a chair and sat beside him, picking up the photographs one after another as he examined them and laid them aside. When she came to the shots taken in the study, she remarked, "I know you said the dog followed a scent in there, but nothing seemed disturbed."

"It does seem odd. The wall safe, the one behind the books, is opened with a combination lock, but the one let into the floor under the desk is opened with a key. The dog was interested in both locations, but as you say, nothing appeared to have been touched. We'll have to see what the fingerprints tell us."

"Mrs Chant probably disturbed her killer before he had time to tackle either of the safes."

"So it would seem, on the face of it." It was clear from his tone that Jim had his doubts. He began to gather the pictures together, a frown rumpling his high forehead, a look of concentration in his greenish eyes above the slightly aquiline nose. "It's odd," he repeated. "An experienced thief would expect to find a safe in that kind of household and know the sort of place where it would be concealed, but the fact that the scent was so strong around the spot where the floor safe was fitted suggests that he knew that one was there as well."

"Do you know where the key was kept?"

"In a drawer in the wall safe. Chant checked in our presence – it was still in its usual place."

"What else did he keep in the wall safe?"

"His wife's jewellery, some documents, the usual stuff."

43

"And nothing was missing?"

"So he says." Jim returned the pictures to their folder and laid it aside.

"You don't sound convinced."

"I just had the feeling he was holding something back. I asked him why he had the second safe installed, and he said there was always a chance that an expert cracksman could open the one in the wall so he'd had the other put in as a kind of back-up. From time to time he keeps fairly large sums of money in the house. His company manages a string of amusement arcades and of course they handle a lot of cash."

"Was there much in it on the day of the murder."

"On the contrary, it was empty."

"So perhaps he'd just paid the last lot into the bank?"

"Or he'd emptied it before we came on the scene."

"Why would he do that?"

Jim shrugged. "It's only a hypothesis, of course, but suppose he was hiding the proceeds of some dodgy business deals – in drugs, perhaps. Money he wouldn't want us, or the Inland Revenue, to know about."

It was Sukey's turn to look doubtful. "Assuming you're right, d'you reckon he'd have had the presence of mind to stash the evidence away somewhere before calling for help, when he was in shock after finding his wife's body?"

"It's true he seems genuinely broken up by her murder, but we can't discount anything at this stage." Jim made an impatient gesture, as if mentally sweeping the problem to one side for the time being. "I'm sorry, I'm off duty, I shouldn't be inflicting all this on you."

"Don't talk rot, I've got a professional interest as well."

"So you have." He put a hand on hers and gave it a squeeze. Something in her nervous system went zing. "I'm sorry about our lunch date, Sook."

"That's OK." She let her hand lie under his, enjoying the

dangerously pleasant messages it sent to remoter parts of her body.

"What about dinner? I don't know about you, but I'm starving."

"Me too, but I can't go out, I'm on standby again until ten o'clock." Against her inclination, she drew her hand away. He stood up awkwardly and his chair almost toppled over. As he grabbed it, the packet of photographs slipped from his grasp. She leaned forward and fielded it. "Clumsy ox," she teased.

He gave a sheepish grin as he took the packet from her. "Well, if we can't eat out, I'll get something from the takeaway. Indian, Chinese, pizza—?"

"I'll have a pizza, I think."

"Me too. What topping would you like?"

They discussed details, agreed on a dessert and he left. Fifteen minutes later he was back with cartons of food. Despite a resolution not to talk shop, the case was still uppermost in both their minds. It was Sukey who reverted to it. "Tell me," she said as she put plates and cutlery on the table, "did Chant's statement take you any further forward?"

"Not really. He says he left for his office as usual at around nine o'clock yesterday morning. His wife had arranged to go to London to attend a friend's wedding and wasn't expected back until next day. Soon after he got to the office he realised he'd forgotten a file that he was going to need at a meeting later on, so he went back home to fetch it. His wife was still there. She was in good time, and his meeting wasn't until twelve, so they had a cup of coffee together before he returned to his office. When he came home at about six o'clock, he found the place in a mess and realised someone had broken in. He went upstairs to see what other damage was done and found her body. He had the presence of mind to call the police and an ambulance, and then went into complete shock. Thought of something?" he enquired as Sukey put down the dish of salad she was holding and reached for the packet of photographs.

"I'm not sure. What time did Chant come back the first time?"

"Shortly before ten o'clock, as far as he remembers. Why?"

"And where was the file he says he forgot?"

Jim thought for a moment. "I think he said he left it on the hall table. He just forgot to pick it up when leaving the house."

"In which case—" Sukey rummaged through the prints and picked out one of the en suite bathroom. She held it up for Jim to see. "What does that tell you?"

"That the last person to use the toilet was a man," he said, after noting the position of the seat. "So what? He probably popped in for a quick pee after his cup of coffee."

"Wouldn't he have been more likely to use the downstairs loo?"

"He would indeed." Jim was quick to spot what she was driving at. "And his wife almost certainly used the toilet after he left home the first time, so any prints other than Chant's on the underside of that seat will probably have been left by her killer. Well spotted, Sook. Now, let's get on with this food before it gets cold."

They ate in silence for a few minutes. Then she asked, "Do we know how much stuff was taken?"

He shook his head. "Not yet. We've asked Chant for a list and when we have it we'll be circulating details through the usual channels."

She nodded and chewed thoughtfully on a mouthful of pizza for a few seconds before asking, "I assume you've had his story checked?" In such cases, she knew, the murder victim's nearest and dearest was always a suspect until eliminated.

"Naturally," said Jim. "Independent witnesses have confirmed the times of his movements, but of course we've only his word for it that his wife was still alive when he left her."

"D'you reckon she could have been planning to leave him?"

"That's an obvious possibility, but nothing he said suggested anything of the kind. On the contrary, he kept on about how close they were, how much in love – but he would say that, of course, whatever the truth of the matter."

"This wedding she was supposed to be going to, where exactly was it?"

"That's another question we can't answer at the moment. Chant claims they were friends of his wife that he's never met, he doesn't even remember their names, and he has no idea where the wedding was taking place except it was somewhere in London. It's significant that no one's called to enquire why she never showed up."

"I suppose they could have phoned before he came home, but got no answer."

"It's possible. In which case presumably they'll call again sometime, but it might not be for ages, after the honeymoon for example. We're working through Mrs Chant's address book to see if we can trace them that way."

"You didn't find an invitation anywhere . . . in her handbag, for example, or her overnight bag?"

"We didn't find an overnight bag, which seems to indicate that she was killed shortly after her husband left for the second time, before she'd started packing. It's a point though." Jim laid down his fork. "I suppose it's just possible that she packed the bag and put it in her car some time before she was ready to leave."

"Where was her car?"

"In the garage, I guess. I should have checked at the time. I'll see to it first thing tomorrow." Jim rumpled his hair with his fingers. "There's something not quite straightforward about this case. On the face of it, we're looking at an opportunist break-in by someone assuming the house was empty, who panicked and committed murder when confronted. But it's hard to see how a casual thief would go to both safes, one concealed by books and the other by a rug, and yet leave everything apparently untouched."

"It is odd," Sukey agreed. "Was anyone seen hanging around?"

"The woman who keeps the village shop says she saw a white van driving up the lane towards the Chants' house at about half-past ten. She doesn't remember seeing it again that day, but she says it's been in the village before and thinks it belongs to a man who does odd jobs around the place. We're following that up as well. Oh, hell, let's talk about something else!" Jim picked up their empty plates and carried them to the sink. A fork fell on the floor and Sukey retrieved it. He took it from her and put it down with exaggerated care. They laughed as their eyes met.

"What time did you say your shift ends?" he asked softly.

She glanced at her watch. "In ten minutes."

"And Fergus is with his father until tomorrow?"

"That's right."

The space between them was a magnetic field, drawing them together, invading every corner of their bodies. Common sense, stern resolution, the responsibilities of single parenthood, all fled from Sukey's mind. She was on the brink of surrender when the telephone rang. Fergus was on the line, and he sounded distressed.

"Mum, I want to come home," he said, his voice unsteady. "Can you fetch me?"

"What is it? What's happened? Are you ill?" One dire possibility after another chased through Sukey's head.

"It's Dad and Myrna. They're having a row – it's awful! Please Mum, I can't stay . . . oh, Dad! I'm sorry!"

Paul had evidently grabbed the telephone from his son. His voice came over the wire, harsh and angry. "He's right, it would be better for him to be with you tonight."

"Paul, what's going on?"

"Nothing I can't handle, but the boy's better out of it. OK if I drop him off? Say in half an hour?"

"Yes, of course, I'll be here but—"

The line went dead. Sukey put down the receiver and turned to Jim. He read her expression and without a word went to pick up his jacket. "Some other time, maybe," he said dully.

"There's some trouble between Paul and Myrna. Fergus sounded really upset."

"And he's coming home." Jim's voice was flat, final.

"What else could I do but agree? He hates scenes – I remember when Paul and I—"

"You don't have to explain. I know he comes first and I understand."

"I'm sorry, I know how you must feel."

"Do you?" They had reached the front door, his hand was on the latch. He turned suddenly and grabbed her in a fierce, almost angry embrace, his mouth crushing hers. "Just tell me one thing," he said hoarsely. "Tell me you want it too."

She put her arms round him, returning the pressure. "You know I do."

"I'll see you soon," he whispered, his voice gentle again. He released her, opened the door and was gone. She went into the front room and watched from the window as he drove away. There was still light in the western sky.

Less than half an hour later she heard a key in the lock and Fergus walked in. He dumped his overnight bag in the hall and came into the kitchen, where she was just putting away the supper things.

"Something smells good," he said, sniffing the air. "Is there any left?" His eye fell on the empty cartons lying on a worktop. "Have you had a takeaway? Did you eat a whole pizza by yourself?"

There was no point in concealment. "Inspector Castle called round with some photographs. Neither of us had eaten so he fetched something for us both. He was just leaving when you

49

called." A white lie did no harm, and it would be reassuring for Fergus.

"He seems a top chap. D'you like him?"

"Very much. I'm glad you do. Do you want anything to eat, by the way?"

"Wouldn't mind." He was at the age of perpetual hunger. "Any baked beans going?"

"Of course." Sukey fetched the tin and Fergus opened it and tipped the contents into a saucepan while she got out some bread for toast. She was curious to know what had caused the rumpus between Paul and Myrna, but felt it better to let Fergus be the one to raise it if he felt like it. She watched him as he lit the gas under the beans, reached for a wooden spoon and began stirring them. His expression gave little away, except for a tightening of the jawline that suggested suppressed tension.

When the food was ready he sat and wolfed it as if he was starving. "Didn't you get any supper?" Sukey asked.

He shook his head. "Myrna was sulking because there was this do on somewhere she'd wanted to go to and Dad had said no. She screamed that it was always the same, he put me before her. He said it was nothing to do with me being there, it was just that he didn't want to waste an evening with a load of bloody boring airheads. She told him not to insult her friends – and then they really tore into each other." Fergus put down his knife and fork and looked at his mother, his expression almost beseeching, begging for help in understanding the complexity of human relationships. His eyes were bright. On the verge of manhood, he was struggling against the tears that would have branded him as still a child.

Sukey felt her own eyes smarting as she sat beside him and put an arm round his shoulders. "Don't let it upset you, love," she said gently. "They've had rows before – it'll blow over."

"You reckon?" He sat hunched over his plate, his mouth working. Then he raised his head and looked at her. This time, the tears won. He buried his face in her shoulder. "I think he regrets the divorce," he said, his voice muffled. "Mum, d'you think you could ever have him back?"

Sukey heaved a sigh. Once, she would have killed for the knowledge that Paul still cared for her. Things were different now. "I'm afraid not," she said. "I don't think Myrna would let him go without a fight, and in any case—"

Fergus sat up and brushed a hand across his eyes. He was back in control. "I guess you'd find it hard to trust him again," he said.

He was learning fast. Sukey gave his shoulder a squeeze before taking her arm away. "I guess I would," she said sadly.

It was not until Monday morning, shortly before Fergus was due to leave for school, that Sukey noticed that the letter about the school trip to France was missing from the front of the refrigerator door.

"I chucked it," said Fergus when she asked him about it. He concentrated on spreading marmalade on a slice of toast, not looking at her. "No point in keeping it. We have to give in our names and the deposit this week if we're going."

"Did Dad say he wouldn't contribute, then?" Sukey sat down at the kitchen table opposite him. Still he avoided her eye. "You did ask him, didn't you?"

"Couldn't very well, not with things the way they were."

"So where is the letter?"

"In the bin." He finished his toast, gulped the rest of his tea, wiped his mouth and stood up. "Forget it," he said gruffly. "There's several others not going." He dropped a kiss on her forehead. "Have a good day, Mum."

"You too. You'll find your supper in the fridge if I'm going to be out when you get home."

"Sure, no problem."

After he had left, Sukey dived into the bin and retrieved the crumpled sheet of paper. She smoothed it out and did some calculations in her head. It wasn't all that much, really, when you came to work it out. The deposit was only fifty pounds, she could manage that, and the rest of the money didn't have to be in for several weeks. It would mean dipping into her reserves, which weren't all that flush at the moment anyway, but . . .

Then she remembered something. That man Gary she'd met at the health club had asked her to do a photo session at his house. He'd said something about paying whatever she asked. From the car he drove and the quality of his sports gear it was obvious he wasn't short of a bob or two. She reckoned she could charge him a fee that would go a long way towards the cost of the trip. It was against the rules and she could be in trouble if anyone down at the nick heard about it, but that was pretty unlikely. Of course, if – as she suspected – the man's interest in her wasn't confined to her professional skills, things could get tricky, but she reckoned she could handle any funny business. It might be worth the risk.

He'd said he used the club most Monday mornings – and today was Monday.

Chapter Six

All Reg Hodson had been able to tell Terry was that the registered keeper of the car he'd seen Charlie Foss driving was a company calling itself Bodywise Systems Ltd with an address in Cheltenham. That meant Terry would have to do a bit of on-the-spot detective work himself. It appealed to his sense of humour to think he was on the point of succeeding where the police had failed. With all their resources, they'd never managed to trace the driver of the getaway car after the raid that had ended so disastrously. Terry and Frank had both grassed on Charlie, of course. They didn't owe him any loyalty, not after the way he'd sodded off and left them to take the rap. It hadn't done them much good; Charlie had covered his tracks so well that it was obvious he'd been plotting the double-cross for weeks, probably from the moment they first started planning the job – or even before that, knowing that sooner or later they'd want his services again.

It had crossed Terry's mind to wonder whether Brenda Foss's Auntie Gwen had known at the time what neck of the woods she and Charlie had gone to. She'd never have grassed to the filth, though, whatever her opinion of Charlie which, as Terry recalled, wasn't very high. It wouldn't be, not the way he treated her niece. But she wasn't all that bright, and when Terry had gone to see her after he came out of prison, she was happy to tell him what she knew because he was an old mate of Brenda's husband. Not that it had amounted to much, when all was said and done. Still, she'd pointed him in the right direction and he'd been confident he'd pick up Charlie's trail in the end. Which, at last, he had.

As luck would have it, Terry's first job on the Monday morning after Lorraine Chant's murder was on an industrial estate midway between Cheltenham and Gloucester, so he left home an hour early, brushing aside Rita's anxious questions, and went to suss out his quarry. He didn't know Cheltenham very well – it was a little off his patch, although he'd taken Rita and Billy there last Christmas to see the lights – but he'd checked the town map and eventually, after twice going astray round the one-way system, he found the address where Bodywise Systems had their head office. It was close to the town centre in a new building which had evidently only recently been completed, for a board outside proclaimed that there was still luxury office accommodation available in 'this prestigious new development'. It was just gone seven and the traffic was still light. He parked the van a little way down the road and strolled back to investigate.

The façade of the building was finished in dazzling white and glistened like icing sugar in the early morning sun. There were rows of elegant sash windows and stone steps up to the front door, which was under a portico with fluted columns, flanked on either side by a bay tree standing upright in its white-painted tub like a dark green toffee-apple. The forecourt was laid out as a car park with spaces marked by parallel white lines and small noticeboards indicating which ones were allocated to individual tenants. Bodywise Systems had four and the registration number of the car Charlie Foss had been driving was painted on one of them. 'Posh' was the word that came to Terry's mind. Charlie had gone all posh. He wouldn't mind betting the creep had even put on a posh accent. *Done all right for yourself haven't you, you double-crossing shit,* he thought. *Well, I've got news for you: it won't be long before you get your comeuppance.*

So far, apart from a van bearing the name of a firm of

contract cleaners, the forecourt was empty. Too early for office staff to show their faces, Terry thought. They'd come swanning in around nine o'clock when the likes of him had been grafting away for an hour or more. He wondered what time Charlie would show up. He couldn't hang about here for long, not with a job of his own to go to. He couldn't afford to be late as it was for a new customer and if the bloke was satisfied it might lead to other things. He was about to return to his van when a woman came out of the front door of the building with a duster and a tin of Brasso in her hand and began polishing one of the brass nameplates. Terry strolled over to speak to her.

"Looking for Bodywise Systems," he said. "Any idea what time the boss gets in?"

She gave him a wary glance. "Who wants to know?" she asked.

"Supposed to be doing a job at one of his clubs." Terry had recognised the name when Reg called and remembered seeing advertisements in the local paper. "Lost the chit and can't remember which one."

The woman's slightly contemptuous smile suggested that in her opinion losing an important bit of paper was just the sort of thing an incompetent male could be expected to do. "Well, I can't help you," she said, rubbing vigorously at a plate engraved with the words Regency Investments Ltd. "You'll have to wait till he comes in. Or maybe one of the others will know – but none of *them* gets in much before half-past eight," she added with a certain malicious relish.

Terry considered, wondering how to prise more information out of her. "I'll have to do another job first and give the boss a ring later," he said after a moment. "Is he the bloke who drives the red Jag, by the way?"

"That's right. Mr Bayliss."

He nodded, affecting recognition of the name. "Yeah, Mr Bayliss, that's the gentleman I spoke to."

"You want to leave a message for him?" The woman's earlier hostility seemed to be thawing a little.

After a second's hesitation, he said, "Yeah, why not? Say Terry Holland called round and will be in touch." He went back to the van, whistling. *That should set old Charlie looking over his shoulder*, he said to himself.

Hugo was in a good mood on Monday morning. He'd just laid his hands on a small fortune, enough to get him out of what could have turned into a tricky situation and leave him on easy street for the foreseeable future. All kinds of possibilities lay open, he could treat himself to almost anything he wanted. He'd change his car for the latest model, order some new suits and that set of fancy golf clubs he had his eye on. He could spend some of it on Sukey, take her to the best restaurants, fancy clubs, weekends in London hotels. That'd impress her. Judging by the battered old car she drove to the Bodywise Club she wasn't exactly flush. Later on he'd maybe take Barbie on a cruise to the Bahamas. She'd enjoy that, she could have loads of new clothes for the trip and join in all the organised fun while he sized up the available talent. There were always plenty of spare women on these cruises, so he'd heard, simply asking for it. He'd have to be careful though, not start chucking too much cash around too soon. Folks might start asking questions. But he wasn't likely to make that kind of mistake. He was too smart, wasn't he? He sat down to breakfast with the *Financial Times* – he always read the FT because it fitted his image – happy in the knowledge that all was right in his particular world.

Barbie was reading one of the tabloids, rustling the pages as she turned them over. Normally he'd have shouted at her to keep quiet when he was trying to read, but in his present mood it didn't bother him. Usually he didn't encourage her to talk at the breakfast table either, but he didn't even snap at her when she exclaimed, "Ooh! Char . . . I mean Hugo, there's been a murder in a village just the other side of Gloucester. A big house burgled and the woman strangled!" Encouraged by his silence, she read the story aloud, lingering with some relish over the more sensational details.

Hugo sat very still, making no comment, his brain racing. The story had been hyped up of course, to give readers the shudders and make them thank their lucky stars it had all happened to someone else. There were references to the house being ransacked and the desperate struggle for life the victim had put up but, to Hugo's intense relief, no mention of any large amount of missing cash. That confirmed his suspicions; Arthur Chant had kept quiet about its loss rather than have to explain where it came from and why he hadn't paid tax on it. By the same token, he'd probably said nothing about the jewellery either, as the chances were that some or all of it had been acquired with money that should have gone to the Treasury.

Hugo wondered how long it would be before the police paid Terry Holland a visit. With any luck, someone would have reported seeing the van and Arthur Chant would remember employing Terry to install the floor safe. Then the possibility that he'd had a spare key cut before doing the job would occur to one of the investigating officers. Once Terry was in the frame, enquiries would be made and his previous record would come to light. If not, there was always the anonymous tip-off to point them in the right direction. Hugo flattered himself that laying that false trail had been a stroke of genius, especially now it was a murder hunt. That hadn't been part of the original plan and it meant he'd have to be more careful than ever to keep his own tracks well covered.

He finished his breakfast and got up from the table. Barbie was deep in the latest royal scandal and didn't raise her eyes from her paper. Not that he noticed; he had other fish to fry. He really fancied Sukey and he was banking on her being at the club again this morning. Before leaving the house he checked in the bathroom mirror to make sure he'd shaved properly and then gave himself an extra splash of Chanel.

He collected his exercise gear, went back to the breakfast room and gave Barbie her routine goodbye kiss, sliding a hand inside her robe and giving her breast a playful squeeze. To his annoyance, instead of putting her own hand over his in response, as was expected of her, she pushed him aside, stood up and began clearing the table.

"What's up with you, then?" he demanded.

"Nothing," she said, her voice flat, her face blank. "Have a good day – and don't forget your check-up."

"Sod it!" In the excitement of planning the robbery he'd totally overlooked his six-monthly appointment. He'd been feeling so fit lately he'd almost forgotten he was supposed to have a heart condition. Nothing to get alarmed about, the consultant had explained, just follow a few sensible rules . . . regular exercise . . . watch your diet . . . blah, blah, blah . . . and come and see me twice a year. *And pay you a fat fee for the privilege of telling me that everything's OK*, Hugo thought irritably as he got into his car. The reminder had taken the shine off his feeling of self-satisfaction. He saw nothing illogical in blaming Barbie for his change of mood.

Sukey, pedalling away on one of the exercise bikes, had been keeping an eye open, half hoping, half fearing that the man who called himself Gary would show. She knew that what she was planning was risky. There was something about the man that she instinctively mistrusted. He was just too good-looking, too well-groomed, too smarmily charming to be genuine. It wouldn't surprise her to learn that Gary wasn't his real name, but uppermost in her mind at the moment was the fact that he had offered her the chance to do a job on the side and earn a bit of extra cash. She was confident she could look after herself; she hadn't been to karate classes for nothing. Of course, on account of her job she shouldn't even be considering it, but she kept seeing the expression on Fergus's face when he told her to forget about the school trip because he couldn't ask his father to help with the cost and he knew his mother couldn't afford all of it. If he'd whined and whinged and said it wasn't fair, she could have pointed out that it wasn't a fair world and she had to do without things she wanted as well – but he hadn't. It was his stoical acceptance of the situation that had wrung her heart.

Sukey concentrated on keeping a steady rhythm on the bike. It was early, and so far she was the only person there apart from Rick, the young instructor who was normally on duty on Monday mornings. He was making some adjustment to the treadmill and when he had finished he stopped for a word with her on his way back to the front desk. He was a nice boy, fresh out of college, with a clean, wholesome look that made him an ideal advertisement for a health club. Sometimes he had a remote, almost sad expression, but there was nothing sad about him this morning as he stood chatting while Sukey pedalled away.

They were interrupted by a man's voice calling out, "Here you, get out my programme, will you?" It was Gary. There had been an aggressive quality about that peremptory summons and it was plain from the way Rick's smile faded and his jaw tightened that he resented the older man's attitude, but he hesitated for only a fraction of a second before going to do as he was asked. Sukey felt considerable sympathy with the lad as she watched him brush past Gary without looking at him. As a former police recruit, she had had some experience of bullying superiors.

Hugo arrived at his office after his workout in a high good humour. Sukey, after an initial hesitation that he felt sure was put on for effect, had agreed to come out to his place on Wednesday morning to do a series of shots of his house and garden. In the car park, he'd scribbled his home address on the back of his business card, explaining that he used a 'nomm dee ploom' when visiting his clubs because he liked to keep an eye on things without his employees knowing who he really was. Sukey had seemed impressed and promised not to tell.

He had, of course, repeated his story that it was his wife who wanted the photos and let it be understood that she'd be there to supervise, but the reason he'd suggested Wednesday was that he knew Barbie was spending the day shopping in Oxford with a friend. He had boasted to Sukey about the pool – which was bigger than either of his neighbours' and had a Jacuzzi – and the sauna he'd recently installed. He had plans to entice her into the sauna. He pictured her half-naked body close to his in the warm, steamy twilight – the prospect excited him so much that he had to stay in the car for several minutes after parking until things calmed down.

Thinking of the sauna reminded him of a less pleasant prospect: the appointment with his consultant. The pompous twit had frowned and shaken his head when he mentioned it and gone on at some length about excessive heat being risky. Such a load of rot. He swam and did his workouts without any ill-effects, and the occasional twinge of discomfort in his chest was probably nothing more than wind. But of course, a consultant couldn't charge a fat fee every six months for telling a man he had indigestion. If it hadn't been for the rules of his pension scheme he'd have cut out the regular check-ups altogether. He was still feeling disgruntled when he reached his desk.

His temper was not improved when his secretary mentioned that a certain Terry Holland had been looking for him. How the hell, he wondered, had the bugger tracked him down? It had given him a jolt to see the name on the side of the van parked outside the mean little house in the Gloucester side street. Terry and Rita had been in the front garden with the kid at the time, but they'd been looking the other way as he cruised past and he was certain they hadn't spotted him. And

An Inconsiderate Death

when he thought about it, he realised that by carrying out the
plan he'd already hit on, he'd be killing two birds with one
stone. Instead of a complete stranger being stitched up for
what he'd done, it meant that a man who was a potential
threat to himself would be removed at the same time. All in
all, things had worked out pretty well according to plan.

Until now. Now there was the problem of Terry being on
Hugo's track, and there could be only one reason for that: he
wanted his share of the money. He couldn't prove a thing, of
course. He hadn't been able to at the trial and he didn't have
a cat in hell's chance of doing so now. Just the same, it would
be as well to set things moving right away, instead of waiting
to see if the police picked up the trail without his help. On the
way home that evening, Hugo stopped at a phone box, called
the local nick and left a message for the officer in charge of
the investigation into the Lorraine Chant murder. When they
asked for his name, he hung up. *That'll take young Terry's
mind off any ideas of outsmarting Charlie Foss*, he thought.
He almost chuckled as he got back into the Jag. He was feeling
so pleased at his own cleverness that he never noticed the white
van following discreetly a few vehicles behind him.

"So what's the verdict?" asked Barbie as she handed him his
gin and tonic.

"The check-up, you mean?"

"What else?"

He took a mouthful from his glass before replying. It was
a warm, sunny evening and they were sitting beside the pool,
he fully relaxed on a lounger, Barbie in an upright chair at his
side, her own drink in her hand. She'd been to the hairdresser
and had her face done, and she was wearing a figure-flattering
new dress and the gold necklet he'd given her the other evening.
Looking at her, he reflected that on the whole he hadn't done
too badly by marrying her. Some birds – Lorraine had been
a classic example – were too smart for their own good, while

61

others were so dim it was embarrassing. Barbie was somewhere in between, apart from a tiresome habit of now and again forgetting to call him Hugo instead of Charlie. So far, apart from that one lapse – and he'd given her something to remind her not to repeat it – she'd managed not to do it in company. She was still a reasonably good lay as well, he thought lazily, running his eye over the cleavage revealed by her low neckline, although naturally, after fifteen years of marriage, she lacked novelty.

He smacked his lips, picked up a handful of nuts from a dish on the cocktail trolley beside him and stuffed them into his mouth. "OK," he said, in response to her question. "Nothing to report, just the usual rabbit about avoiding stress and not overdoing it."

He sipped his drink while contemplating his property, the fruit of six years of steady improvement in his fortunes. From the time when, recognising that his luck couldn't hold forever, he had made the decision to pack in the precarious profession of bank robber and sink a sizeable slice of the money he'd stashed away in a firm of swimming pool installers on the point of bankruptcy, he'd never looked back.

The house wasn't large – it only had four bedrooms – but it stood in a half-acre plot in one of the most exclusive parts of Cheltenham and he'd picked it up at a bargain price from the executors of the late owner, who were anxious for a quick sale. It had been neglected, but he'd soon had all that put right, calling in professional help with the garden and putting Barbie in charge of the decorations and furnishing. After days spent browsing through glossy magazines she'd gone for what she declared was 'a real up-market look'. When he'd expressed misgivings at the result she'd pointed out that the jazzy carpets, curtains and wallpapers that he'd have gone for, the sort of stuff they'd had in their London flat that all their old friends used to admire, would look all wrong in what the estate agent's blurb had described as 'an elegant, architect-designed residence'.

It had taken a bit of getting used to, but in the end he had to admit she was right.

Finally, he'd had his own workforce in to install the pool and, just a couple of months ago, the sauna. Thinking of the sauna reminded him of Sukey and that made him feel randy again. He held out his empty glass for a refill and when Barbie brought it he put his hand round her calf and slid it up her thigh. "Don't worry, girl, the medics never told me to lay off the other," he said with a leer. "I'll give you a good time later on."

She moved away, po-faced. He recalled her similar lack of response that morning and felt a stab of irritation. "What's up with you?" he asked for the second time that day and, as before, she replied, "Nothing."

His eye fell on the evening paper lying on the ground at her side. Black headlines screamed of the hunt for Lorraine's killer. "Hey!" he said, "you scared of that happening to you? Is that what's on your mind?"

"I've told you, there's nothing on my mind. I must go and see to the dinner."

It seemed to Hugo that she deliberately avoided looking at him as she went into the house. His irritation increased. Here he was, trying to be nice and considerate and getting the cold-shoulder for his pains. He had problems of his own, but he wasn't moaning about them to her. He was about to follow her indoors to have it out with her when he heard the sound of wheels on the drive. A few moments later the doorbell rang.

"Answer that, will you," he shouted over his shoulder before settling back to finish his second drink and admire the expert arrangement of trees and flowering shrubs that screened him from his neighbours. He put down the empty glass and closed his eyes, only vaguely aware of the voices coming from inside the house. He yawned, hoping it wasn't anything that would disrupt the evening. It had been quite a day and all he wanted now was the chance to unwind.

63

The voices came nearer – mostly Barbie's, with the occasional monosyllabic reply from a man. She sounded animated, almost excited. Her high-heeled shoes clicked on the patio as she stepped out of the house.

"You'll never guess who's here!" she said.

Reluctantly, Hugo opened his eyes, squinting upwards, momentarily blinded by the evening sun so that for an instant he was aware only of the figure of a man behind Barbie, a man whose feet had made no sound on the flagstones surrounding the pool and who towered almost menacingly over his own recumbent form. Then a familiar voice said, "Nice place you've got here, Charlie."

Chapter Seven

"Guess you're surprised to see me, Charlie," Terry remarked as Hugo, slow to react and momentarily speechless, struggled into a sitting position. A hand like a slab of concrete landed, none too gently, on his chest and forced him back among the cushions, where he lay staring up into eyes like grey pebbles set in flesh-coloured granite. He was unhappily aware that he had been completely wrong-footed and as his mind grappled with the unwelcome turn of events, astonishment turned to anger. Characteristically, he found a scapegoat in his wife.

"What the hell did you let him in for, you stupid cow!" he shouted. The hand pressed down harder on his chest, the fingers knotted round the front of his shirt. He found himself labouring for air. "For Chrissake Tel, let me breathe, will you," he gasped.

Terry's face loomed close to his. "That ain't no way to talk to your wife and it ain't no way to greet an old friend neither," he informed his unwilling host. "Maybe you should apologise."

"You've got a fucking nerve—"

The fingers shifted their grip and settled round Hugo's throat. "Tell Bren you're sorry."

"OK, OK. Sorry Bar . . . Bren." Instinct warned Hugo just in time that to call his wife by her assumed name would undoubtedly cause derision and possibly increased discomfort. He began to bluster. "No offence meant, Tel, it was just the shock at seeing you . . . I had no idea . . . how d'you know where I live?"

"Well now, that'd be a good story for a winter's night, wouldn't it?" There was an underlying hint of intimidation in the almost jocular tone, but at least the almost unbearable pressure on Hugo's windpipe was released – slowly and deliberately, as if to remind him that it could be renewed at any time.

Terry reached behind him to grab a chair, dragged it to within a couple of feet of Hugo's lounger and sat down. His eyes never left his victim's face and their expression left no doubt that any attempt to move would be asking for trouble. He leaned forward, his hands on his knees, his face grim. "This ain't no social visit, Charlie boy," he said softly. "But you already know why I'm here, don't you – *Mister Hugo bleeding Bayliss!*" The final words were uttered in a contemptuous snarl. "What fancy name did he give you, Bren?" he added over his shoulder to Barbie, who had been standing behind him, motionless. Hugo saw her mouth twitch, her eyes wide with apprehension.

"I'm called Barbie now," she faltered. "We just thought, when Charlie decided to go straight, it'd be nice to have new names, so's we could forget the old days. We was trying to make a new life here, wasn't we Charlie?" Nervousness made her forget the grammar she had studied so diligently and the middle-class accent she had tried to acquire in an attempt to feel at ease among the people Hugo made a point of cultivating. "We was ever so sorry when the bank job went wrong and you and Frank got sent down, but there wasn't nothing we could do."

"No?" A sneer spread from Terry's mouth to his eyes. "Didn't he tell you how it happened that *he* never got caught and sent down?"

"How could he . . . he wasn't even there . . . was you, Charlie?" She rounded on him, her eyes pleading for reassurance, but with a hint of desperation in her voice as if in her heart she already knew the truth.

"That what he told you?" said Terry. She nodded, dumbly,

staring at the ground. "And you believed him, of course. You always was a bit soft. Must have been, to marry him." He cast a withering look at Hugo, who glowered back at him. "Well," he went on, "since Charlie here never seems to have mentioned it, I'm sure you'll be interested to know that he owes Frank and me a little matter of forty grand between us." He turned back to Hugo and his voice took on a note of mock apology. "That's why I've took the liberty of dropping in on your cocktail hour without an invite, just to collect my cut of the bank job that me and Frank got sent down for – after you left us to take the rap, you double-crossing shit!"

He raised his voice on the final words and they seemed to echo and re-echo in the soft evening air, bouncing off the flagstones, skating like flung pebbles across the smooth surface of the pool and out into the garden beyond. Hugo licked his lips and glanced nervously from side to side as if fearful that at any moment curious neighbours would appear, hoping to hear more of the sensational drama so unexpectedly unfolding on their doorsteps.

It was Barbie who broke the silence that followed Terry's denunciation of her husband. "Charlie, is this true?" she demanded, her voice a thin wail. "You told me you had nothing to do with that bank job – was you lying to me? Is that why we left London and all our friends in such a hurry?"

"I've told you before not to go poking your nose in what don't concern you," said Hugo through his teeth, "but if you must know, the lads got round me to do that drive for them so—"

"So he decided to be nice and obliging, and then keep all the cash for himself instead of sharing it with his mates," Terry broke in. "Nice bloke, your Charlie."

"I never meant to," Hugo protested. "I just panicked when I heard Frank had clobbered that punter. I'd have got your share to you once the heat was off. Then it turned into a murder rap and I couldn't do nothing, could I?"

"Bullshit! You planned all along to keep the lot."

"Honest, Tel! I meant to pay you back – and Frank. I didn't know you was out." Little by little, Hugo was recovering his nerve. If he could bluff things out, stall Terry for a day or two until the police got on to him about the Chant job, he figured he could get away with it. Soon there'd be the knock on the door, the questions about the planted evidence, the enquiries and checks that would reveal how Terry Holland had done time for his part in a violent crime . . . that gentleman would soon have something more serious than twenty grand on his mind. Cautiously, feeling more confident by the minute, Hugo shifted into a more upright position on the lounger.

Terry appeared for the moment to have lost interest in him. He got up and put his hands in his pockets. He was wearing overalls and grubby trainers, as if he'd come straight from his last job of the day. Hugo thought of the smart suit he wore to the office and glanced down with a feeling of superiority at the cream linen jacket and slacks he liked to change into on summer evenings. He patted his lapels and smoothed out the creases that Terry's grip had left on the front of his made-to-measure shirt – all the time keeping a wary eye on his former partner in crime, who stood looking around, directing his gaze this way and that, taking everything in: the house, the garden, the pool, the sauna, the ornamental tubs brimming with flowers, for all the world like a prospective buyer sizing the place up.

"Well, now, I wouldn't mind living somewhere like this, Charlie," he observed, and a stranger listening in would have been hard put to it to detect anything but a friendly admiration in the comment. "Sauna too," he added, as if he had only just noticed. "Really done yourself proud, ain't you? Sexy things, saunas, so I hear. You go in it with him, Bren?"

"No." The monosyllable was a faint whisper.

"You want to watch he don't take some other bird in there

– and mind you don't have it too hot, Charlie, not with your dodgy ticker. Or is it OK now you're living the high life? There don't seem much wrong with you at the moment."

"I'm fine, thank you," said Hugo icily.

"Glad to hear it. Wouldn't be good for business if you got sick, would it? I particularly want your business to do well – till you've paid your debts, that is. After that, I don't give a monkey's. Unless you feel like taking me on as a partner. You could do worse – we've worked together before. It'd be nice for Bren and Rita as well, they always used to hit it off."

"Well now, that's something we could talk about," Hugo replied, affecting interest in a proposal which privately filled him with horror. "I'd have to discuss it with my fellow directors, of course. Why don't you give us time to think it over? Come and see me again in a week or two."

Abruptly, Terry's demeanour changed. He swung on his heel, grabbed the startled Hugo by his lapels and yanked him to his feet. "I'll be back all right, you rat," he hissed. "You pay me every penny of what you owe me, or I'll make sure all your posh friends know how Mister Hugo fucking Bayliss used to be one Charlie Foss whose name cropped up at a certain trial and who used to keep some very dodgy company. You might not be welcome at the golf club, Charlie boy, if that got around."

"No need to take that line, Terry old son." The notion flew into Hugo's head that it might be a good idea to offer to hand over a few hundred right away. There was a good chance the police would find it and, like the other planted evidence, it would be very difficult to explain. There was plenty of cash in the house, courtesy of the late but unlamented Lorraine. "I was just going to say, if you're short, I can let you have a bit to be going on with."

The offer appeared to take Terry by surprise. He released his grip and gave Hugo a shove in the direction of the house. "Good idea, why didn't I think of it? Go on then – fetch!"

Inwardly seething, but doing his best to retain some shreds

69

of dignity, Hugo went indoors. Barbie started to follow, but he stopped her with a gesture, saying in his best, polite society manner, "You stay here and entertain our guest – perhaps he'd like a drink." The last thing he wanted was for Barbie to see him go to the bag of money and jewels hidden in the back of his wardrobe. He hurried to the bedroom, got out one of the bundles of fifties that Lorraine had taken from her unsuspecting husband's safe and went back downstairs. Terry was standing at the edge of the pool. His hands were still in his pockets; evidently he had declined the offer of a drink. Barbie was a short distance away, staring out at the garden, her hands clasped in front of her, her face expressionless.

"OK, here's something on account," Hugo said, offering the notes with the air of a philanthropist distributing largesse. "It'll take a week or two to arrange the rest, of course – a large sum like that." *By which time you'll have more pressing problems to worry about*, he thought to himself.

"Week or two be buggered." The semblance of good humour faded from Terry's expression as he pocketed the money. "I want at least five grand by Wednesday or there'll be trouble." He glanced down at the blue water a couple of feet away and added casually, "Think it over while you're having your swim."

Before Hugo realised what was happening he was picked up as if he weighed no more than a child and dumped into the pool. As he struggled to the surface, Terry squatted down and said, in an almost conversational tone, "That was just a warning. Any funny business and I'll cook you in your own sauna." He stood up, brushing his hands together in a symbolic gesture of triumph. Then he turned to Barbie, reached out a hand and fingered the gold necklace. "*Very* nice," he said with a nod of approval. "Rita'd like one of those. Guess I'll soon be able to afford to get her one. It's OK, Bren, I'll see meself out. I think Charlie needs a hand." There was a blend of mockery and contempt in his smile as his eyes rested briefly on the figure floundering in the water before he turned and vanished into the house.

Shocked and bemused by the events and revelations of the past few minutes, Barbie stared dumbly after his retreating back until a furious shout from behind her brought her back to reality. Hugo had reached the side of the pool and was heaving himself up the ladder. He stood grasping the rails, coughing and spluttering, looking down at his sodden, ruined suit with a mixture of fury and disbelief. Then his eyes focused on Barbie; he grabbed her by the arm, twisting it behind her, and propelled her towards the open patio door. "Inside, you!" he rasped.

"What are you doing? You're hurting me," she pleaded, but his only response was to wrench her arm further backwards until she screamed.

He marched her into the kitchen, spun her round and pinned her against a cupboard. "How did he know where to find me?" he snarled. "Tell me that."

"I don't know," she stammered. Her throat was so constricted by fear of what was to come that she could hardly speak. Whether it was her fault or not, she was the one who was going to pay the penalty for the humiliation he had just suffered. "Honest, Charlie," she pleaded.

"*Hugo*! How many times do I have to tell you . . . my name's Hugo!" He slapped her twice, hard, across the face. Bright lights flashed in front of her eyes.

"I'm sorry . . . Hugo," she whimpered.

"Did you tell him?" He took her by the shoulders and slammed her hard against the cupboard door. "Did you?" Dumbly, she shook her head. "So it must have been your fucking big-mouthed Auntie Gwen. And there's only one way she could have found out, and that's through you, you two-faced bitch!"

"But I never—"

"You're lying!"

71

She raised her arms to protect her face from further blows. She could taste the blood flowing from her cut lips. "Please, Hugo, don't—"

"Shut up!" He punched her in the ribs and she lurched sideways, gasping with the shock and pain of it. "You've been to see that old cow – admit it! I told you to keep away from her! A fine bloody mess you've landed me in now. Get out of my sight!"

With a final box on the ears, he released her and she slithered, moaning, to the floor. Her head was swimming and there was blood in her eyes. On hands and knees she groped her way to the door and felt a fresh stab of agony as he kicked her in the buttocks. Reaching the hall, she clawed her way upstairs and collapsed onto the bed. Moments later she became aware that Hugo had followed her into the room and she rolled over and buried her face in a pillow to stifle her sobs, knowing from experience that they would only infuriate him further. She braced herself for further punishment, but mercifully it never came. She could hear him moving about, swearing, banging cupboard doors, running the taps in the bathroom. Then, without a word to her, he went out, slamming the door behind him.

It was a long time before she dared to move. She had a vague recollection of hearing the front door close, of the sound of his car starting up. She struggled to her feet, aware that the light outside was fading but with no clear idea of how long she had been lying on the bed or of the time it took her to stand up, stagger to the bathroom and switch on the light. She knew only that each movement sent stabs of pain to every part of her body. Slowly and unsteadily, supporting herself by grasping at furniture, the door handle, the towel rail, she reached the washbasin. When she caught sight of herself in the mirror, more sobs welled up in her throat and tears of pain and misery trickled from her swollen eyes, down her inflamed cheeks and into her blood-encrusted mouth.

A prolonged hot shower brought some relief to her body, but did little to assuage her despair. She dabbed the bruises with witch hazel, put on a robe and went downstairs. Hugo's linen suit and underwear lay in a sodden heap on the kitchen floor – waiting, no doubt, for her to arrange for them to be laundered. In a spasm of fury she kicked them into a corner and trampled on them, hating them, hating him, wishing he was still inside them so that she could hurt him the way he had so many times hurt her. There was a litter of used plates and cutlery on the table, evidence that he had eaten some of the food she had prepared earlier. He had changed into dry clothes, had a meal and gone out without giving her a thought, probably in search of entertainment. She peered at the clock on the wall. It was almost nine, nearly two hours since Terry's visit and its violent aftermath.

She went to a cupboard, found a bottle of painkillers and swallowed three with a drink of water. She sat turning the bottle between her fingers, toying with the idea of taking the lot, of putting an end to it once and for all. Then she slammed it down on the table in a gesture of rage and defiance, thinking, *Why should I kill myself for you, you bastard!*

The thought of food made her retch, but she brewed some coffee and drank two cups of it, black and scalding. There was only one thought in her mind: this time he had gone too far. It wasn't the first beating he'd given her, not by a long way, but it was far and away the most savage. All these years she had stuck with him, fearing him, longing for freedom. She would have given anything at that moment to be able to pack her bags and walk out, go anywhere so long as she never set eyes on her husband again, go back to Auntie Gwen and the old crowd she missed so much. They would give her moral support, love, protection . . . but the one thing they couldn't give her was the life of luxury that she was loth to forgo.

It might have been easier to bear if she had a close woman friend, someone she could open her heart to, but there was no one. She felt no affinity with the wives of Hugo's business and golfing cronies and she suspected that they despised them both, probably laughed behind their backs at his pretensions and her efforts to copy their speech and manners. She could never confide in any of them, not in a million years.

Then a thought occurred to her. Perhaps there was someone after all. She went to the telephone and tapped out a number.

Chapter Eight

Terry sang along with the van radio as he drove home. He felt he had won the first skirmish with Charlie Foss very handsomely. Not only had the bastard ended up with a well-deserved ducking – Terry broke off in mid-warble to have a prolonged chuckle at the memory – but he'd capitulated hands down, handed over a nice little fistful (a quick count had revealed exactly five hundred smackers, all in used fifties), and even promised to consider taking him into partnership. That hadn't been a serious suggestion. The last thing Terry wanted was to get mixed up with a crowd of toffee-nosed yuppies, but it warmed his heart to think that he had enough hold over Charlie to make him feel under pressure to arrange it. He couldn't wait to get home and tell Rita. She'd have to take back all her gloomy predictions. He took one hand off the wheel and patted his pocket, enjoying the feel of the roll of banknotes. *Wait till you get an eyeful of these, my girl,* he thought. *And this is only a fleabite compared with what's to follow.*

His ebullient mood was only slightly dented when, on arrival in his home street, he found a strange car parked outside his house. It wasn't one he recognised so he couldn't blame any of his neighbours. It meant he had to park several yards farther down, but he told himself it wasn't important, it was all going too well to let himself get narked over a little thing like that. He was in such a hurry to tell Rita the news that he went straight indoors in his working gear. She hated him coming into the house looking scruffy and dirty, so he normally took off his overalls and the shabby old trainers he wore on the job and left them in the van. She wouldn't nag him today, not when she heard what he had to tell her.

She must have been listening for the sound of his key in the lock because the second he opened the front door she was there.

"Sorry I'm a bit late," he began, "but wait till you hear what I—" He broke off, feeling a stab of alarm at the look on her face. "What's up, love? Is something wrong with Billy?"

"No, Billy's fine. He's having tea with one of his mates." She lowered her voice and cast a fearful glance behind her. "Tel, the police are here. What've you been up to?"

"I ain't been up to nothing." The denial was automatic, but the news was like a punch in the stomach. Charlie must have shopped him after all, but how had he known what address to give? There was the phone book, of course, but there must be any number of Hollands, so how would he know which was the right one? He wasn't listed in Yellow Pages – couldn't afford it, not yet. He was on the verge of panic when a thought struck him. "How long've they been here?" he asked.

"Nearly half an hour. I told them you'd be home any time and they said they'd wait."

Terry blew out a huge breath of relief. It couldn't be anything to do with Charlie, there hadn't been time. His brain began to function more calmly.

"Did they say what it's about?"

"I asked them, but they wouldn't tell me. Tel, are you sure you haven't – I mean, you're awfully late."

"It's all OK. Tell you later," he whispered. "It's probably to do with the van," he continued in his normal voice, taking her by the arm and leading her along the tiny passage. "Maybe they found out who nicked it."

There were two plain-clothes detectives in the sitting room and they stood up when Terry and Rita entered. They showed

76

him their identity badges: Detective Sergeant Radcliffe, grey-haired and middle-aged, and his younger, fresh-faced colleague Detective Constable Hill of Gloucester CID.

"We understand you recently reported the theft of a white Ford van, registration number DF 191 X," said the sergeant.

"That's right." Terry sat down on the shabby settee with Rita beside him and indicated with a nonchalant wave of a hand that the two officers should resume their seats. When they were all settled he said affably, "Last Friday it was, and your boys found it the same day. Brilliant – must be a record!"

"It wasn't even damaged," Rita put in eagerly.

"I'm glad we managed to trace it so quickly." Radcliffe gave a benign smile. "We like to give service to honest citizens."

Terry felt a twinge of unease at the final words. Was the guy taking the piss? Had someone turned up his record? He tried to keep up his relaxed attitude as he asked, "So what's the problem? The tax and insurance are OK and it's passed its MOT."

"We have no reason to think there are problems in that direction, sir." There was something about the politeness of Radcliffe's manner and the bland quality of his voice that made Terry uneasy. He wasn't used to this sort of treatment from the police. "The fact is, Mr Holland," the sergeant continued, "we *do* have reason to believe that during the period when you say the vehicle was out of your possession, it was used in furtherance of a crime."

Terry's mouth fell open. Had he imagined the faintest of emphasis on the words 'you say the vehicle was out of your possession', as if the man was hinting he'd only pretended the van had been nicked? It was an old trick, too obvious to be seriously relied on by an old lag like him – except, of course, that they didn't *know* he was an old lag and he'd no intention of letting on. He'd have to be bloody careful what he said.

77

Out of the corner of his eye he saw Rita's head twist sharply in his direction. It wasn't difficult to guess what she was thinking, but he knew he had nothing to hide on that score. "A crime?" he repeated. "What sort of crime?"

"Murder," said Radcliffe. "We're conducting a murder inquiry, Mr Holland, and we're hoping you may be able to help us." He spoke softly, deliberately, his eyes never leaving Terry's face. The technique was all too familiar. Watching for a reaction, that's what the man was up to. Well, he wouldn't learn anything about a murder by looking at Terry Holland. More confidently than at any time since he'd been picked up and questioned about his first burglary at the age of fifteen, he could look straight back and speak with a clear conscience.

"How'm I supposed to know what the van was used for after it'd been nicked?" he demanded, perhaps a little too aggressively.

Radcliffe did not appear to have heard the question. He dropped his eyes briefly to his notebook before asking, "Have you ever done work for anyone living on The Hill in Marsdean? A village about five miles south of Gloucester," he added helpfully as Terry hesitated.

"Yeah, I know where Marsdean is. I'm not sure I ever . . . I'd have to check. The log's in the van, I'll go and get it."

"Thank you." Radcliffe flicked a glance at the constable, who stood up and followed him as he made for the door.

"What's up?" he asked resentfully. "Think I'm going to do a runner?"

"Just routine, sir."

"Suit yourself." In silence, the two men walked the short distance to the van. Terry unlocked the passenger door, took a thick loose-leaf notebook out of the glove compartment and thrust it under the constable's nose. "You'd better carry it back, just in case I tear out the odd incriminating sheet," he said sarcastically.

"No one's suggesting you'd do that sir," the young officer

replied politely, but he took the book and waited while Terry relocked the van.

When they were back indoors, Terry asked, "Any idea when it would have been?" and began flipping through the pages. "Or who the job was for?"

"Try early May," suggested Radcliffe. "Mr Arthur Chant."

"Oh yeah, I remember him – owns all the amusement arcades. I done a repair job for him after some yobbos smashed a window. Then he asked me to do a private job at his house."

"What sort of job would that be, sir?"

"He wanted a floor safe installed in his study." As he spoke, Terry found the relevant page in the log. "Here it is – tenth of May. I charged him twenty quid plus the cost of the safe." He handed the book over for verification and both officers looked at it and nodded. The young constable wrote the details in his own notebook and the log was returned to Terry, who looked from one to the other and asked, "Anything happened to Mr Chant? Was it him as got topped?"

"You don't read the newspapers, Mr Holland?"

"Can't say I do."

"Then you may not have heard that Mr Chant came home on Friday evening and found his wife's body in the bedroom. She had been strangled."

"No kidding!" Terry exclaimed in genuine astonishment.

"No kidding," the sergeant assured him gravely.

"Poor cow. I remember her . . . she came in while I was doing the job. Good-looking bird."

"So I understand." Radcliffe paused, then said, "There were signs of forced entry; we think she may have disturbed an intruder."

"So what's all this got to do with me?" Terry didn't like the way this conversation was going, not one little bit. The sergeant's next words did nothing to allay his anxiety.

"The thing is, Mr Holland, our information is that your

van was seen in the vicinity of Mr Chant's residence at about ten thirty on the morning in question. Did you by any chance have another job in Marsdean last Friday?"

Terry spotted the trap and avoided it. "How the hell could I without the van and all me gear?"

"Of course not, I was forgetting," said the sergeant smoothly. "You reported the theft at," there was more consultation of notebooks, "half-past seven that morning."

"You saying whoever took it topped Mrs Chant? Bloody hell!" There was nothing contrived about Terry's expression of shock and revulsion. Violence was nothing new in his life – he'd grown up in one of the toughest areas in South London – and he'd made threats more than once in the course of a robbery, although he'd never had occasion to carry them out. Mostly the victims were too scared to do anything but hand over. But ever since that terrible scene in the bank when Frank had lost his nerve and brought the sawn-off shotgun down on the old man's head, the thought of actual, deliberate violence sickened him. Putting the wind up someone, roughing them up a bit like he'd just done to Charlie Foss – there were times when circumstances called for that. Murder was something else.

Radcliffe broke into his thoughts with a question. "Have you any idea at all who might have taken your vehicle?" he asked.

"Course not, I'd have said. But if there's anything I can do to help—" He meant it, too.

"We appreciate that, Mr Holland. For a start, we'd like to have the van down at the station so that our people can go over it again, a bit more thoroughly." His tone was respectful, almost conciliatory. "We realise you use it for your business, so we'll keep it no longer than absolutely necessary. I understand your fingerprints have already been taken for elimination purposes so we won't need to go through that again. I take it you have no objection?" he added, his eyes searching Terry's in a way that did nothing to put that gentleman at ease.

"Er, no, course not." It would be inconvenient to have to part with the van, even for a short time, but that wasn't his main worry. If some smart-arse of a copper who wasn't too bothered about sticking to the rules compared his elims with national records and found he had form, he could be in deep trouble. They hadn't asked him what he'd been doing on the day of the murder and if they did, all he could say was that he'd been kicking his heels at home because without so much as a screwdriver left to his name he'd had to cancel the jobs he'd lined up. He hadn't stuck his nose outside the door all day. The nearest thing he had to an alibi was Reg Hodson's phone call and he couldn't say for sure what time that had come through. In any case, the word of an old lag like Reg wouldn't count for much.

"Right, shall we go?" The sergeant turned to Rita, who had been sitting silently on the couch throughout the interview. "My apologies for the inconvenience, Mrs Holland. One of our officers will give your husband a lift home – it shouldn't take long."

When they were outside, Radcliffe said, "Constable Hill will go with you so he can give you directions."

"No need. I know me way round Gloucester."

"He'll show you the quickest route." The tone was courteous but firm. The sergeant was taking no chances.

Terry shrugged and unlocked the van. "If you insist."

They reached the central police station and drove into the yard. DC Hill showed Terry where to park the van, took charge of the key and accompanied him into the building. A young woman with dark hair and pale, sharp features was at the counter talking to Sergeant Radcliffe and another man who, like the woman, was in plain clothes. They broke off their conversation as Terry and the constable approached.

"Ah, Mr Holland – this is Detective Inspector Castle," said Radcliffe. "Mr Holland is the owner of the vehicle we've been speaking about, sir," he explained. "He's very kindly agreed to allow us to examine it and to cooperate in any way he can."

"We appreciate that, thank you," said Castle. He turned to the young woman and said, "OK, Sukey, it's all yours."

She took the key from DC Hill, but said to the Inspector, "Could I have a word first, Mr Castle?"

"Sure." They moved a short distance away and spoke for a few moments in low tones. Although neither of them glanced in his direction, Terry had an uncomfortable feeling that they were talking about him. Then the woman called Sukey picked up a case from the counter and went out. Terry felt her eyes on him as she passed, as if she was mentally taking his photograph.

"What happens now?" Terry asked the sergeant. "I mean, do I have to stay here and wait for the van, or what?"

"I believe Inspector Castle would like a word with you before you go, if you wouldn't mind following me." Without giving Terry a chance to say whether he minded or not, Radcliffe opened a door and beckoned him through.

He was left cooling his heels for a good ten minutes before DI Castle entered the room where Radcliffe had left him. To Terry, becoming more fidgety by the minute, it seemed a hell of a lot longer. When the Inspector finally appeared, he pulled up a chair and sat for a second or two without speaking, his hands slowly massaging his thighs. His greenish eyes had a steady, unwavering stare, his nose had a distinct hook to it and his thin fingers curved like talons over his kneecaps. Terry was reminded of a bird of prey. He had once remarked to Rita that he reckoned it was part of police training to fix people in the eye as if trying to hypnotise them into owning up to whatever crime they were suspected of committing. But he wasn't suspected of anything today – was he?

"We're most grateful to you for being so cooperative, Mr Holland," Castle began. "We hope to return your vehicle later this evening."

"Make sure you do. I need it – it's me living." During his

enforced wait, Terry had decided that, as an upright and public spirited citizen whose ready cooperation with the police was causing him considerable inconvenience, it would be quite in order for him to make it known that his patience was wearing a little thin. "And how'm I supposed to get home without it?" he added aggrievedly. "I haven't even had me tea yet."

"I realise you're being put to considerable inconvenience," said Castle. "One of my officers will give you a lift home shortly. Meanwhile, I have one more small request to make."

"Oh yeah, what's that?"

"Those overalls you're wearing – are they the ones you said were in your van when it was stolen?"

"Yeah, what of it?"

"My Scene of Crime Officer has reminded me that a piece of green thread was found on bushes at the point where an intruder entered Mr Chant's house. We'd like to have forensics compare it with those overalls."

"You reckon this guy actually dressed up in my gear to do the job?" Terry was affronted. It was bad enough pinching his van and losing him a day's work without having the cheek to wear his clothes.

"We think it's possible. If you wouldn't mind—?" Evidently, he was expected to hand over the overalls there and then. He stood up, undid the Velcro fastening and stepped out of them, dragging the legs awkwardly over his trainers. As he handed them over, the hawk-eyes switched to his feet.

"He might even have worn your shoes," said Castle. "Are those—?"

"Yeah, so what? There must be hundreds of trainers like these knocking around."

"There are always small differences. Perhaps when you get home, you wouldn't mind putting on another pair so that—"

"Yeah, OK, anything you say, only please, can I go home now? The wife'll be worried sick."

"Please give her my personal apologies."

As Castle began stuffing the overalls into a brown paper bag, Terry remembered what was in the pocket. "Hang on a minute," he said hurriedly. "I've just remembered, I've left some cash in there."

"Oh, right." The inspector pulled the garment out again, but to Terry's dismay, instead of passing it back, he put his own hand into the pocket and brought out the roll of Charlie's fifties. He riffled casually through the notes before handing them over. "That's rather a large sum to carry around," he commented blandly, his eyebrows climbing up his high forehead.

"Yeah, well, some people like to settle in cash," Terry muttered as he stuffed the roll into his jeans pocket.

"Very true," Castle agreed, adding casually, "and I believe some people like to be paid in cash – something to do with income tax."

"Here, what are you suggesting?" This time, Terry's indignation was spontaneous and genuine. He knew that robbing banks wasn't the only thing a bloke could be sent down for and ever since he started his one-man business he'd done his best, with Rita's help, to keep his accounts in some sort of order. "You're welcome to check my books any time," he said huffily.

"I assure you, Mr Holland, I'm not accusing *you* of tax evasion."

"I should bloody well hope not!" Terry looked Castle straight in the eye and saw the hawk-like features relax into something approaching a smile. As he told Rita afterwards, it made the guy look almost human.

Chapter Nine

Sukey was alone in the SOCOs' office when DI Castle looked in and asked, "Did you find anything interesting in the van?" She took a heavy duty envelope from her pigeonhole and handed it to him. He ran his eye down the list of exhibits written on the outside in her neat printing. "Gravel from the tyres . . . did you take a sample from Chant's drive?"

"Sure – all in there. They look the same to the naked eye, but I understand the owner of the van went to the house on legitimate business quite recently."

"Over four weeks ago, according to his own records."

"It's hardly likely to have remained in the treads that long. We had some quite heavy rain towards the end of May."

"What do the shoeprints tell us?"

"The ones we found in the house gave traces of white powder. There was white powder on the floor of the van and on some of the tools – probably plaster or paint particles. I took samples of both. This is interesting." Sukey held up a brown paper bag. "Terry Holland's overalls. I'm almost a hundred per cent certain our man was wearing them. There's all sorts of dust on them – a lot of it sawdust by the looks of it – but see here." She pulled the garment out and pointed to a tear in the fabric. "Remember the scrap of green cotton that I found outside the window? That little tear is on the seat . . . and you see these yellowish smudges? There are more on the legs. Where the intruder entered there are roses up to window height and yellow lichen growing on the concrete sill. The tear

85

and the marks suggest he scrambled to a sitting position on the outside sill, catching his overalls on a thorn in the process. Then he probably swung himself round and jumped down into the room, leaving the prints we found on the carpet."

Castle gave a grunt of satisfaction. "It fits so far. What else?"

"Fingerprints galore, of course. Probably mostly Mr Holland's, although on things like tins of paint there'd be others from the place where he bought them. Unless we can match any of them with prints found in the house, they won't tell us much. And then there's this." She placed a plastic envelope containing something that glittered on the desk.

Castle held it up to the light. It was a pendant earring set with diamonds; through the clear film, the stones flashed with a myriad bright colours. He gave a soft whistle. "That never came out of a Christmas cracker," he observed.

"No chance," Sukey agreed.

"Where did you find it?"

"At the bottom of the tool box. It must have fallen out of the bag where our man put the rest of his haul."

"No surface large enough to get a print, but if Mr Chant recognises it as belonging to his wife—" Castle put the earring aside. "Anything else?"

"When Janice checked the van after it was recovered, she found a partial thumb-print on the rear-view mirror. Holland was quite definite that when he adjusts it, he holds it by the frame the way most of us do."

"You reckon it was left by whoever nicked the van?"

"Looks like it, don't you think?"

"I have my doubts." Castle frowned and drummed on the desk with the long, sensitive fingers that Terry Holland had mentally compared to talons. "Is that it?"

"There's the trainers DC Hill brought back after taking Holland home." Sukey indicated a second brown paper bag. "From a visual comparison of the soles with the photos of the

An Inconsiderate Death

shoeprints in the house, they could be the same, but obviously they need going over in the lab."

"Right. Get that lot on its way first thing in the morning and ask for it to have priority treatment."

"Will do." Sukey glanced behind her to make sure the door was closed before adding, "If that's all, Jim, I'd like to get home. I haven't eaten yet and—"

"Nor have I. Why don't we both grab something now?"

It was tempting, but . . . "Not this evening, thanks all the same. Fergus is on his own."

"Oh, right."

It always seemed to be like this. They were seldom free at the same time and when they were, other responsibilities got in the way. Sometimes Sukey felt resentful and, because she made no attempt to kid herself that she wasn't attracted to Jim Castle, frustrated. At others, she was grateful for an excuse to avoid situations that might lead to a commitment. Her love for Paul was long since dead, but the sense of betrayal remained and the memory of the pain made her shrink from the possibility of repeating the experience. Once you let yourself care for someone, you handed them the power to hurt you.

Castle was staring out of the window. He had taken his car keys from his pocket and was holding them balanced on his palm. Several times he tossed them an inch or two in the air and then caught them again. It was a habit of his when he was concentrating. If it wasn't keys, it was whatever else happened to be around: coins, an apple, a pencil sharpener or an eraser from his desk, anything to occupy his hand while his brain wrestled with a problem.

"Is something bothering you?" Sukey asked.

He swung round to face her. "A couple of things. One, Chant told us none of his wife's jewellery was missing. If he's telling the truth, where did that earring come from?"

"He could have been mistaken. Or maybe his wife was wearing the earrings when she was attacked and this one

87

fell off in the struggle . . . no, come to think of it, she was wearing gold ones and they were still on the body."

Castle put the keys away, sat down at one of the empty desks and took out his notebook. "Maybe there were some loose pieces lying around that she hadn't bothered to put back in the safe. I'll call on Chant tomorrow and ask if he recognises the one you found, and also whether he's done the complete check he promised. He said he had photographs of all the valuable items, so it shouldn't be difficult."

"You said there were a couple of things," Sukey reminded him after a pause during which he appeared deep in further thought.

"So I did. Chant insisted no money had been taken. Now, it may be a coincidence, but Holland had a wad of notes in his overall pocket. Ten or a dozen fifties, much more than you'd expect a self-employed handyman to be carrying."

"Did he say where it came from?"

"He claims he'd been collecting payments owing to him from people who preferred to deal in cash."

"That could be true. I assume you let him keep it?"

"I didn't have a valid excuse to hang on to it."

Sukey sat down again, her brain busy with various possibilities. "Just supposing Chant did have money in that safe that he wouldn't like us – or the Revenue – to know about, and assuming the safe was locked, is there any way Holland could have got into it?"

"He's the one who installed it . . . he told us so quite openly. But he could have had an extra key cut beforehand that he didn't bother to mention."

"In which case, the story about the van being nicked could be a fake?"

"It's not the most original of alibis, is it? I got the impression, and so did Radcliffe, that he wasn't entirely comfortable answering our questions – although to be fair, he seemed quite anxious to help us find Mrs Chant's killer. I'd still like to know how he came by that cash, though." Castle yawned and got to his feet. "That's enough for one day. I think I'll sleep on it." He took Sukey's camera bag from her and opened the door. "Come on, I'll walk you to the car park."

It was getting on for ten o'clock when Sukey got home. She found Fergus watching a film on the television in the living room, slumped low on the couch with his back to the door so that all she could see of him was the top of his head with its crown of glossy fair hair. His father's had been like that when he was in his twenties, thick and silky under her caressing fingers. For a long time after Paul left home, when Fergus was still young enough to be shampooed and bathed by his mother, she had found something almost unbearably poignant in the sight of his curly, golden mop. It had been short in those days; now, like so many of his peers, he wore it long and it wasn't always tidy. She had given up nagging him about the tidiness, so long as he kept it clean.

He craned his head when she entered and raised a hand to greet her. "Have you had anything to eat?" she asked.

"I took a chicken pie out of the freezer. There's some left if you're hungry."

"I'm starving. D'you want tea?"

"I'll come and make it." He switched off the television and stood up.

"Weren't you watching that?"

"It was a load of rubbish, really."

They went into the kitchen together and Fergus filled the kettle while she took the remains of the pie from the fridge. "This was supposed to last us two days," she said accusingly, staring at the microscopic portion that remained.

"Ah, well, Anita came round to ask about our science homework and, er, I said she could stay for supper." Fergus turned away to reach the tea caddy down from the cupboard, but not quickly enough to hide the wave of rich crimson

89

spreading over his face. "I didn't think you'd mind," he said, his voice squeaky with embarrassment.

Sukey put the pie in the microwave and set the timer. This was one of the occasions when a mother's rôle was to sound laid back and unconcerned. Resisting the impulse to enquire how long the girl had stayed, she said, "Of course I don't mind. I hope you saw her home."

"Sure." He spooned tea into the pot and poured on boiling water. "What kept you so late?"

"Something came up. I left a message on the machine – didn't you get it?"

"Yeah, we . . . I got it. What job was it?"

"Checking a van we think may have been used in a crime." The pinger sounded and Sukey brought her supper to the table and sat down.

"What sort of crime? Was there any blood?" The lad's eyes lit up in anticipation of gruesome details.

His mother grinned at him over a forkful of pie. "No blood, I'm afraid, only a load of boring old prints and a torn pair of overalls."

Fergus put two cups of tea on the table and sat down. "Mum," he said after a pause, "you are free this Saturday, aren't you?"

"Hopefully, yes. Why?"

"There's a home match against New Park and I've been picked for the school team. Will you come and watch?"

"Of course I will. Morning or afternoon?"

"Afternoon." There was a pause, then he said, "D'you think Jim would come as well?"

Sukey cocked an eyebrow over the rim of her teacup. "Jim who?"

"Your policeman friend. He said I could call him Jim, when I met him that time at the football match. That's what you call him, isn't it?"

"When we're off duty."

"Anyway, d'you think he'd come?"

"Oughtn't you to mention it to Dad first? You know how keen he is on your school sports."

The lad's face clouded. "Used to be. He hasn't watched a match in ages. Petal thinks cricket's a stupid game anyhow."

And what Petal says, goes, Sukey thought. Aloud, she said, "OK, I'll ask Jim if you want me to."

"Great. Perhaps you could invite him back for tea or something. Then you wouldn't be on your own all evening." The last two sentences tumbled out in a rush.

"Do I take it you're going out on Saturday?"

"Anita and I are going to a party."

"Where?"

"At Maisie Evans's house. It's her birthday. She'll be seventeen."

"Well, that's nice." *Was it?* Sukey wondered. *Would I like to be seventeen again? Not unless I could keep all the wisdom I've acquired during the past twenty years.* She got up from the table and carried her empty plate to the draining board. "These can wait till the morning. I'm going to bed."

"Yes, why don't you? I'll do this bit of washing up." Fergus squeezed his mother's shoulders and gave her a peck on the cheek before running hot water into the sink. "Goodnight, Mum."

Halfway up the stairs, she remembered something and went back to the kitchen. "By the way," she said, "I've been thinking it over . . . I reckon it'll be OK for you to go on that trip."

"Really?" He swung round, his expression a mixture of surprise and delight. "Are you sure?"

"I can just about manage it, even if Dad won't contribute, but I think he probably will. You'll have to pick the right time to ask him."

"Brilliant!"

"I'll give you a cheque for the deposit tomorrow, all right?"

"Thanks, Mum."

He deserved it, she thought as she went slowly up to her room, her feet dragging a little with weariness. He was a good kid in so many ways. Unusually considerate for his age, too, especially so this evening. If he'd been a bit older, she'd have wondered what he'd been up to. She undressed, put on a robe and slippers and went to the bathroom. Here at least were all the normal signs of male teenage occupation: splashes on the mirror, a damp towel on the floor, the cap off the toothpaste. And, inevitably, the toilet seat left up. She gave a resigned sigh as she lowered it, then paused as her eye was caught by something lying in the water at the bottom of the pan. She drew a quick, startled breath of recognition. "Oh, Fergus," she muttered as she pressed the lever to flush the condom away. "I knew you were growing up, but I hadn't realised how fast."

Her mind went back to their conversation of a few minutes ago. Fergus had suggested that she invite Jim Castle for the evening on Saturday, knowing he would be out of the house. Was that his way of telling her that his own first experience of sex – she was certain from his demeanour that it was the first – had taught him that she was not simply his mother, but a woman who needed a life of her own?

Despite her tiredness, she lay awake for some time, wondering whether to speak to Fergus in the morning and if so, what she should say; whether it was her duty to tell Anita's mother what her sixteen-year-old daughter was up to; whether to tell Paul and ask him to deal with it. She dismissed the last option out of hand. He would simply laugh and tell her to forget it, saying that all young people were at it nowadays. The final thought that drifted through her mind before she fell asleep was that asking Jim Castle for his opinion mightn't be a bad idea.

*   *   *

Sukey was not the only one to whom sleep did not come readily that night. A few miles away, Rita Holland lay staring into the darkness. One of the bitterest quarrels she could remember had ended with Terry storming off to the pub on his own. It was after midnight before he came home and fell into bed without saying a word to her. Now he lay snoring at her side, dead to the world and heedless of the anxiety and foreboding that tormented her.

The trouble had started soon after his return from the police station. Having assured her that there was nothing for her to worry about because he'd done nothing wrong, that this time he was on the right side of the law and smelling of roses, he'd boasted about how he'd tracked down and browbeaten Charlie Foss into handing over five hundred pounds and promising more. He'd thrust the money into her hand, obviously expecting her to be thrilled to death and tell him how clever he'd been. Terrified at what might come of his determination to go after his share of the spoils from the bank robbery, her nerves further shaken by the appearance of the police, she had thrown the money back at him, accusing him of putting it before her happiness and Billy's, saying that nothing but trouble could come from contact with Charlie. "Get mixed up with that snake and you'll end up back inside," she had screamed at him, "and this time, don't expect me to wait for you to come out." It had all ended in a slanging match that half the neighbourhood must have heard. Their lives could never be the same again.

Chapter Ten

After lying awake for what seemed a very long time, Sukey finally fell into a heavy sleep and knew nothing more until Fergus banged on her door shouting, "Mum, it's half-past eight and I'm off to school," before clattering down the stairs without waiting for an answer. She was still trying to gather her wits when she heard the front door slam and by the time she had dragged herself out of bed, pulled on her dressing gown and gone to the window to draw back the curtains, he had wheeled his bicycle out of the garage and was preparing to ride off. She noticed with interest that he was strapping his school bag to the saddle instead of slinging it carelessly over his shoulder, something she had been nagging him to do for a long time in the interests of road safety. There was a subtle difference in his demeanour as well – less of the gangling adolescent, more the purposeful, self-confident young man. When she leaned out and called his name he looked up, smiled, gave a jaunty wave and pedalled energetically away. She made her way to the bathroom, a little relieved that she had not had to face him before deciding what to do about her discovery of the night before. She wondered if it had occurred to him that she might have guessed his secret. In any case, the half-hour before he left for school would not have been the best moment to raise the subject and it would have been difficult to appear relaxed and natural with that uncertainty hanging between them.

Fergus had, judging by the debris left in the kitchen, enjoyed a hasty but reasonably substantial breakfast. Sukey cleared the table, made some coffee and toast and settled down to read the morning paper. A political scandal and a motorway pile-up shared the headlines while the report on the hunt for Lorraine Chant's killer had been relegated to an inside page. It referred to the possibility of the deceased's husband appearing later that day at a press conference to appeal to the public for information. Sukey felt a wave of pity for Arthur Chant at having to face such an ordeal and wondered whether it was under serious consideration or mere speculation on the part of an imaginative reporter. Jim had said nothing about it, only that he was planning to talk to Chant again today. She found herself wishing she could be present at that interview and how much Jim would tell her about it later. There were times when she felt frustrated by the limitations of her job and wished she could become a fully fledged detective. At least Jim discussed his cases with her; once she had spotted a flaw in a suspect's alibi which he and the other officers on the investigation had missed. She wondered when she would see him again without other people being present.

The last question was provisionally answered just as she was about to step into a hot bath. He called to say that he would shortly be on his way to Marsdean to see Chant, that he hoped to be free at around eleven and could they meet for a cup of tea or coffee in the village? If things didn't go according to plan he'd be in touch. Three cheers for mobile phones, she thought as she lowered herself into the steaming water, feeling lighter of heart than she had done for several hours.

When Detective Inspector Castle arrived at Priory View, Marsdean on Tuesday morning, there was a sleek, champagne-coloured Bentley standing outside the front door. He recognised it as belonging to Chant, having noticed it there on his previous visit on the day of the murder. As he parked his own car at a respectful distance, it crossed his mind that it had been left there deliberately to reinforce the impression, given over the telephone when he called to make the appointment, that Chant had pressing matters to attend to once the interview was over.

A thin, elderly woman with snow-white hair answered his ring. She showed no surprise or concern at the sight of his official badge, merely saying in a pleasant Gloucestershire accent, "Mr Chant is expecting you sir, this way if you please," and leading him up the stairs into the study. She tapped on the door, opened it in reply to a voice calling "Come in", ushered the visitor inside and withdrew.

Castle's first impression, as Chant rose to greet him, was of an altogether taller and more commanding presence than the sad, crumpled figure, numbed with shock at finding the murdered body of his wife, whom he had interviewed a few days ago. His face was drawn, and his deep-set eyes under their heavy brows had an almost haunted expression, but his "Good morning, Inspector, please sit down," was spoken in a courteous but businesslike tone and his manner was that of a man with many calls on his time and important affairs on his mind. It reinforced Castle's earlier impression and he pitched his approach accordingly.

"I'm aware that you're a busy man, Mr Chant, so I won't take up any more of your time than is absolutely necessary," he began.

"I appreciate that." Chant opened a silver cigarette box that stood on a corner of his desk and offered it to Castle, who declined with a movement of his hand. "You have no objection if I do?"

"Of course not." Chant lit a cigarette with a matching lighter which he replaced carefully alongside the box. His hands were perfectly steady. "As a matter of interest," the detective said, "were those items on the desk on the day of the . . . burglary?"

"You mean, the day my wife was murdered? There is no need to beat about the bush, Inspector, although I appreciate your delicacy. Yes, both these were exactly where you see them now. I am an orderly person, you see. If an ornament or a piece of furniture has been moved only a couple of inches, I notice it immediately. Why do you ask?"

"I find it surprising that the killer didn't take them, along with the things he stole from downstairs. They must be quite valuable."

"It is surprising, now you mention it. I suppose his thoughts were directed towards finding the safe."

"The safes," Castle corrected, with emphasis on the final 's'. Chant, drawing deeply on his cigarette and exhaling through his nostrils, made no comment. "Mr Chant, who besides yourself knows of the existence of that second safe?"

"So far as I know, only the man who installed it."

"And that was—?"

"A chap called Holland who does odd jobs for me."

"That would be Mr Terry Holland, of Exeter Road, Gloucester?"

"That's right." A slight lift of the eyebrow indicated surprise. "How did you know?"

Castle affected not to hear the question. "What about Mrs Chant?"

"No." The monosyllable was curt to the point of rudeness.

"Or your housekeeper?"

"You mean Mrs Hapwood, the woman who let you in? Of course not. She's not the housekeeper, by the way, she just comes in two or three times a week to do the cleaning."

"I see. We've already established that she wasn't here on the day of the murder. Now, Mr Chant, you told me that you are in the habit of keeping quite large sums in cash in the floor safe. About how much is in it at any one time?"

If the question surprised Chant, he gave no sign. "It depends. A couple of thousand, perhaps."

"Is there any particular reason why you need to have so much cash in the house?"

"I don't keep it here for long. As I told you, I own a string of amusement arcades. Each manager holds a substantial float in small change to issue to the punters to enable them to play the machines. The notes he receives in return are kept in his safe until I and my assistant come to collect them. For security reasons, we vary the collection times. In daylight hours we pay the money straight into the bank, but an attempt was made to mug us once when we were putting it into the night safe. It was then that I decided to have the second safe installed here."

"Enabling you to bank the money at a more convenient time?"

"That's right."

"And you are absolutely certain that it was empty on Friday?"

There was a hint of impatience in Chant's voice as he replied, "Haven't I already said so, in my statement?"

"Yes sir, but at the time you were in a serious state of shock. It occurred to me that you might have been mistaken."

"I was not mistaken."

"Then that settles that. Now sir, I wonder if you can help me on another matter." Castle took from his pocket the envelope containing the earring that Sukey had found in Terry Holland's van and placed it on the desk. "Do you recognise this?"

Chant's face underwent a dramatic change. He crushed out his cigarette with a hand that trembled. Almost reverently, he picked up the jewel and laid it in his palm. His features crumpled and his mouth puckered; his voice was thick with emotion as he whispered, "It's one of a pair I bought for my wife a few months ago." Tears welled from his eyes, his shoulders heaved and the envelope slipped from his grasp as he covered his face with his hands. After a few moments he pulled a handkerchief from his pocket and blew his nose. "Forgive me, Inspector, I—"

"I'm sorry to cause you additional distress, sir, but I have to ask you . . . you told us that none of your wife's jewellery was missing."

"She . . . must have forgotten to put the earrings in the safe. Or perhaps they were on her dressing table. She might have been planning to wear them to the wedding."

"Ah yes, the wedding. I take it you have no further information about that?"

"I'm afraid not."

"I believe she intended to be away overnight."

"Just one night, she said."

"The officer who searched the bedroom mentioned that she did not appear to have packed an overnight bag. Our original assumption was that she was killed before she had time to do it. It occurs to me that she might have packed it earlier and put it in the car before she was killed. Have you checked, by any chance?"

"I haven't been to the garage since . . . I can't bring myself to. I don't even put my own car away." Chant's eyes filled again and he gnawed furiously at his lower lip.

"Perhaps I could have a look before I leave. If it's there, it might contain some clue as to where she was going." Chant nodded without speaking, spreading his hands in a vague gesture that the Inspector took as permission. "Back to this earring, sir. You haven't seen the other one lying around?"

"No, I haven't. Where did you find this one?"

"In a van which we have reason to believe was used by the killer."

Chant's head jerked up as if invisible hands had grabbed him by his thick silvery hair. "You've traced it?"

"Actually, we had a tip-off. The van belongs to your handyman, Mr Holland."

"Terry Holland!" A look of concern crossed Chant's face. "Inspector, you aren't suggesting that it was he who robbed me and then killed my wife?"

"He reported his van stolen on the day of the murder and so far we have learned nothing to disprove his story. What do you know about him, sir?"

"Not a great deal. The manager at one of our premises got him to do some repairs after we had a break-in. He did a reasonable job at a fair price, so we've used him again, several times. That's how I came to get him to install the safe. Oh, my God, what does it all mean?" Once again, the tide of grief became too much for the man to bear.

Castle waited patiently until he had recovered before saying casually, "Holland's not a local man, is he?"

Chant shrugged. "I've no idea where he comes from. I know he has a wife and child – he mentioned something once about having to collect the youngster from school."

"When we questioned him, he had a bundle of notes in his pocket. That's why I wanted to make certain that nothing like that was missing from your house."

Castle could not be sure, but he thought he detected a certain tightening of Chant's mouth and a wariness in his expression as he replied, a little sharply, "I've already reassured you on that point."

"Quite so. By coincidence, the bundle was held together with one of these." Castle reached across and picked up a rubber band of a particularly lurid shade of pink, one of a number piled up in a tray on the desk. "I'd say it was the same colour, too."

Chant's eyes seemed to retreat even further into their sockets as he said, a little too quickly, it seemed to Castle, "There's nothing strange about that, surely. There must be thousands of those knocking about, you can buy them anywhere."

"I dare say you're right. Well, I won't take up any more of your time, Mr Chant." Castle reached forward and picked up the earring. "I'm afraid I have to keep this for the time being as evidence, but it will of course be returned to you eventually."

Chant swallowed hard, then abruptly swung round to stare out of the window. With his back to Castle, he said in a tremulous voice, "Inspector, do you really believe that young man murdered my wife?"

100

"You mean, Terry Holland? We haven't eliminated anyone yet, but our enquiries are at an early stage, Mr Chant. And I would ask you to treat everything that has passed between us this morning as strictly confidential."

"Naturally."

"And if I could check your wife's car on the way out?"

"Yes, of course. It'll be locked. Lolly's keys must be still in her handbag, but I have a spare set here." Chant turned back to the desk, took a small leather pouch from one of the drawers and without another word walked out of the room and headed downstairs with Castle at his heels. Outside, he operated a radio-controlled mechanism to open the door of the double garage adjoining the house. One half was empty; in the other stood a silver-grey Mercedes.

Castle peered through the car windows, grasped the handle of the driver's door and found it locked. Without a word, Chant handed him the key. "There's nothing inside," the detective remarked after a rapid inspection. "Better check the boot."

Seconds later, the two men were staring down at a full-sized dark blue suitcase bearing the initials L.C.

Sitting alone in a corner of the Marsdean village tearoom, Sukey was beginning to feel uncomfortable. Several times she noticed the proprietress, a fiercely-frowning lady who presided over the counter and dispensed hot drinks, pastries and light snacks to order, shooting disapproving glances at her. Whenever the pale-faced, slightly downtrodden-looking waiter approached the counter with an order, she whispered in his ear and swivelled her rather prominent eyes towards Sukey, who began to wonder whether her explanation that she was waiting for a friend and would prefer not to order until he arrived was being interpreted as suspicious behaviour.

She was on the point of giving up when her mobile phone began warbling. She grabbed it from the pocket of the cotton jacket slung over the back of her chair and spoke in a whisper into the mouthpiece, aware that the chatter had subsided while a dozen or so pairs of ears were cocked in her direction. Evidently, such advanced technology was not often encountered by the establishment's regular clientele.

"Where are you?" she demanded in response to Jim Castle's greeting. "I've been here nearly half an hour without ordering and I'm getting some filthy looks from the management."

"Got held up. Thought you'd like to know I'm on my way. I've no time for coffee, I'm afraid."

"Well thank you very much," she snapped, but he had already switched off.

His car pulled up outside a couple of minutes later. She could tell the moment he entered that the interview had produced results. He perched on the edge of the chair opposite her like a man with only moments to spare before catching a train. "Can't talk here," he said in a low voice. "Come and sit in the car for five minutes while I tell you the latest. Let me pay for your coffee."

"What coffee? I haven't had any, I've been waiting for you."

He appeared only mildly disconcerted. "Well, like I said, there's no time now, I've got to get back to the incident room."

"Sorry . . . something urgent . . . another time . . ." Sukey stammered apologetically as they passed the accusing stare of the proprietress on the way to the door.

Jim unlocked the passenger door of his maroon Mondeo, waited while she got in, and closed it before climbing into the driver's seat. "This had better be good," she said. "I could have killed for some coffee, and those cakes looked absolutely scrumptious."

He gave her a brief account of his interview with Chant, ending with the discovery of the suitcase, in which they had found the dead woman's passport as well as a substantial part of her wardrobe. "I'll have it checked, but I doubt if it'll tell us much."

"So she was planning to leave him?"

"Almost certainly. And as if that wasn't enough, her jewellery was gone. When he checked again he found that all that was left in the safe, apparently untouched, was a pile of empty cases."

"Presumably, so that she wouldn't be missed for a couple of days at least. I wonder where she was really going."

"More important, who was she going with?" Castle wondered. "Not Holland, surely?"

"Why not? Maybe she likes a bit of rough. She was obviously a lot younger than her husband."

"And a bit of a sexpot too, according to Mrs Hapwood, the domestic help."

"Oh?"

"She nobbled me as I was letting myself out. Chant was too upset to come down."

"What did she say?"

"She claims the dead woman used to make and receive a lot of phone calls from what she called her 'fancy men'."

"Fancy *men*? More than one?"

"So it would appear. Mrs Hapwood made no secret of the fact that she used to listen in on the conversations."

"You mean on an extension phone?"

"No, just eavesdropping outside the door. She says Mrs Chant had several lovers at various times."

"Anything to suggest who they might have been?"

"Only that the latest seems to have been the hottest thing so far. Mrs H says she used to fairly drool over the phone to her 'Walter Baby'."

"Yuk!" Sukey pulled a face.

"I went back to ask Chant if he knew anyone called Walter or Wal, but he said not." Jim gave a sympathetic shake of the head. "Poor chap. If you could have seen his face when he opened that suitcase . . . I left him in much the same state as the day he found his wife's body."

"You said he seemed uneasy when you asked about the money. Maybe there was some there, possibly quite a substantial sum. Maybe the wife had the safe open to help herself when she was attacked and the killer made off with the lot."

"Very possibly. I'm going to have to talk to Chant again. I'm almost certain the money that we found on Holland came from that safe." Jim fumbled in his pocket and pulled out the rubber band he had purloined from Arthur Chant's desk. "It was held together with one exactly like this."

Sukey blinked and held her hands in front of her eyes in a pretence of being dazzled by the vivid, fluorescent colour. "Heavens! You could find anything held together by that in the dark," she exclaimed.

"The money, the earring, the van being spotted in the village at the critical time – they all point to Holland being our man. According to Radcliffe, his wife was like a cat on hot bricks while they were waiting for him to come home, almost as if she knew he'd been up to something. And I'm convinced he wasn't telling the whole truth about where that money came from. I think I'll send Radcliffe round to have another go at him."

"But if he sticks to his story that his van was stolen—"

"That's the snag, there's no proof either way. What we need is a witness who can identify the driver. Hill's pressing on with the house-to-house enquiries, but he's had no luck so far." In a fit of frustration, Jim thumped the steering wheel with his fist. "It's all so bloody circumstantial at present. We've no hard evidence that Holland was actually there and yet everything else seems to fit."

"What sort of a guy is he?"

"Fairly tall, just under six feet and heavily built. Londoner, by his accent. Now, that's interesting—" Jim broke off as if a thought had struck him.

"What is?" Sukey asked.

He turned to look at her. "Remember that anonymous tip-off I told you about? The officer who passed the message to me mentioned that the caller 'seemed to be putting on a Cockney accent'. She thought he might be trying to disguise his voice."

"Well, that's not unusual." Sukey could remember occasions when informants had taken extraordinary measures to conceal their identity. "What did he say?"

"That he'd seen Terry Holland's van in Marsdean, heading in the direction of the Chants' place."

"Which you already knew from the house-to-house enquiries."

"Yes, but the caller might not have been aware of that. He also hinted that Holland had a record."

"And has he?"

"We've got nothing on him. My first reaction was that the suggestion was malicious – we get quite a lot of that, as you know – but if that accent wasn't assumed, then maybe the caller is someone from Holland's past, someone who knows his background." Jim gave the steering wheel another thump, but this time it was prompted by excitement rather than irritation. "We've got a spot on the TV news this evening . . . I'll put out an appeal for this man to come forward . . . promise absolute confidentiality, the usual stuff."

"If he knows Holland from way back he may have form himself, in which case he's hardly likely to—"

"It's worth a try." Jim glanced at his watch. "I ought to be getting back – the Super wants a progress report. Sorry about the coffee."

"Can you spare another couple of minutes?"

"Something on your mind?"

"Yes, Fergus." Briefly, she told him of her discovery. Jim's pragmatic, down-to-earth response to the situation gave her considerable comfort – and food for much heart-searching.

Chapter Eleven

Leaving Detective Inspector Jim Castle to report to his superiors, Sukey went back to her ten-year-old Astra, which she had parked a short distance from the tearooms. It was overdue for servicing and not entirely reliable, so she was using it as little as possible until she could afford to have it seen to. Money again! It crossed her mind that it had been rash to promise Fergus that he could go on that trip. Still, there was always the chance that Paul would help with the cost, if Fergus managed to find the right moment to tackle him. And tomorrow she had the photographic assignment from Gary, whose actual identity according to his business card was Hugo Bayliss, Managing Director of Bodywise Systems Ltd, and on whom she was counting for a substantial contribution.

Sukey drove slowly, hoping that the rattle from the engine didn't mean that something expensive needed doing. Reaching home without mishap, she parked outside the house and went indoors. She tried to concentrate on rehearsing what she would say to Fergus that evening – assuming she wasn't landed with a job that would carry over into the small hours, as occasionally happened. Her son had taken a significant step forward into manhood, a step which could have an effect on her own future as well as his. It was a situation that demanded her full attention and yet, despite the fact that her part in the hunt for Lorraine Chant's killer was over – at any rate for the time being – it was to that case that she found her mind constantly harking back.

On the face of it, it was a pointless exercise. Within a couple of hours she would be busy on fresh assignments, helping her police colleagues to track down other villains – small-time burglars mostly, breaking into houses while the occupants were out at work, leaving a scene of damage and disorder for them to face on their return home. More often than not it was an opportunist burglary, with entry effected through a door or window carelessly left unfastened. At this point Sukey stopped short, the egg she had been about to crack for her lunch poised an inch above the rim of the frying pan.

Jim had mentioned in passing Arthur Chant's passion for order and neatness, and his apparently high regard for security which, presumably, had been shared by his wife, since she kept her car locked even when it was inside a locked garage. When the house was checked after the discovery of the body, every door and window had been securely fastened except the one through which the intruder had entered. The fact that the burglar alarm system had not been set was not significant, that was something one normally did just before leaving the house, but to leave a ground-floor window open was not the sort of thing a security-conscious person would be expected to do, even when at home and especially when alone in the house.

Unless it had been done deliberately. Several possible scenarios raced through Sukey's mind as she fried her egg, made coffee and toast and settled down to a hasty lunch. She found a sheet of paper and made notes while she ate, becoming so absorbed that her coffee grew cold and she forgot about the time until a glance at the clock reminded her that unless she left the house within ten minutes she would be late reporting for duty. She hastily took a casserole out of the freezer, scribbled some instructions for Fergus about supper and set off.

Her first assignment was at a flat on a council estate. The policewoman who opened the door in answer to her knock greeted her with a cheery, "Hi, Sukey!" and a welcoming gesture with the teapot she held in her other hand.

107

"Hi, Maddy. What have we got here?"

"Domestic. The kids' father – or rather, the father of the two eldest – has just come home after eighteen months in the slammer to find he's got a six-week-old baby. He gave the mother a going over, smashed the place up and scarpered. A couple of officers are out looking for him."

"He didn't touch the kids?"

"No, thank God, they're all OK."

"So what am I doing here, if you know who's responsible?"

"We want evidence of the damage and the injuries . . . a few of his prints on stuff she bought or had given to her while he was inside . . . the kids' toys maybe – anything else you can find to pin it on the bastard. You know how things are nowadays, the bench doesn't take our word for anything. I'm just making a cup of tea. Julie's in there." Maddy gestured with the teapot towards the front room, from which came the sound of a baby's fretful wailing. She disappeared into the kitchen and Sukey pushed the door open and went in.

The victim was a young woman barely out of her teens, wearing a shabby, sleeveless and none too clean cotton dress. She was thin and pale, with lank, mousey hair badly in need of a wash, and bruises on both cheeks and on one arm. She was seated on a rickety settee, which appeared to be the only undamaged item in the room, making half-hearted efforts to comfort the baby on her lap and seemingly oblivious to the activities of two toddlers, a boy and a girl, who were exploring the wreckage of ripped-down curtains, trampled clothing, scattered toys, overturned furniture and smashed ornaments that surrounded them.

"Julie?" The girl raised her eyes and nodded. "I'm Sukey. I've come to take some pictures. Is that OK with you?"

"You the police?"

"No, a Scene of Crime Officer."

Julie gave a faint, cynical smile. "A SOCO. I know all about them. They helped to put Clyde away last time – only not for long enough." She spat out the final words through clenched teeth as she surveyed the ruins of her home.

"Have you got anywhere else to go?" Julie shrugged and shook her head. "What about the baby's dad?"

"Dumped me, didn't he?"

"How about a cuppa?" said Maddy breezily, entering with three chipped mugs on a battered enamel tray. Somewhat reluctantly, Sukey accepted one, only partially reassured by Maddy's whispered, "It's OK, I washed 'em first."

"What about a drink for the kids? Have you any more milk?" Julie shook her head, sipping her tea with a blank, hopeless expression in her red-rimmed eyes. "Fruit juice?"

"There's some Coke in the cupboard out there."

"I hope she means the stuff you drink," Maddy muttered as she went off on another foray in the kitchen. By the time she returned with a can and a couple of plastic beakers, Sukey had unpacked her camera and started work. After taking shots of the damage, she went over to where Julie was sitting with the baby.

"I'd like some photos of those bruises," she said gently.

Julie gave another shrug. "If you like. Won't do no good, he'll be back."

"Not if we can help it," said Maddy. She had given a half-filled beaker of Coke to the three-year-old, who was slurping it with every sign of enjoyment, and was now sitting on the floor with the little boy in her lap, holding the second beaker to his mouth. Despite the surrounding squalor, the children looked healthy and were reasonably dressed.

"You know, they shouldn't drink too much of this." Maddy indicated the Coca Cola can with the toe of her shoe. "Milk or fruit juice does them more good and they're cheaper."

"That's what the Social tell me, but the kids like it."

As if to confirm her statement, the two toddlers began clamouring for their beakers to be replenished. With a grimace

109

of resignation, Maddy reached for the can while Sukey packed her camera away and got out her fingerprint kit. "Was Clyde wearing gloves when he did this?" she asked.

"You kidding?" The suggestion brought another wan smile to Julie's face.

"That's good. Makes our job a lot easier."

"They won't give him bail, will they?" A flicker of apprehension crossed the young mother's face.

"That'll be up to the magistrate, but we'll do what we can to protect you," Maddy promised. "Maybe we can fix you up in sheltered accommodation, somewhere he can't find you."

When she had finished, Sukey repacked her equipment. "I'll be on my way now," she said.

There was no response from Julie. Maddy said, "I'll see you out."

At the door, Sukey asked, "How long are you staying?"

"Till her social worker gets here. Can't leave her alone, just in case matey comes back for more."

"You reckon she'll press charges?"

Maddy shrugged. "You never know."

Sukey's next assignment was an aggravated burglary. A pensioner and his wife had returned from a visit to their allotment to find a youth in their sitting room with their video and the wife's handbag in his hands. The husband had tried to wrest the articles from him and been punched in the face; when the wife intervened to protect him she had been pushed to the floor, where she was still lying, obviously in excruciating pain, when Sukey arrived. The house was in a normally quiet neighbourhood, but the sound of police sirens as a patrol car attended the incident, followed by an ambulance, seemed to have brought every resident in the street out to stare. Two uniformed officers were in attendance; one urged the crowd to stand back while the injured woman was lifted onto a stretcher and put into the ambulance, accompanied by her badly shaken husband; the other was inside the house inspecting the damage.

"Any idea how he got in?" Sukey asked when the ambulance had departed and the sightseers persuaded that the excitement was over.

"Back door, broken window. You should get some prints. The husband was too shaken to give much of a description, but he was sure the intruder wasn't wearing gloves."

"Not very bright, are they?" Sukey commented, and set to work.

After a hectic four hours, during which all the SOCOs currently on duty were kept almost continuously busy, things went quiet. Sukey's latest job was at a house only a couple of minutes' drive from her own home so she decided to nip back to have a cup of tea and, if he was there on his own, a quiet word with Fergus. She was relieved to find him alone in the kitchen, about to sit down before a plate piled high with beef stew and vegetables. He greeted her with a cheery grin.

"Hi, Mum! You've finished early!"

"I haven't finished – I just happened to be doing a job round the corner. You tuck in."

"Right." He set to as if he'd been starving for a week. Sukey made a cup of tea and sat opposite him. "Anything exciting happened today?" he asked between mouthfuls.

"Not what you'd call exciting, I guess. A couple of break-ins, one aggravated, and a young mother beaten up and her home damaged by her partner." A sudden vision of Julie, seated among the debris with the baby on her lap and a look of utter defeat on her young face, made Sukey pause with her cup halfway to her mouth. "She only looked about eighteen. She must have had her first baby while she was still at school."

"Umm," said Fergus, his mouth full of potato.

"Younger than Anita," Sukey went on. "She's sixteen already, isn't she?"

Her son's eyes swivelled sharply in her direction, then dropped to his plate. His face reddened. "You know she is. I went to her birthday party a couple of weeks ago."

"So you did. She's hoping to go to university after doing her A levels, I understand."

"That's right." Fergus's blush deepened, highlighting the faint shadow on his upper lip.

"Do you know," Sukey went on, "I thought of her when I was in that poor kid's flat this afternoon. I was comparing her situation with Anita's and thinking to myself what a tragedy that she'd allowed herself to be used and her life blighted by some yobbo who couldn't care less about the consequences for her." She paused before adding softly, "It made me so thankful, and proud, that my son had more consideration for *his* girl."

Fergus looked up, his jaw dropping and the rich colour ebbing from his cheeks. "How did you—?" he began, his voice thick with embarrassment.

"You should have been a little more careful about flushing away the evidence," said Sukey drily.

"Oh, Mum—" He seemed to be unable to decide how to react. He put down his knife and fork and pushed his empty plate away, avoiding her gaze.

"Was that the first time?" she asked him gently. He nodded. "Will you promise me something, Gus?"

"What?"

"That you will always be as careful as you were the other night. That you'll never, ever, put a girl – or yourself – at risk."

This time his eyes met hers. He looked dumbfounded. "You're not angry?"

"No, just a little sad that you couldn't have waited a bit longer."

"Are you going to tell Anita's mum?" His tone was sharp with anxiety.

Sukey shook her head and saw the muscles round his mouth relax in relief. "I don't think that's up to me," she said. "Just make sure you don't take any chances . . . you promise?"

"I promise." He got up, went round to her side of the table and gave her a hug. "Thanks for being such a sport, Mum."

She put her hands on his shoulders, holding him at arm's length. "I'm not being a sport and it isn't a game," she told him earnestly. "Relationships are tricky things, Gus. It's so easy to hurt someone badly, and to get hurt yourself. You've seen what happened to Dad and me . . . and now Dad and Myrna."

"Yes." His expression became sombre, then brightened. "That won't happen to Anita and me . . . we care about each other."

"That's fine. Keep it that way as long as you can. And Gus—"

"Yes?"

"You know, don't you . . . there hasn't been anyone for me since Dad and I separated—" She broke off, uncertain how to go on. It was her turn to feel embarrassed.

His response, and the insight that lay behind it, took her by surprise. "You like Jim, don't you?" he said.

"We haven't . . . I mean, there hasn't been anything between us," she blurted out, feeling as self-conscious as a schoolgirl.

"But there might be?" Fergus sat down again, facing her, his clear blue eyes, so like Paul's, looking straight into hers. In these past few moments their relationship had changed forever. His first sexual experience, that could so easily have raised a barrier between them, had instead provided common ground where they could communicate, if not entirely as equals, at least without restraint. Some things would remain the same – there would still be times when she would have to scold him for coming home late, for not tidying his bedroom, for not doing his homework, for leaving toenail clippings all over the bathroom floor – but the one subject she had

113

instinctively avoided could now be spoken of openly and honestly.

"Mum?" He was waiting for the reply to his question.

She responded with one of her own. "Do you think you could handle it, if we – Jim and I—?"

"I told you the other day, I reckon he's tops." As if there was no more to be said, he got up and went to the door.

"Are you going out? Don't you want anything more to eat?"

"Not now, thanks. I'm going to see Anita."

"OK. Enjoy your evening."

"Thanks. And Mum . . ."

"Yes?"

"If you want my advice, and if that's what you and Jim want, go for it."

It was Sukey's turn to sit open-mouthed as her teenage son went clattering upstairs to get ready for his date with his teenage lover.

Chapter Twelve

Hugo awoke on Wednesday morning with the comfortable feeling that, after a brief period when things had been looking decidedly dodgy, they appeared to be back on the rails again. The unexpected appearance of Terry Holland on Monday evening had shaken him badly, but the report in Tuesday's *Gazette*, that the police had been questioning the owner of a white van seen in Marsdean on the day of Lorraine Chant's murder, had been reassuring. Obviously, his message had reached the right ears. He'd had a good laugh when the inspector assigned to the investigation had appeared on the telly, appealing for the anonymous caller to come forward. Barbie had forgotten her sulks for a moment out of curiosity to know what the joke was, but he didn't dare tell her. She couldn't be trusted to keep her stupid mouth shut, not any more.

Barbie was still asleep, lying on her back, as far away from him as she could be without falling out of bed. Still a bit miffed at him, he supposed. She'd slept in the spare room on Monday night and as he was still mad at her he'd let her get on with it, but he'd brought her back to their own bed the following night because he'd needed sex. She'd made a fuss at first, complaining it was hurting her sore ribs, but she'd given in in the end, even seemed to enjoy it after a fashion. Not quite so much as usual, perhaps, but what the hell? She was always a bit off after a row; she'd get over it.

He leaned up on one elbow to look at her. The bruises had

started to fade, but her face still looked a bit of a mess. He hadn't meant to hit her that hard, but he reckoned she'd asked for it after deliberately disobeying his orders. It was all her fault that Terry Holland had caught up with him, threatened him and wound up ducking him in his own pool and ruining his new Hugo Boss summer suit. Still, he'd cooked old Terry's goose for him, hadn't he? Things were back on track, Lorraine was dead – and he, Hugo, had all that lovely money and a lot of valuable rocks to dispose of. And this morning, at ten o'clock, Sukey would be along to take the photos he'd commissioned.

Thinking of Sukey reminded him that it was important to make sure Barbie kept her shopping date. It was up to him to keep her sweet, check there was plenty of spare credit on all her plastic. He shook her by the shoulder and she opened her eyes.

"What is it?" she asked sleepily.

"It's nearly eight o'clock. How about a cuppa?"

"Oh, all right." She pushed back the duvet and sat up on the edge of the bed with her back to him, reaching for her white satin robe. She stood up and put it on before slipping her feet into matching mules. Her nightdress was white satin as well. It was what he liked to see her in . . . and what he enjoyed taking off her. Some blokes preferred black lacy stuff, but Hugo reckoned wives should stick to white. Black – or red maybe – was OK for your bit on the side. He wondered what Sukey favoured. With luck, he'd soon be finding out.

"Sleep well, did you?" he asked.

Barbie didn't look at him, but she answered quietly enough, "Yes, thank you," as she tied the sash on her robe and went over to the window to draw back the curtains. Sunlight poured into the room.

"Going to be a nice day for your shopping trip. Got plenty of elbow room on your cards?"

"Yes, thank you."

116

"Catching the nine fifty train, I think you said?"

"There isn't a nine fifty any more, it's ten thirty. I've ordered a taxi for ten past." She disappeared into the bathroom.

"Shit!" he muttered under his breath at her retreating back. He'd asked Sukey to be there by ten, thinking Barbie would be out of the way by half-past nine at the latest. As things were, there was a fair chance that the pair of them would bump into each other. He'd have to do some fast talking if that happened, but he wasn't unduly worried. He'd bullshitted his way out of trickier spots before now. He switched on the radio and settled back onto the pillows. When Barbie emerged from the bathroom a minute or two later he was lying there with his eyes closed, a picture of a man entirely at his ease.

"I'll go and get the tea now," she said.

"Great."

"You know something," he said when she reappeared with the tray. "I fancy a dip in the pool before breakfast." He drank his tea and held out the cup for more. "On second thoughts," he went on, almost thinking aloud, "I'll have half an hour in the sauna first, then a swim and a shower. That'll set me up for the day's work . . . and the night's fun, eh, girl?" With his free hand, he reached out and squeezed her bottom as, having refilled his cup, she sat down on the edge of the bed. Her own cup rattled in its saucer.

"Careful, you're making me spill my tea," she said. He noticed that her hands were shaking slightly.

"Sorry. Just nip down and switch the sauna on for me, there's a good girl. Usual setting."

"All right." She put her untouched tea back on the tray and went out.

"I'll have breakfast after me swim," he told her when she came back. "Just make me some coffee first. Hot, strong and sweet – you know how I like it."

"All right," she said again.

"That's my girl." He was glad she'd got over her sulks.

He stayed in bed and listened to the radio while she had her shower. She took her time, but there was no rush. The sauna needed thirty minutes or so to warm up. When she came out of the bathroom she was wearing the satin robe again and smelling of some of the expensive body lotion he'd given her recently. Apart from the marks on her face, she looked pretty appetizing. If there had been time, he'd have dragged her back into bed.

"I'll go and make your coffee now," she said. "I'll get dressed later."

"Cheers! With you in a few minutes."

When he went downstairs he found her in the kitchen, drinking orange juice. On the table was a tray with a mug, a sugar basin and a jug of coffee.

"Are you going to have that here or by the pool?" she asked.

"By the pool, I think. Too good to be indoors this morning, innit?"

He wandered into the sitting room, slid back the patio doors and stepped outside, flexing his arms and taking a few deep breaths. Barbie followed him with the tray, put it on the table and poured coffee into the mug. She stirred in two large spoonfuls of sugar and handed it to him.

"Ta." He took a mouthful, swallowed, took another. "Boy, that's good." He strolled along the edge of the pool, mug in hand, admiring his property. The light seemed perfect for photography. Not that he knew much about it. He'd get Sukey to teach him – and then maybe he could teach *her* a thing or two.

Behind him, Barbie called, "I'm going to get dressed now, and then I've got a few things to see to before I leave."

"That's OK, there's nothing else I want for the moment."

She went back indoors and Hugo checked the sauna. Not quite up to temperature yet. Never mind, it was only a quarter to nine. He'd spend twenty minutes or so in the heat, swim a

118

few lengths of the pool and then have a quick shower, there was
plenty of time. It was pleasant out here in the early morning
sunshine. He refilled his mug with coffee, drank it, settled
down in a chair and closed his eyes. Conscious of a faint
movement close at hand, he opened them again. He sat up,
scowling, as he recognised the newcomer.

"What the fuck are you doing here?" he demanded.

"I want to talk to you . . . privately."

"You've got a bleeding nerve. I've got nothing to say
to you."

"But I've got one or two things to say to you."

"I'm not listening." Hugo got up and entered the sauna
cabin. "Just piss off and don't ever show your face here
again," he shouted as he slammed the door behind him.
It was a bad start to the promising little programme he'd
planned for the morning.

It was getting hot in the sauna. Much too hot. Hugo's head
was swimming and his heart pounding; his entire body had
become lethargic and heavy. He must have dozed off and
stayed too long in the heat. His parched mouth was desperate
for water, his body running with sweat. Dimly aware that he
had slumped against the wall of the cabin, he struggled to a
sitting position and tried to stand up. His knees buckled and he
lurched forward and fell, striking his head on the door. Panic
set in. The consultant's advice and the warning signals that
he had so lightly dismissed were like burning darts taunting
his befuddled brain. He was being roasted alive . . . he must
get out of this oven . . . out of this soundproof box where his
calls for help would go unheeded . . . into the air . . . fresh air
. . . dear God let me breathe sweet fresh air again. He managed
to struggle into a kneeling position and reached up, blindly
groping for the handle. His outstretched fingers touched it,
closed round it, gave it a feeble downward tug. It moved a
fraction, but not enough to unfasten the latch. His hand was

slippery with sweat and his grip failed. His strength was ebbing by the second, the blood was boiling in his veins, his head was a raging inferno. The dim light in the cabin seemed to blaze like a bonfire that engulfed him, consumed him . . . and sent him sliding at last into oblivion.

Gary's house – Sukey still thought of Hugo Bayliss as Gary even though she now knew his real name – was in the Charlton Kings area of Cheltenham. Had he lived on her own patch, she doubted whether she would have agreed to his suggestion. If by an unlucky chance her visit had coincided with a burglary in the neighbourhood she would have risked being spotted by one or more of her police colleagues and questions might have been asked. She could hardly admit to moonlighting and it certainly wouldn't do much for her relationship with Jim Castle if she gave as her explanation an invitation to share a sauna or a dip in the private pool of a handsome and wealthy businessman who had picked her up in one of his health clubs.

She calculated that the journey would take twenty minutes, but decided to allow half an hour to be on the safe side. At nine thirty, after making sure all the doors and windows in the house were locked and checking that she had everything she was likely to need in the capacious pockets of her denim jacket, she opened the garage, got in the car and switched on the ignition. The starter motor churned energetically, but the engine failed to respond. Normally, it fired first time. She tried again, jabbing her foot impatiently on the throttle. Nothing. She turned the key a third time, and a fourth. Still no response.

"I don't believe it!" she exclaimed aloud through gritted teeth. "I just . . . don't . . . believe it!" She got out of the car in a fury, slamming the door behind her.

Her next door neighbour emerged and called a cheerful "Good morning!" He was a pleasant, sandy-haired individual who had recently moved in with his wife and two small children.

"What's good about it?" said Sukey crossly.

"Something wrong?"

"My car won't start," she replied despondently. "I've got an important appointment at ten – I'll have to call a taxi."

He stepped over the low fence separating their front gardens. "Let's see if I can help."

"Would you? I know it needs a service, but I've never had this trouble before."

He got into the car and sniffed. "I think you've flooded the carburettor."

Sukey grimaced. Why hadn't she thought of that? "You're probably right. I was in a hurry and—"

He grinned. "Too much throttle. I know – we've all done it at some time or other." His tact made her feel better, less like a novice who had only just passed her test. He got out of the car, helped her to push it out of the garage and lifted the bonnet. "Yep, that's your problem. Give it a few minutes to evaporate and then it should start OK. Not too much gas, remember!"

She gave him a grateful, if slightly embarrassed smile. "I'll remember. Thank you so much."

"No trouble." He hopped back across the fence, got out his own car and drove off, leaving Sukey to wait and fume as the minutes ticked past. Her prospective client had not struck her as the kind of man who appreciated being kept waiting, even for a short time, and there was no way she was going to be there by ten o'clock. She was not particularly superstitious, but it crossed her mind that Fate was warning her that what she was doing was ill-advised in more ways than one. She'd had reservations from the beginning. Maybe she should just phone and cancel the arrangement. The trouble was, she didn't have his home number. Then she told herself not to be stupid, closed the bonnet lid and got back into the car. She held her breath as she turned the key, this time more cautiously. As if it had never given any trouble in its life, the engine turned over and fired first time. From that moment, Fate seemed to give up on being perverse and obstructive and became positively obliging. Gaps appeared in the traffic and red lights changed to green at Sukey's approach. When she reached her destination, she was only a few minutes late.

The Bayliss residence was in a private road, set well back behind a tall laurel hedge. It had a semi-circular drive flanked at either end by a pair of white stone pillars, each pair adorned with the words 'The Laurels' in painted black letters. Not a very imaginative name, thought Sukey as she swung the wheel, parked the Astra behind the hedge and went to the front door. The house was white and, like the pillars at the entrance, appeared freshly painted. It was built in a neo-Georgian style, with sash windows below which multicoloured petunias sprouted from window boxes concealed by little wrought-iron balconies. There was more wrought iron in the form of a gate in the white stone wall which linked the main building to a large double garage.

Before Sukey reached the front door, which was approached by a low flight of stone steps, it was opened by a woman wearing a stylish dress and jacket of flowered silk with a small hat in the same material. The white kid gloves that she held in one hand and the white leather purse dangling by a gilt chain from one shoulder suggested that she was on the point of going out. At the sight of Sukey, she appeared disconcerted. "I thought you were someone else," she said. Her eye went to the Astra and back again. "I heard a car and I thought it was the taxi," she went on.

"I have an appointment with Mr Bayliss for ten o'clock," Sukey said. "I'm sorry if I've kept him waiting, my car was playing up."

"An appointment? With my husband?" The woman looked flustered. Her lacquered fingertips moved from her gold necklet to the matching earrings just visible under her carefully coiffured blonde hair, as if she was reassuring herself that they were still in place. "He didn't say nothing . . . anything to me."

"He asked me to do a series of photos of your house and garden. He said you wanted them."

The woman seemed even more bewildered. "He didn't say," she repeated. She spoke with the same compressed vowels and the slightly nasal tone of voice as her husband. "I don't know nothing . . . anything about it."

"Perhaps he wanted it to be a surprise for you," said Sukey.

The smile that greeted the suggestion, and the tone in which Mrs Bayliss replied, "I dare say he did", held a trace of weary cynicism, as if she was unimpressed by the excuse offered for her presence by this unexpected – and clearly unwelcome – visitor. It tended to confirm Sukey's own impression that 'Gary' was a womaniser, something that could well have caused trouble between him and his wife in the past . . . quite possibly the very recent past, judging by the bruising round the eyes, only partially concealed by dark sunglasses, and the discoloration on the cheekbones that was clearly visible despite the careful make-up.

"My husband's not here," Mrs Bayliss said. "He must've forgotten you was . . . were coming. There's no point in waiting, I'm sorry." She spoke hesitantly at first, then with nervous haste. She was plainly relieved when a taxi turned into the drive and pulled up, leaving the engine running. "Won't be a minute!" she called to the driver. She ran into the house, pushing the door to behind her as if to make it quite clear that Sukey was not to be admitted. Emerging a minute or two later, she shut it with a bang, brushed past Sukey and got into the cab. As it moved away, she wound down the window and repeated, "There's no point in waiting."

"Well, sod that for a waste of time," Sukey muttered irritably. She was on the point of going back to the car when it occurred to her that Mrs Bayliss, suspicious of her husband's motive in inviting a strange woman to the house, might have deliberately lied to her. 'Gary' might be there all the time, unaware that she had arrived. From one point of view, this might be no bad thing. She had started out with certain misgivings and the encounter with Bayliss's wife offered the perfect excuse to call the whole thing off. On the other hand, the streak of stubbornness in her nature that had seen her through far more serious setbacks than this made her reluctant to give up that easily. After a moment's hesitation, she climbed the steps to the front door and pressed the bellpush.

There was no movement inside the house. She rang again with the same result. She could hear the sound of the bell quite distinctly; anyone indoors could not fail to hear it. It seemed, after all, that she had come on an abortive errand. She would have to find the money for Fergus's school trip some other way. She was halfway back to the car when she remembered the side entrance to the garden. Perhaps 'Gary' was waiting for her there, out of earshot of the doorbell. She tried the latch on the gate, found it unfastened and went through.

A short passage between the house and the garage gave on to a paved area dotted with stone containers overflowing with flowering shrubs. A fair-sized swimming pool, surrounded by an assortment of luxury garden furniture, lay in the angle created by a single-storey extension which, Sukey guessed, had been built to accommodate the changing rooms, shower and sauna of which the owner had boasted. The smooth water glistened in the sunshine like pale blue satin and beyond it was a wide, velvety green lawn fringed by trees and herbacious borders. At the far end, a summer house nestled in the shelter of another tree-lined boundary behind which rose the distant backdrop of the Cotswold Hills. No neighbouring houses were visible; the overall effect was one of total seclusion and considerable affluence. Sukey figured that Bodywise Systems must be doing very well indeed. There was no sign of life and no response to her call of, "Is anyone there?" Mrs Bayliss had obviously been telling the truth after all.

It crossed her mind that if she went ahead and took some pictures, she could show them to 'Gary' next time she saw him at the health club. He might, of course, pretend they were not exactly what he wanted and try to persuade her to make another appointment, which would confirm her suspicions of an ulterior motive. And if he wouldn't come across with the money, all she stood to lose was a roll of film and the cost of processing it.

She wandered about for several minutes, but the extensive grounds appeared as deserted as the house. Since there was no one there to challenge her, she got out her camera and went to work. She began with the area round the pool before turning her attention to the garden. It had obviously been designed by a professional, someone with horticultural expertise combined with an artist's eye for form and colour. Whichever way she turned she found perfect examples of imaginative planting. Memories of what she had been taught at college about composition, angles, contrast and the effects of light and shade came back to her as she worked. It was a long time since she had had such an opportunity to use her creative skills and she soon became absorbed, enjoying the change from her normal job where accuracy rather than artistic achievement was the watchword.

She saved her last few exposures for the patio area. She had already covered it pretty thoroughly, but the sun had gone round in the meantime and there was no longer the glare off the sliding glass door that had hampered one or two of the shots that she wanted. There was something else different as well. The door had been closed when she arrived. Now it was open. There must be someone in the house after all. She stowed the camera in her pocket and stepped indoors.

She found herself in a sitting room that looked as if it had been lifted bodily from a furniture store. It was clear that no expense had been spared; everything had been carefully chosen and colour coordinated, but the overall effect was of a show house rather than a home. There were no books, no fresh flowers or plants, no personal items of any kind. The few pictures were somewhat garish reproductions of hackneyed pastoral scenes in over-bright gilded frames.

The door into the hall was ajar. She went over to it and called, "Excuse me, is anyone there?" No one answered. She called again, and this time she thought she detected a faint sound overhead. She listened intently for a few moments, but it was not repeated. She hesitated, uncertain whether to investigate further or to go quietly away. Whoever was up there might be no one more sinister than a hard of hearing domestic help. But, on the other hand . . . her instinct, coupled with her police training, told her that all was not as it should be. Since she was, after all, on the premises by invitation of the owner, a quick, systematic check would surely be in order.

None of the ground-floor rooms showed any sign of disturbance. Sukey was about to go upstairs when she spotted a cast-iron stand by the front door containing a couple of umbrellas and a stout walking stick which would, she decided, make a handy defensive weapon in case of need. She picked it up and made her way cautiously to the upper landing, where all the doors were closed except one, which was wide open. It was evidently the main bedroom, with built-in furniture covering the wall to her left, a glimpse of an en suite bathroom opposite and a king-sized bed on which lay a bulky holdall, its flap partially unfastened as if someone had been disturbed in the act of searching it. Holding the stick firmly at the ready, Sukey moved forward to take a closer look.

She sensed rather than heard the movement behind her. Before she had time to turn round an arm was hooked round her throat, dragging her backwards, while a hand wrenched the stick from her grasp and then clamped firmly over her mouth, stifling her cry of alarm. For a second she was paralysed with

126

shock and terror. It was the kind of situation that she had been trained to deal with in her karate classes, but the suddenness and unexpectedness of the attack had taken her completely off guard. Then, as the pressure on her windpipe increased, threatening to cut off the air to her lungs, her brain cleared. This was no practice session. This was the real thing.

She kicked backwards with her right foot, felt it connect with a leg and dragged her heel downward, pressing with all her weight against the shin-bone and at the same time jabbing her elbows into her assailant's stomach. There was a muffled grunt of pain and the grip on her throat slackened. Bending forward from the waist, she thrust her backside against him, seized him by the wrists and heaved. A figure in blue denim surmounted by a motorcyclist's helmet shot over her shoulder and crash-landed against the wardrobe.

Sukey fled from the room and pelted down the stairs, clearing the last three in a single jump. Dashing across the hall on her way to the sitting room, she heard the thud of her would-be assassin's boots as he came charging after her. She glanced over her shoulder as she stumbled through the open patio door; he was almost on her. Any minute now and she would once more be fighting for her life. At the edge of the pool she stopped short, swerved and ducked, grabbing desperately at an ankle. Caught off balance, her pursuer toppled forward. Dodging his outstretched hand, she gave a hefty, sideways shove which sent him spinning helplessly towards the water, where he landed on his back with a resounding splash. Her last sight of him was of a bobbing helmet and flailing arms as he struggled to his feet.

At least, she thought as she tore back to her car, it was the shallow end – he wasn't going to drown even if he couldn't swim. She thrust the key into the ignition with a shaking hand, praying that the engine would start first time and sending up a heartfelt message of thanks as it fired. There was no sign of the machine on which, presumably, the intruder had arrived,

127

but it couldn't be far away. He was probably out of the water already, but with luck his ignition key would be in his pocket and need drying off before he could use it. That gave her a few seconds' advantage. He had not appeared when she shot out of the drive and raced along the mercifully deserted street towards the main road, keeping an anxious eye on her rear-view mirror. There was still no sign of pursuit when she joined the stream of traffic heading for the centre of town.

She was trembling from shock and her heart was thudding in her chest like a stampeding elephant, but her brain was crystal clear. Whatever that holdall contained was so valuable that someone was prepared to commit murder rather than allow anyone else to get their hands on it. When at last she was confident that she was not being pursued by a helmeted motorcyclist in soaking denims, she stopped, pulled out her mobile phone and dialled 999.

Chapter Thirteen

When the ten thirty train from Cheltenham Spa pulled into Reading station, Oxford-bound passengers alighted for their connections, but Barbie Bayliss stayed in her seat until the end of the line at Paddington. There, she went down the steps to the Underground and boarded a westbound train on the Bakerloo Line. During the journey, she had started to think of herself as Brenda Foss. By the time she stepped out at Willesden Junction, her mental metamorphosis was complete.

It was only a short distance from the station to the block of council flats where her late mother's sister had spent most of her married life and the long widowhood brought about by her husband's untimely death in a brawl during one of his numerous spells in prison. During the few minutes' walk the memories that flitted through Brenda's mind spanned thirty years. She had lived with Auntie Gwen from the day her mother died when she was ten years old until her marriage to Charlie Foss. During her teenage years her appearance, pop music and boys had been her main preoccupations; she spent her wages as a shop assistant on clothes and make-up and her evenings in discos and bars. Many of her friends had police records by the time they left school, but good luck and a certain native shrewdness, coupled with a respect for the weight of Auntie Gwen's right hand, had kept her out of serious trouble.

She was just under nineteen when she met Charlie at a local disco and fell for him at first sight. He made a pass at her right away and from that day on she thought of no one else. Handsome, well-dressed, never short of money and a lavish spender, she found him utterly irresistible. He was a passionate lover and she joyfully gave in to his every demand. All her girlfriends were jealous of her, but Auntie Gwen had been dead against the relationship. Time after time she had warned her niece not to be taken in by his superficial charm, always ending her lecture with, "Got a cruel streak, that one, you mark my words." But her advice was like writing in the sand, swept away by the crashing breakers of desire that surged over Brenda at Charlie's lightest touch.

Charlie left her in no doubt from day one of their married life that he expected her to submit to his will in all things. He became violent if he thought she had stepped out of line, but always – as she reminded herself while soothing away the aches and pains in hot baths and disguising the bruises with make-up – there were plenty of compensations. She had no financial worries, they ate in posh restaurants and took holidays on the Costa Brava, and she was better dressed and had more fancy gadgets and expensive furniture in her home than any of their friends. And in any case, by the time she at last faced up to the fact that Charlie's good looks and personal charm concealed the soul of a tyrant, a bully and a heartless womaniser, she had become so accustomed to the comfortable lifestyle he provided that she could not bring herself to cut her losses and return to Auntie Gwen's poky little flat. She never knew for certain how Charlie came by his money, although she had a shrewd idea that the law would not approve. The only time she had asked him, he'd told her it was none of her bloody business and made it clear that further questions would be unwise. A fist held a couple of inches from her nose drove the point home.

Brenda had grown up in an environment where practically everyone either had some sort of racket going or knew plenty of people who had. Keeping one jump ahead of the law was a constant preoccupation for most of them and failure to do so regularly caused separation from friends and families for long periods. Charlie was the exception. Whatever he dabbled in, he aways came up smelling of roses, with plenty of cash up front and even more salted away. Brenda had once come across a stash of banknotes hidden away in a drawer. He had caught her with some of it in her hand and gone ballistic, given her the worst hiding she could remember, and told her it was a slap on the wrist compared to what she'd get if she ever poked her nose into his affairs again. Shortly after that he spirited her away to Gloucestershire, cut all ties with his former associates and ordered his wife to do the same. He bought an ailing company, turned it round and became a respectable member of the Cheltenham business community. Five years later, they had moved out of their modest semi into their present home.

Auntie Gwen lived in a four-storey block, one of several built round an open area, referred to by the council as 'the garden', but known to the police as 'the rat run' on account of the narrow interconnecting alleys which led out of it, making ideal escape routes for suspected villains. It was covered with worn turf and surrounded by an informal hedge of tired-looking shrubs, home to an assortment of discarded rubbish, with gaps where the youth of the estate rode through it on stolen bicycles. The flat was on the top floor and if you stood on tiptoe on the balcony you could catch a glimpse of the trees in Gladstone Park, but it was a long time since Auntie Gwen herself had seen them. An arthritic hip made standing on tiptoe a distant memory. Because she couldn't manage the stairs and was afraid of lifts and being mugged she hardly ever went out except when one of her late husband's nephews took her for a spin at weekends. She had married into a close-knit clan whose members saw she was all right, sent their kids round after school to do her shopping and run errands for her, and topped up her pension whenever they could afford it.

They had some pretty hard things to say about Brenda: too stuck up and too mean, now she was rich and living in a posh area, to do anything for the aunt who'd treated her like her own daughter. They never believed she had hardly any ready cash of her own, or that Charlie had threatened to knock the living daylights out of her if she had any contact with them or anyone else from the old days. Only Auntie Gwen herself defended her and bore her no grudge. "There's an 'ome for you with me any time if you feel you can't take it no more," she'd say whenever her niece managed to sneak up to town and pay her a flying visit. "If that bugger steps out of line once too often, you know where to come." And Brenda would give her a hug and say, "Yes, I know", aware in her heart that, faced with the stark choice, the pull of money and luxury would always outweigh the occasional beatings.

The entrance to the flats was a gloomy cavern. Brenda wrinkled her nose in disgust at the smell of stale urine and averted her gaze from the graffiti on the walls and the litter in the corners. Never, she thought as she climbed the stone stairs – as usual, the lifts were out of action – could I come back to this. She walked along the open balcony, stepped over a couple of children scuffling on the ground and knocked at her aunt's front door. Several moments passed before she heard the familiar dragging footsteps and the tap of a stick on the floor of the passage, and felt rather than saw the eye that inspected her through the spy-hole let into the door-panel. There was the sound of bolts being undone and the rattle of a safety chain before the door opened to reveal the dumpy body and apple-cheeked countenance, surmounted by an abundance of white hair, of the one person in Brenda's life whom she truly loved.

The old woman's face lit up and she took her niece by both hands and drew her inside. "Bren, love, 'ow are you?" she exclaimed. "That's a fancy outfit you've got on . . . but . . . Jesus, 'e gave you a right goin' over this time!" she went on as she reached up with her free hand and removed Brenda's sunglasses. "What was the excuse for that? No, tell me later. Come and sit down – you look knackered." She led the

An Inconsiderate Death

way into her tiny living room as she rattled on. "Fancy a cuppa tea?"

"Let me make it," said Brenda.

"'S all right, I can manage." Independent as always, leaning heavily on her stick, Auntie Gwen shuffled out of the room and into the kitchen. Brenda sat down and closed her eyes, listening to the sound of the gas hissing under the kettle and the clatter of cups and saucers being set out on a tin tray. The room had the familiar smell that she remembered from her childhood, a mixture of cigarette smoke and lavender-scented polish. Auntie Gwen had always smoked like a chimney and even nowadays, when moving around was painful, still spent much of her time obsessively waxing her furniture. It was nothing out of the way for her to get up in the middle of watching a television programme to take a duster to some fancied finger-mark or dull patch on her sideboard. Always been very houseproud, had Auntie Gwen, kept her home shining like a new pin.

This enthusiasm for housework had never rubbed off on Brenda, who was only too happy nowadays to leave it to a domestic help who came in several times a week. Charlie liked the arrangement because it enabled him to refer to 'our housekeeper' when they were in company and it suited Brenda in more ways than one because it meant she could wangle some extra cash out of her husband with no questions asked. She paid Mrs Parsons the minimum rate and put the rest of what he gave her in her own pocket. What with that and using the 'cash-back' facility in the supermarket from time to time, she'd managed over the years to stash a little away. It was a paltry sum compared with what Charlie spent, but she knew what it would mean if ever he found out. She'd got away with it so far because he never asked to see the till receipts or quibbled over the size of her credit card accounts. He might be all sorts of a bastard, but he was generous to the point of munificence in that respect. It was all part of the image he had created for himself.

133

Auntie Gwen brought the tea and their conversation went on the usual lines: Brenda enquiring about the old crowd, her aunt grumbling about her aches and pains and not being able to manage the stairs, Brenda saying why didn't she ask the council to give her a ground-floor flat and receiving the inevitable response that after living in this one for forty years she wasn't going to move out until she was carried feet first. Presently, as usual, Brenda went out and bought cigarettes for her aunt and fish and chips for both of them for lunch. It wasn't until they had finished their meal and were sitting together with a second brew of tea that Auntie Gwen lit up her umpteenth cigarette, waved it in the direction of Brenda's face and said, "You goin' to tell me why that swine done that to you?"

"It was because of Terry Holland," said Brenda. "He turned up at the house on Monday." She looked her aunt straight in the eye. "Charlie reckons you must have told him where to find us. Did you?"

The old lady was seized with a fit of coughing. When it was over, she said indignantly, "Course I never – 'ow could I? All I knew was, you'd gone somewhere near Gloucester. I said you'd changed yer name but I didn't know what to and that was all I could tell 'im."

"I asked you not to tell anyone even that much," said Brenda wearily. During the journey to London she had planned to scold her well-loved but over-loquacious relative, but it hardly seemed worth it now; the damage was done.

"I thought it'd be all right. Terry and Charlie was good mates, wasn't they?" Through the cloud of smoke, Auntie Gwen's watery eyes pleaded for forgiveness. "Tel said there was something 'e wanted to give Charlie, most particular. They was good mates," she repeated. "I didn't think it'd do no 'arm."

"They're not mates any more," said Brenda. "And you know why?" Auntie Gwen shook her head. "Remember why Terry and Frank got sent down?"

134

"Course I do – the bank job. What's that got to do with Charlie? Wasn't there, was 'e?"

"Yes, he was. He was driving the getaway. When they were switching cars, he drove off with the money and left the others to get caught."

Auntie Gwen was outraged at such blatant treachery. "The bleedin' 'crook!" she said furiously. "No wonder Terry was keen to contact 'im. Wanted 'is share of the takings – an' I don't blame 'im neither. 'Ow long did 'e go down for?"

"Can't remember exactly. He's been out on licence for twelve months after getting full remission. Frank's still inside – he's the one that clobbered the old boy."

"No wonder Charlie done a disappearing act!"

"I'd no idea at the time, but thinking back – he had the move all planned and only told me the day before we left. Said he'd kept it as a surprise and we was . . . were going to start a new life together, just the two of us. He said we were going to be rich and we had to break away completely or one or other of the old gang'd be on the scrounge as soon as they knew he was making a bob or two." Brenda heaved a sigh and her voice became tremulous as she added, "Made it sound so lovely and romantic, he did."

"An' you swallowed every word of what the lyin' sod told you," sniffed her aunt contemptuously. "Won't you never learn?"

"It wasn't all lies," Brenda protested. "He did what he promised. He's running a legit business, and we've got a lovely home and know all sorts of posh people."

"You told me you couldn't stand the toffee-nosed lot."

"Some of them are OK."

"Knew all along there was something else behind the flit," muttered Auntie Gwen. "Said so at the time. You was just too blind – an' too soft in the 'ead – to see it."

Brenda sighed again, but said nothing. In those days she had still been under Charlie's spell, able to forgive if not to

135

forget. Secretly keeping in touch with her aunt after their hasty move had been her one act of defiance. She stared out of the window into the distance. Earlier, the trees had been hidden under a veil of haze. Now they were clearly visible. That was how things had been in her life. Only in her case, it was the unpalatable truths that had emerged, inexorably, from the mists of self-delusion.

"What about Terry – 'ow's 'e doin'?" asked Auntie Gwen after a pause.

"OK, I think. But he's different. He's turned real hard. He threatened Charlie and guess what he done . . . did, just before he left. Picked him up like a baby and chucked him in the pool."

"Get away!" Auntie Gwen nearly choked on her cigarette smoke as she broke into gales of wheezy laughter.

For the first time, Brenda saw the funny side of the episode and joined in, but it was not long before her own mirth turned into hysterical weeping. "Beat me up something rotten once he got out of the water," she sobbed. "Said it was all my fault Terry found us."

"Spiteful bleeder!" Auntie Gwen gave the heaving shoulders a consoling pat. "Wonder 'ow 'e did manage it, though," she mused.

Brenda stopped crying and dried her eyes. "I dunno, just got lucky, I suppose. Spotted Charlie in a pub or something and followed him. What's it matter?"

"You can't go on like this, girl. Why don't you just leave 'im?"

Brenda made a helpless gesture. "Where do I go? No, don't tell me to come back here . . . I couldn't, honest. It'd be like living in a cage, and the family'd laugh and say it served me right . . . I couldn't face it."

"What about those posh friends of yours?" A sly look crept over the old woman's face. "Can't you find yerself a rich fancy man among that lot?"

"It's a nice idea, but—" Brenda thought fleetingly of Steven Lovett before adding, "none of them's as well loaded as Charlie."

"So back you goes for more punishment." Auntie Gwen stubbed her cigarette out as viciously as if the face of Charlie Foss was painted on the bottom of the ashtray instead of a picture of the Brighton Pavilion. She lit another, coughed, and croaked, "You always was wet as a duck's arse."

"It's not all bad," Brenda protested, almost believing it. She glanced at the clock on the tiled mantelpiece. "I must be going or I'll miss my train. Here, let me give you this." She opened her purse and took out some notes. "Take it, I can spare it."

Her aunt said, "I thought you was still 'elping out Ivy Palmer's boy," but her gnarled fingers closed greedily over the money.

"Not any more – he's got a job."

"Doin' what?"

"I dunno, do I? I haven't seen him lately."

"You 'eard Ivy was dead?"

"Yes, I heard. I tried to get Charlie to cough up for her funeral, but he said it was nothing to do with him. You know he always said the kid wasn't his."

"Well, we know who to believe, don't we?"

"I guess so. Well, goodbye Auntie. See you again."

"Believe it when it 'appens." It was the old woman's invariable response.

During the train journey back to Cheltenham, Brenda Foss concentrated on thinking herself back into the persona of Barbie Bayliss, married to Hugo, Managing Director of Bodywise Systems Ltd. By the time the taxi dropped her at The Laurels she had succeeded in pushing all thoughts of her London visit to the back of her mind.

Chapter Fourteen

At about the same time as Barbie Bayliss was getting off the train at Cheltenham Spa station, Sergeant Radcliffe informed DI Castle that the manager of the Gloucester branch of the Western Building Society had asked to speak to a senior detective.

"Any idea what it's about?" asked Castle.

"No, Guv. The lady says it's confidential – won't speak to anyone lower than a DI."

Castle sighed. He had only just returned to his office from the Lorraine Chant incident room, where a considerable time spent sifting through reports of the house-to-house enquiries had added little to the information previously gathered. Because the three dwellings comprising the enclave known as The Hill had been built on clearings in a small area of established woodland, visitors and residents alike could come and go in virtual privacy. Whereas anyone approaching along the main road from Gloucester would normally drive through the centre of Marsdean to reach The Hill, anyone wishing to do so unobserved could use a narrow lane skirting the village from the opposite direction. This route led past only a handful of dwellings, most of them owned by commuters and empty during working hours. Although one or two reports of cars seen approaching The Hill might be worth following up, if only for elimination, the one firm sighting during the crucial period was that of Terry Holland's white van. Unfortunately, no one had been able

An Inconsiderate Death

to give anything approaching a recognisable description of
the driver.

Castle studied the business card Radcliffe had given him
with no particular enthusiasm. Previous experience of people
who considered their business too important, too delicate, or
merely too complicated to be dealt with by the lower ranks
had taught him that in most cases the significance of what
they had to say varied inversely with the amount of fuss they
made. He had the feeling that Ms Katherine Percival would
be no exception, but could think of no valid excuse to avoid
talking to her.

"All right, I'll deal with it," he said resignedly. "Then I'm off
to get something to eat." For some reason, his thoughts turned
to Sukey. He had hardly set eyes on her since their conversation
of the previous morning. Around midday he had received a
message that she had been trying to contact him, but he had
been too busy to do anything about it. Not that it would have
been possible to discuss anything personal but he felt a sudden,
illogical need to hear her voice, to be reassured that everything
was all right with her. He made up his mind to call her at the
first opportunity, when he was away from the station, after
he had listened to whatever Ms Percival had to tell him.

He was expecting an aggressively businesslike personality,
but instead found himself shaking hands with a slim, well-
groomed brunette with a gentle voice and a friendly smile.
She was neatly dressed in a light grey coat and skirt over a
grey blouse patterned all over with the initials WBS in tiny
blue characters. He showed her into an interview room and
offered her a seat.

"Can anyone overhear us?" she asked as he closed the door
behind them.

"I assure you, anything that passes between us will be entirely
confidential," he said, taking a chair opposite hers. "Unless,
of course, you have reason to believe that a crime has been
committed."

139

Betty Rowlands

"That's the trouble. There may be nothing to it. Just the same, I decided it was my duty to report it." She fiddled with the clasp of her dark blue leather handbag.

"Report what?" prompted Castle, as she appeared uncertain how to continue.

"The fact is, all our staff were recently instructed by Head Office to bring to their manager's attention any case of unusually large sums of cash being deposited in one of our customer's accounts – especially where only comparatively modest amounts had previously been put in or drawn out."

Castle nodded. "That's right. It's part of a national effort to crack down on money laundering through banks and building societies, particularly by drug dealers."

"Yes, so I understand."

"Has something like this occurred in your branch?"

"No, in our Cheltenham branch. The manager there telephoned me to say that a customer went in today and deposited five thousand pounds in cash, mostly in fifty pound notes, into an account which is held here in Gloucester."

"I take it this person was a stranger to the Cheltenham staff?"

"The employee who dealt with him couldn't remember seeing him before and our records show that all previous transactions, both in and out, have been made in the Gloucester branch."

"How long has the account been open?"

"About a year. The holder uses it principally for business purposes. Deposits are mostly in cash but occasionally by cheque. When Mr Merrivale told me the amount of the deposit, I was very surprised as no previous transactions on the account have been for more than a hundred pounds or so either way."

"Can you give me some idea of the man's line of business?"

Ms Percival hesitated for a moment, as if asking herself whether this was confidential information or not. Then she said, "I can't give you full details, you understand—"

140

"Quite. I'm only trying to establish the type of person he deals with."

"Well, I don't see why I shouldn't tell you that. He sometimes draws cheques payable to builders' merchants – all well-established and respectable firms, so far as I'm aware."

"And that's all you have to tell me?"

"Well . . . yes." She gave a nervous cough, covering her mouth with one hand, before hurrying on. "I thought perhaps, if you spoke to the employee who handled the transaction, and got a description . . . and perhaps saw the film from the security camera . . . you might recognise the man. I thought it possible – I mean, he could be a known criminal, someone you suspect of dealing in drugs, for example . . ." Her words trailed off as she caught Castle's eye. Faced with his unrevealing stare, she began to flounder. He could see her mentally asking herself whether she wasn't making something out of nothing. "I suppose he could have got the money selling a car, or maybe won it on a horse," she finished lamely. "I'm sorry if you think I've been wasting your time."

"Not at all," Castle assured her. "It's quite possible, of course, that the man came by the money honestly, but you did the right thing by telling us about it. Will the employee in question be at work tomorrow morning?"

"Yes. Her name's Donna Jupp. I've written it down for you." Ms Percival took a slip of paper from her bag and handed it to him.

"I'll send an officer round to have a word with her. What would be the best time?"

"I suggest nine o'clock, that's half an hour before the branch opens for business. I'll telephone Mr Merrivale first thing and let him know." She stood up and held out her hand. "Goodbye, Inspector, and thank you for listening to me."

Castle went back to his office and wrote up the interview. Then he sat for a few moments chewing the end of his pen and considering the facts. A man whose account was held in Gloucester had used a different branch to deposit an unusually large amount of cash. A number of his regular dealings were with builders' merchants. Terry Holland was a jobbing builder and he lived in Gloucester. And although Arthur Chant had been adamant that no cash had been stolen from the safe that Holland had installed in his study, Castle was by no means satisfied that he was telling the truth. Coincidence? Probably. There must be scores of men in and around the city running similar one-man businesses. Just the same, it was worth looking into. He instructed DC Hill, who was just going off duty, to be at the Cheltenham branch of the Western Building Society the following morning at nine on the dot and to ask for Donna Jupp. Then he left the station and made for a small café in Westgate where he regularly ate. On the way, he stepped into the doorway of a deserted shop and called Sukey on his mobile phone.

"Sorry I couldn't get back to you earlier," he said when she answered. "Is everything OK?"

"Oh, Jim!" she said, and from her tone he knew that something was up.

"What's wrong?"

"I can't talk about it now. Can you come round this evening after my shift finishes . . . say about half-past ten?"

"Sure."

"Bless you!" The relief in her voice and the knowledge that it was to him that she had turned with her problem gave him a warm feeling, even while it increased his anxiety. He tried to imagine what the trouble might be and concluded it was probably something to do with Fergus. He went into the café and ordered steak and kidney pie and chips.

When he got back to the station, he went in search of Sergeant Radcliffe and gave him a brief account of the interview with Katherine Percival. "It might have no bearing on our case but you never know – it's time we got lucky." He glanced at his watch. "Holland is probably at home now, watching the telly. I think I'll go and have a word with him."

"You aren't going to question him about the cash, Guv?"

Castle shook his head. "Not directly, not until – and unless – we get a positive connection. I'll play it softly softly for the time being, see what I can tease out of him. I've got the photographs of the stuff that was pinched from the Chants' place – they'll be my excuse for calling. Maybe our Terry'll recognise some of it."

"Hardly likely to admit it, is he?"

"No, but he might show some reaction. Straws in the wind and all that." Castle heaved a sigh. "It's a pity our anonymous caller never came back to us. I'd give a lot to know whether Holland really has got form."

Radcliffe grinned. "Ask him when his birthday is, then you can run a check on the PNC," he suggested with a twinkle. "Say you'd like to send him a card, in appreciation of his kind cooperation!"

By half-past six, Barbie had everything prepared for the evening meal. She never began the actual cooking until Hugo got home; he'd made it clear from day one of their marriage that he hated food that had been kept hot in the oven. Straight from the pot to the table, that was how he wanted it. She poured a gin and tonic and took it into the sitting room, opened the sliding door and stepped out onto the patio. After the polluted atmosphere of London, the air was sweet and fresh in her nostrils.

At a quarter to seven she called the office of Bodywise Systems but got no reply. At a quarter past she poured herself another drink before calling Steven Lovett at his home in Battledown.

"Steve? It's Barbie Bayliss."

"Barbie! I've been trying to contact you. I left a message on the answering machine. Didn't you get it?"

"Hugo's the only one who uses that thing. Is something wrong?"

"I don't know. There's been a report of an intruder in your house."

"What? How do you know?"

"A police officer came round to the office this morning, looking for Hugo. I explained that he wasn't expected in the office today. When I asked what it was about, I was told there had been an emergency call from a woman who'd seen someone acting suspiciously at The Laurels, gone to investigate and been attacked."

"What woman? What did she look like?"

"I've no idea – why do you ask?"

"A youngish woman came to the door this morning, just as I was leaving the house. She said she'd arranged with Hugo to take some photographs of the garden, but I told her I knew nothing about it. I said he'd gone out and she'd better phone the office to make another appointment." There was a pause, during which Barbie tried desperately to figure out what it all meant. She experienced a creeping fear that something was terribly wrong. A tinkling sound nearby made her heart thump until she realised that it was the ice vibrating in her glass. She took a gulp from her drink, tightening her grip on the tumbler in an effort to steady her shaking hand.

"Barbie?" Steven's voice sounded anxious. "Barbie, are you there?"

"Yes, I'm here. Did the police come to the house?"

"Yes, but they didn't find anything – or anyone. They said they'd like a word with Hugo or you, but I couldn't tell them when either of you'd be available. Maybe they've been trying to get in touch. Why don't you check the answering machine?"

"I've never used it. I'm not even sure how the thing works."

"And you haven't seen Hugo?"

Barbie felt the fear all about her, cold but intangible. She drew a deep breath before whispering, "No."

There was a pause. Then Steven said, "I think perhaps I'd better come round."

"Yes, please do."

It was Steven Lovett who led the ambulance crew to the sauna, where he and Barbie had discovered Hugo lying slumped on the floor. Barbie had almost passed out at the sight and he'd had to carry her back into the house and lay her on the couch. While waiting for the ambulance to arrive, he fetched her some brandy. "Just lie there quietly and leave everything to me," he said. "If he really is dead, I don't think the paramedics will move him until he's been seen by a doctor."

She gave him a grateful glance as she took the glass from him, holding it in both hands and taking quick, nervous sips. "Give them Dr Frayle's number, he knows Hugo's history," she said. "It's on a pad by the phone."

When the doctor arrived, he shook his head sadly as he knelt by the body saying, "I warned him something like this could happen, but he wouldn't listen." He glanced at his watch and made a note of the time. "I'm afraid I'll have to notify the police."

"The police?" Lovett looked at him in surprise. "Why?"

"It's routine in any case of sudden death, but it shouldn't be a problem. I'll have a word with Mrs Bayliss and tell her not to worry. Can you arrange for someone to stay with her, by the way . . . your wife, perhaps? She shouldn't be left on her own."

"I don't have a wife, I'm a widower."

"I see. Is there a relative you could contact on her behalf?"

"I believe there's an aunt in London, but it's too late to do anything tonight. I'll see what else I can organise."

"Good. I'll leave it with you." The doctor packed his bag and went indoors to deliver his message.

Barbie had no idea how long she lay on the couch after

everyone had gone. The doctor had come with Steven to tell her that Hugo was dead and that his body would be taken away 'as soon as the formalities were over'. In her slightly befuddled state she could not quite grasp what those formalities were and it came as a shock when Steven brought a policeman to see her and explained gently that he would like to ask her a few questions, if she felt up to it. The officer was very kind and she told him in a weak, unsteady voice how she had been getting ready to go out for the day, that the last time she had spoken to her husband he was standing by the pool drinking coffee while waiting for the sauna to warm up, that when she went to tell him she was leaving he was in the sauna and she had tapped on the glass and waved to him. No, they hadn't spoken, the cabin was pretty well soundproof. Yes, he had seemed perfectly all right. No, he hadn't complained recently of feeling unwell, in fact, he'd only just had his regular check-up and the consultant had said he was fine. The officer took the name of the consultant and then went away, expressing his sympathy and saying he hoped it wouldn't be necessary to trouble her again.

When he had gone she shut her eyes and tried to get her head round what had happened. Hugo was dead – a heart attack, the doctor said. Surely, she should be feeling something, some emotion? All she could think of was that tonight, and every night for the rest of her life, she would be able to go to bed and sleep without having her body plundered against her will.

Chapter Fifteen

After a fortnight of dry weather, clouds had built up throughout the afternoon. The light drizzle that had been falling for the past half-hour became a steady downpour as DI Castle turned out of the police station car park and headed for Exeter Street. The traffic was heavy and the usual crawl through the congested city centre was made worse by temporary traffic lights at roadworks. By the time he reached his destination, after taking several wrong turns in a fruitless attempt to find a short cut, his spirits had sunk to a point where he began to believe that the visit would probably turn out to be a complete waste of time. Still, now he was here he might as well go through with it. He locked the car, turned up his collar and hurried through the rain towards the house, noting with relief that the white van was standing outside. That at least meant he wouldn't have to wait until the owner got home.

His knock was answered by a tired-looking woman whose age might have been anywhere between thirty and forty-five. She had the weary expression of one for whom life was a constant battle. The sight of a stranger evoked only a faint flicker of interest, which quickly changed to apprehension as Castle held up his warrant card.

"Mrs Holland?" She nodded. "Detective Inspector Castle, Gloucester CID. I'd like a word with your husband."

"What about? What's he done—?" She stopped in mid-sentence, like a tape that had been cut off before the end.

Castle sensed that she had been on the point of adding 'now'.

"Nothing that we know of. I'm just making some routine enquiries," he said smoothly.

"You'd better come in." Grudgingly, she stood aside just far enough to admit him, then pushed past him and opened a door on the right of the narrow passage. She stood barring Castle's way as she said, "Tel, it's the police again." Her voice sounded shaky. Over her shoulder, Castle saw Holland scrambling up from the floor, where a boy of about ten was kneeling in front of a toy garage. The two had evidently been playing with the dozen or so miniature cars lined up on the worn carpet.

"Sorry to intrude on your evening," said Castle. "This shouldn't take long."

"Billy!" Holland jerked his head towards the door. "We'll finish the game later."

"But Dad!" the boy protested, but his mother took him by the arm and hauled him to his feet. "You heard what your father said," she snapped. "Go in the kitchen."

"Can't I take my cars?" the child whined.

"No, you—" the mother began, but Castle, who had been doing a rapid inspection of the room, stepped past her and intervened.

"Let the boy take them, I'm in no hurry," he said, in his best public relations manner. He picked up one of two small cardboard boxes lying on a chair. "Do you keep your cars in here, son?" The child nodded, took the box and began filling it with toys. Castle squatted down to help. "And then you fasten the lid with one of these?" he continued, holding up a fluorescent pink rubber band. Billy took it from him, again without speaking, and snapped it round the box he held. "You chose good bright ones, Billy," Castle went on. "No risk of losing anything done up with them, eh?" The boy gave a shy smile. "D'you buy them with your pocket money?"

"No, me Dad gave 'em to me. He's got lots." This time Billy

turned to his father with a broad, affectionate grin, which was not returned.

"All the same lovely bright colour?" Castle went on. He waited for a contradiction, but none came. "Well now, as your Dad's got lots, perhaps you can spare me this one." He picked up a second band lying beside the other box and dangled it between his thumb and forefinger.

Billy glanced up at his father as if seeking approval. Holland scowled at Castle. "Sure you don't want to pinch one of the kid's cars as well?" he demanded belligerently.

"Now, why would I do that?" Castle replied blandly. As he straightened up and slipped the band into his pocket, his eyes slid across the room to the mantelpiece, on which half a dozen or so brightly coloured greetings cards were ranged among an assortment of brass and china ornaments. One of the cards bore the legend, 40 NOT OUT in bright red capitals. Castle felt a flutter of excitement. Was he about to get lucky after all?

He turned to Holland with a genial smile as he enquired, "Your birthday today, is it? Many happy returns!"

"No, it was yesterday," Billy informed him eagerly. "We went to the Pizza Hut for supper and me Mum—"

Before the lad could finish, his father took him by the shoulder and pushed him towards the door. "OK, that's enough for now," he said sharply. "Do as your mum says." Reluctantly, with a backward glance at the remaining cars, the boy left the room. His mother hesitated, looking from the policeman to her husband and back again.

"No need for you to stay, Rita." Holland made it sound like a command and, without a word, she followed her son. As the door closed behind them, he rounded on Castle. "So what's this about?" he demanded in an angry whisper. "If it's Mrs Chant's murder, I told you, I wasn't there – I don't know nothing."

"So you said. Just the same, it's possible you can help us with our enquiries." Castle sat down in one of the shabby armchairs and stretched out his legs. He sensed that Holland's aggressive manner concealed a certain disquiet. "How's business, then?" he asked conversationally.

The question evidently took Holland by surprise and he avoided Castle's eye as he sank into the other armchair and replied, "Not bad. Why d'you ask?"

"Just wondered. You mentioned you collect quite a few cash payments from your customers."

"So?"

"Picked up any large amounts lately?"

"What is this?" Holland's face and neck grew red and he glared at the policeman. "I told you the other day, I keep my accounts straight."

"So you did. Well, maybe we can talk about that some other time." From his inside breast pocket Castle pulled out the photographs of the items Arthur Chant had reported missing. "Ever seen any of these?" He handed the prints over, one at a time. "Look carefully."

Reluctantly, as if suspecting a trap, Holland took each print, scanned it briefly and handed it back. Castle saw his eyes flicker at the sight of a picture of a gold necklet with matching earrings. "Recognise those?" he asked.

"No."

"Sorry, thought you did."

"Well, you was mistaken."

Holland held out the photograph, but Castle made no move to take it from him. "Have another look," he urged. "Take your time. It's a very distinctive design. If it was bought locally and we can track the purchaser down, it would take us a step nearer to Mrs Chant's killer."

Holland gave him a sharp look. "This is her stuff?"

"That's right – didn't I mention it?"

"No, you didn't."

"That necklace and earrings . . . are you quite sure you

never saw them before? Perhaps she was wearing them when you went to the Chants' house to do some work?"

At the suggestion a look of relief replaced Holland's wary expression and he said hurriedly, "Yeah, that must be it."

"Ah! I thought you recognised them. Thank you so much." Castle put the photographs back in his pocket and stood up. "Well, thank you for your time, Mr Holland. I'll see myself out." He paused at the door and turned. "Oh, just one more thing. You did say you'd never been in trouble before?"

Holland glared. Once again, he was on the defensive. "Who says I'm in trouble now?" He got to his feet and thrust his face close to Castle's. "You got nothing on me, so clear out or I'll have you for harassment."

Castle raised both hands in a placatory gesture. "No need to get excited, I just wanted to make sure," he said.

The front door had barely closed behind him when Rita came storming out of the kitchen. "What was all that about?" she demanded in a fierce whisper. "And don't start shooting your mouth off – I don't want Billy upset again."

"Whose fault was it he got upset last time?" Terry hissed back.

She brushed the question aside. "You've been back to see Charlie Foss, ain't you?"

"What if I have? I told you, he owes me."

"And I told you, that guy's pure poison, always was. You know I never liked you working with him and I was right, wasn't I? Well, wasn't I?" she repeated as he remained sullenly silent. "What did that copper want?"

"It ain't nothing for you to worry about," he said insistently, but he knew his voice lacked conviction. Those deceptively casual questions about money and the business over the rubber band . . . that detective wasn't just making polite conversation, he knew something. Had the police been tailing him? Had Charlie called his bluff and grassed after all? If that was the case, why not come out and say so? His palms grew sweaty at the thought, but he did his best to reassure Rita. "It was about some stuff what got pinched from a house where I done some work – it was all legit, honest," he told her. "Whoever nicked my van the other day must have done the job, but you know what coppers are like – never take your word for nothing."

"You swear it's nothing to do with Charlie Foss?" She put a hand on his arm and looked up at him beseechingly. "Tel, promise me you won't go and see him no more – it ain't worth it, not for any money."

"It was my share of sixty grand he made off with, Reet." He stared down at her tired, careworn face, mentally comparing her shabby dress and dowdy appearance to the way Charlie Foss's wife was turned out. His anger at the way he had been treated was like a griping in his guts. "I done time for that, and I want my cut. I managed to screw five grand out of him—"

Her eyes stretched. "You what?"

"He's a posh businessman now, Reet – he won't say nothing." Terry wished he felt as sure of it as he tried to sound. "The last thing he wants is for his past to catch up with him."

"What past? I keep telling you, he's never had a record, he's too smart. Tangle with him and he'll make dogshit of you. For God's sake Tel, what do you use for brains? You can bet your life there's a catch in what he's done. They never found the money you stole from the bank and—"

"The money Charlie stole, you mean."

Rita passed a hand over her forehead, brushing back an untidy wisp of hair that badly needed cutting. "No," she said wearily, "*you* stole it, you and Frank."

"It was Charlie that got his dirty hands on it – he ripped us off rotten."

"You know the jury never bought that story and the police have quite likely been keeping an eye on you since you got out, hoping you'd lead them to it. Suppose they come and search here?"

At this, Terry remembered how smart *he* had been and the thought cheered him up. "Won't find nothing, will they?" he said smugly.

"So what've you done with what you took off Charlie?"

"Put it in the building society, where else?"

She stared at him, wide-eyed and ashen-faced. "You bloody fool!" she gasped. "How're you going to explain it when they check your account?"

He stared back at her in genuine incomprehension. "They can't do that!" he protested. "Bank accounts is private, ain't they?"

"If they think there's hot money in it, of course they can check, you . . . you pratt . . . you stupid—" For a moment she seemed to have difficulty getting her words out. Then, forgetting in her fear, rage and frustration about not upsetting Billy, she screamed, "Why did I ever take up with a half-wit like you?" and rushed out of the room, leaving him scratching his head in hurt bewilderment.

Meanwhile, DI Castle went straight back to his office and wrote up the interview. Then he tackled some more outstanding paperwork until it was time to keep his date with Sukey, but all the time his conversation with Terry Holland was nibbling at the back of his mind.

I'm on the right track, I know I am, he said to himself later as he set off for Sukey's house. Although Holland had admitted nothing, he was certain from the man's demeanour that he was holding something back. Despite his initial denial, he had admitted recognising some of the jewellery, and his eagerness to accept the explanation that Castle had put into his mouth was definitely suspect. The wife, too, seemed scared witless and had been on the point of letting on that her husband had a record. Well, he knew the man's date of birth now and first thing tomorrow he'd put Radcliffe onto the job of tracking him down.

Then there was the little matter of the elastic bands – 'lots of them', Billy had said – that Castle was sure had been used to secure bundles of banknotes similar to the one found in the pocket of Holland's overalls. And he was still not convinced by Arthur Chant's assurance that there had been no money in his safe. Inch by inch, he was getting near to the truth.

Sukey was on her own in the sitting room when he arrived at the little house in Brockworth, although splashing noises and the sound of pop music from upstairs told him that Fergus was at home. She greeted him with her usual warmth, but he could tell that something was worrying her.

"Have you had anything to eat?" she asked as she took his jacket.

"Yes, thanks, but I could murder a cup of tea."

"Me too." She led the way into the kitchen and filled the kettle. "I'm so glad to see you," she said over her shoulder as she plugged it in and reached into a cupboard for cups. "I've . . . been a bit stupid, Jim."

He put his hands on her shoulders and leaned his head against hers. "Tell me," he said.

It all sounded so trivial at first as she ran through the details: her need for extra money to pay for the school trip (*if only she'd asked him, he'd have lent it to her like a shot*); the offer that had seemed like a heaven-sent opportunity; her decision to undertake the commission despite the risk of being spotted; her stubborn determination (*typical!*) not to be put off by unjustified suspicions but to go ahead and take the series of photographs that Hugo Bayliss, the man who called himself Gary, claimed his wife had asked for.

Jim listened in silence as she told her story, breaking off as the water came to the boil for the tea. She made it, poured it out, offered him milk, sugar and biscuits, then sat down at the kitchen table. He took the chair opposite her, reached out and took her hand. "There's more, isn't there?"

"Yes." She told him of the attack by the helmeted intruder and his grip on her hand tightened. There were questions that,

154

as a police officer, he knew he should be asking, but for the moment he felt nothing but horror at the danger she had been in and thankfulness that she had come out of the incident alive and apparently unhurt.

"You're sure you're all right?" he said urgently, and then, "Does Fergus know?"

She shook her head. "It would only upset him. He worries about me."

"He's not the only one."

"I know." She returned the pressure of his hand, then gave a chuckle and said, "But whoever tried to throttle me will have bruised ribs and a nasty graze on his shin for his pains."

He saw another problem and asked, "Did you report it?"

"Of course I did. I called 999 the minute I was sure Chummy wasn't on my tail. I gave all the details I could think of at the time and promised to call in to the station tomorrow and make a full statement."

"Do they know who you are . . . what your job is?"

"Not yet, but I suppose they'll have to." She gave a rueful grimace. "I'm in hot water, aren't I – are you going to report me?"

"As if I would. Just the same, you know what the official attitude is towards moonlighting." Jim played with Sukey's fingers, his brow wrinkled in thought. "I could try having a quiet word with one of my colleagues at HQ – it might not be necessary for it to get back to Gloucester. Unless, of course, you're needed to give evidence in court. It would have to come out then."

"I'd be grateful for anything you can do, Jim. I can't afford to lose my job."

"Oh, I don't think it'll come to that. How about some more tea?" He released her hand and held out his cup. To his consternation, she burst into tears. He was at her side in a moment, pulling her to her feet, putting his arms round her. "It's all right darling, it's just delayed shock ... you've had a nasty experience ... you'll be OK."

"It isn't that," Sukey sobbed. "It's just ... I know that when it comes out there'll be a lot of nudge-nudge wink-wink ... wanted photos of his swimming pool, hee hee ... a likely story. You know how people are. That was what Mrs Bayliss thought, I know she did." She looked up at him through her tears and he stroked her hair, thinking how badly she needed someone to look after her, how much he wanted to be that person. "You do believe me, don't you?" she begged. "I had my suspicions all along, but I took a chance. I do so want to be able to give Fergus that trip – he's such a good kid and he's had so much to put up with – but I'd hate you to think—"

Her mouth puckered like a little girl's and he held her more closely. "You are just plain wet," he murmured in her ear. "That would never have occurred to me. But listen," he pushed her back into her chair and sat down again, "this bloke who attacked you has got to be caught." A thought struck him. "It couldn't be Bayliss himself, could it? Maybe some kind of sexual perversion—?"

She frowned, considering. "It's possible, I suppose, but ... no, I don't think so. He – the bloke who attacked me, I mean – was roughly the same build, but I had the impression that he was younger, although I never saw his face. It all happened so quickly – I never had time to get a description."

"Let's see how much you can remember." Jim's professional instinct took charge and he began asking questions, jotting down her answers in his notebook. "You'll make sure you put all this in your statement, won't you?" he said in his official voice when he had finished.

Sukey, once again her normal, buoyant self, grinned at him. "Of course, Guv," she said. From upstairs came the sound of water cascading through pipes. "Fergus will be down in a minute. You won't mention any of this, will you? By the way, what sort of day have you had?"

156

He outlined the visit from Katherine Percival, his subsequent interview with Terry Holland and the details of the man's birthday that had so fortuitously fallen into his lap. "He's our man, I'm sure of it," he said, "but we desperately need some cast-iron evidence. All I've got at the moment is a couple of Day-Glo elastic bands."

"What about the prints on the loo seat?"

"All they tell us is that it was handled by someone other than Chant or Holland."

"Which seems to confirm the housekeeper's hint that Mrs Chant had more than one lover."

"Exactly. If we could track down 'Walter Baby' it'd be a help. Oh, by the way, we do have this." He put his notebook away, took out the pictures of the missing valuables and showed her the one of the jewellery Holland had recognised.

Sukey glanced at it and was about to hand it back when she exclaimed, "Just a minute! Mrs Bayliss was wearing these – or ones very like it."

"Are you sure?"

She studied the picture more closely. "I couldn't swear to it, but it's an unusual design, not the sort of thing you buy from a high street jeweller. I noticed because she was fiddling with it while we were talking – the earrings as well."

"Brilliant!" His spirits rose again at the prospect of a breakthrough. "If it was a recent present from her husband, maybe he'll remember where he bought it."

"I wonder if it was a peace offering," Sukey commented drily as she handed the photo back. "She had some nasty bruises on her face."

"A wife-beater as well as a womaniser, eh?" Jim was deadly serious again. "You took one hell of a risk, Sook."

"I reckoned I could take care of myself." There was a familiar, obstinate tilt to her chin as she added, "Proved it, didn't I?"

"Don't do anything like that again . . . promise?" She looked

157

so vulnerable sitting there, her fine-boned hands fiddling with her empty tea cup, her sharp features pale and tired under the cap of short, dark curls. "Please, Sook. And about the school trip . . . I can help out if you're short."

She shook her head and her small mouth set in a firm line. "Thanks Jim, but I'd rather not borrow. Anyway, Paul should really fund it, but it's difficult for him . . ." There was no need for her to go on; Jim knew how things were with Myrna.

He glanced at his watch and stood up. "It's getting late and you need some rest. Will I see you at the weekend?"

Her expression brightened. "I hope so. Fergus would like you to come and watch him play cricket, if you're free on Saturday."

"I'd love to. By the way," he added as he put on his jacket, "have you mentioned what we were talking about yesterday?"

"You mean about his sex life?" She gave an odd, secretive smile. "Oh yes, I mentioned it."

"Everything OK?"

"Everything's fine." Her eyes glowed and she stood on tiptoe, putting her hands on his shoulders. Her lips brushed against his ear and he felt his heart thumping as she whispered, "Tell you about it on Saturday evening."

Chapter Sixteen

Before leaving for work the following morning, DI Castle phoned DC Hill at his home and told him to make a point of finding out whether the five thousand pounds paid in at the Cheltenham branch of the Western Building Society had been secured in bundles, and if so, how. On reaching his office, he instructed Sergeant Radcliffe to give priority to a check on Terence Holland, born on the 15th of June 1956. He then called the county headquarters in Cheltenham and spoke to his old friend Inspector David Mahony, saying that he would be in the town shortly and arranging to call in for a brief chat later that morning. Then, after dealing with a few routine matters, he set off for The Laurels.

There was a dark blue Ford Granada parked on the drive. Castle hoped it was Bayliss's car, which would mean he hadn't yet left for his office. He would be more likely than his wife to know where the necklace came from.

A bespectacled, prematurely balding man whom Castle judged to be in his mid-thirties answered his ring. His expression was guarded and he kept one hand on the latch, holding the door less than half-open. Like Rita Holland the previous evening, he gave the impression that the visitor was unwelcome.

"Mr Bayliss?"

The man shook his head. "No, my name's Lovett. I'm the late Mr Bayliss's office manager."

Castle felt his jaw move floorwards. Of all the rotten, lousy breaks – just when he reckoned he was getting somewhere. "The *late* Mr Bayliss?" he repeated. "I'm sorry . . . I had no idea—"

"He was found dead yesterday evening," Lovett informed him. "A heart attack, I understand. What was it you wanted?"

"Detective Inspector Castle, Gloucester CID." Mechanically, he held up his warrant card. "I realise this must be a very inopportune moment to call, but if it's possible, I'd appreciate a word with Mrs Bayliss. It shouldn't take long."

"If it's about the report of an intruder—"

"No, that's being dealt with here in Cheltenham. This is a different matter."

"Can't it wait? She's very shocked. It was so sudden."

Much as Castle hated the thought of intruding on private grief, he had a job to do. "I quite understand, sir, and normally I'd be more than willing to leave it for another time," he said, "but it's in connection with a murder inquiry."

Lovett hesitated, then stood back for Castle to step inside and closed the door behind him. "I'll have a word with her and see if she's up to it," he said. "If you wouldn't mind waiting."

He disappeared into a room leading out of the hall, leaving the door partially open. Castle heard him say "Barbie!" and there followed a brief consultation in low voices before Lovett returned and said, "Would you like to come this way?" and beckoned him into the sitting room.

A petite woman in a white satin robe and matching mules was standing with her back to the door. She was silhouetted against a wide picture window that gave a view over the patio, with the swimming pool and garden beyond. It gave Castle a sensation like a kick in the stomach to realise that it was there that Sukey had fought for her life against her faceless attacker. For a second or two his imagination dwelt on the bleak emptiness that his life would have become had she lost

160

that battle. Then, as the woman turned to face him, he switched his mind back to the job in hand.

"Mrs Bayliss?"

"Yes." She moved away from the window, sat down in an armchair and motioned to Castle to do the same.

He put her age at somewhere in the forties, but possibly shock and grief were making her look older than she actually was. The bruises Sukey had mentioned appeared to be fading, but they didn't help. She had a generally well-groomed appearance; her hair, although slightly dishevelled, had obviously been cut by a first-class stylist and her hands, which she held clasped on her lap, were expertly manicured.

"Mrs Bayliss, I do apologise for troubling you at this sad time," Castle began. "I explained to Mr Lovett—"

"It's all right, but you must excuse the dishabille." She pronounced it 'dizzibiw' and her faint smile and the way she settled the robe to conceal her legs held a hint of coyness. "What can I do for you, Inspector?"

"I'd like you to tell me if you recognise this necklace and earrings."

He handed her the photograph and she gave a little cry as she took it from him. "Of course! It's the set my husband – my *late* husband – gave me the other day. Lovely, innit?" Her smile, half sad, half proud, gave way to an anxious frown and she shot a glance at Lovett, who was sitting apart from them in an upright chair close to the door. "Where d'you get this?"

"You still have this jewellery?" Castle enquired.

"Course I do. But why—?"

"I have reason to believe it was among items stolen from the home of Mr and Mrs Arthur Chant."

Mrs Bayliss appeared shocked. "Wasn't Mrs Chant the woman what . . . who was killed the other day?"

"That's right. Did you know her?"

"No, course not . . . just read about it in the paper."

"Did your husband know her?"

161

She glared at him. "Here, what are you getting at?"

"Really, Inspector—" Lovett half rose from his seat, but she waved him back with an impatient gesture.

"'S all right Steve, I can handle this." She turned back to Castle. "You suggesting my Charlie nicked this?" she demanded.

Castle was taken aback at this sudden show of aggression, but he concealed his surprise as he replied soothingly, "Of course not. Whoever murdered Mrs Chant almost certainly stole her jewellery and disposed of it through a fence. Now, if you happen to know where your husband bought it, it would be a great help to us in our hunt for her killer."

"Sorry, I've no idea."

"Can you remember when he gave it to you?"

"Not exactly, a couple of days ago maybe."

"You can't be more precise than that?"

"Really, Inspector," Lovett interposed for the second time, "can't you see how distressing this is for Mrs Bayliss? Surely these questions can wait?"

This time she shot him a grateful glance. She handed the photo back to Castle and said, "Is that all?"

"Not quite, I'm afraid. I must ask you to let me take the necklace and earrings for identification by Mr Chant."

Her face crumpled as if she was going to cry. "They was the last things he gave me," she whispered. She fished in the pocket of her robe, brought out a lace-edged handkerchief and dabbed her eyes. Then she looked at Lovett. "Do I have to?" she faltered.

"I don't think you can refuse, Barbie, not in such a serious matter," he said gently. "It may turn out to be a mistake. Your necklace may not be the one in the picture after all."

"In that case, it will naturally be returned to you without delay," Castle assured her. "And of course, I'll give you a receipt."

Reluctantly, she got to her feet. "It's upstairs. I'll go and fetch it."

Castle stood up as well. "I'm sorry this had to happen at such an inopportune time," he said, thinking how futile it sounded. She nodded and went out of the room, closing the door behind her. Castle turned back to Lovett. "It must have been very sudden," he said quietly. "Do you know what happened?"

"We found his body in the sauna." Lovett nodded over his shoulder towards the window. "He'd had it installed just a short while ago. He was something of a fitness freak, but he had a heart murmur and he'd been warned against overdoing it. Unfortunately, he tended to ignore his doctor's advice."

"Very foolish," Castle remarked, then said, "You were with her, then?"

"Yes. She was worried because he hadn't returned home and she called me to find out if I knew anything. I was concerned as well because he'd been out of the office all day and there'd been that report of a prowler attacking someone, so I came over. Eventually, that's where we found him."

Further discussion was prevented by the reappearance of Mrs Bayliss holding a small lacquered box. She opened it and held it out to Castle. "Is that the one?"

He took it from her, sensing her reluctance to let go of it. "That's the one," he said gently. He closed the lid and put the box on the arm of his chair while he completed and signed the form of receipt he had brought with him. "Thank you for your cooperation," he said. "I'll see myself out."

Stage one successfully accomplished, Castle thought to himself as he went back to his car. Before driving off he carefully slid the box into a plastic envelope. Then he called Radcliffe and instructed him to arrange an urgent meeting with Mr Arthur Chant before making his way to police headquarters and seeking out his former colleague.

"Nice to see you, Jim," said David Mahony. "Any joy with your enquiry?"

"I think so." He followed Mahony into his office and went over to the window, watching the traffic streaming along Lansdown Road. "I'm pretty sure I've got hold of some of the jewellery missing after the Lorraine Chant murder."

"Congratulations! How did that come about?"

"Pure luck. One of my SOCOs recognised it from a photo of one of the pieces . . . said she'd seen a woman wearing it yesterday. I've just been round to pick it up."

"That *was* lucky. Did the woman say where she bought it?"

"That's where the luck ran out. Her husband gave it to her, and he died yesterday from a heart attack."

"Very inconsiderate of him," Mahony commented, without a ghost of a smile. Gallows humour had always been one of his specialities. "Think of the legwork he could have saved your people by hanging on for another twenty-four hours."

Castle grinned and nodded. "At least this item's turned up quickly," he said. "More chance of a fence remembering who flogged it to him."

"Who was the bloke, anyway?"

"A Mr Bayliss, of The Laurels in Charlton Kings."

"That rings a bell. We had a 999 from there yesterday morning. Some woman said she'd been attacked. A patrol car got there within ten minutes and the officers had a good look round, but found nothing untoward. None of the neighbours saw or heard anything, but one of them knew where the householder worked so we contacted his office and left a message. No one's come back to us so far."

"They got the message all right . . . a chap named Lovett, Bayliss's office manager, was there with Mrs Bayliss when I called. He thought at first that was what I'd come about."

"Was anything else said?"

"Nothing. I thought of asking, but Cheltenham isn't my patch and in any case it was obvious the poor woman had had enough of answering questions."

"We were almost inclined to write it off as a hoax, except that the caller gave her name and promised to call in today to make a full statement." Mahony reached for his notebook. "I'll check in a minute whether she's been. And we should really speak to Mrs Bayliss, to make sure nothing's missing."

"Sure. Now, there's something else I wanted to mention." Castle pulled up a chair and sat down. Lowering his voice to a discreet level, he said, "The woman who made the 999 call is the one who spotted the necklace."

"Your SOCO?" Mahony raised an eyebrow.

"Right. I told her not to call in to make her statement until I'd had a word with you. The fact is, she was at The Laurels doing a bit of moonlighting. This Bayliss character – he owned the Bodywise Health Clubs, but I guess you already know that – pitched her a yarn about wanting some photographs of his garden and swimming pool. Unfortunately she bumped into the wife, who was just going out for the day and who obviously assumed she had an assignation with her husband."

Mahony's brows lifted for the second time. He looked knowing. "Natural mistake," he commented.

"But nevertheless, a mistake." Castle could hear his voice becoming over-emphatic and hastened to cancel any suggestion that he might be personally concerned by adding, "So Mrs Reynolds assures me. Anyway," he went on as Mahony made no further comment, "she went wandering round to the back of the house looking for Mr Bayliss, saw the patio door open and went in. It was then that someone jumped her." It wasn't the complete story, he knew. Sukey would have to fill in the details herself. "She was pretty shaken."

"Understandable," said Mahony. "I take it you'd like me to see that word doesn't filter back to George Barnes in Gloucester?" he added shrewdly.

"If you could. She's a first-class SOCO and I don't want

165

to see her in hot water. She's also anxious not to have it thought that she had any sort of relationship with this Bayliss character."

"I'll do what I can. Tell her to ask for me personally when she calls in."

"Thanks Dave, I appreciate it." Castle stood up. "I must be getting back. I'm hoping to get a positive ID on this jewellery sometime today."

"Nice to see you. Drop in any time."

As soon as Castle arrived back at Gloucester police station, DC Hill followed him into his office, brandishing a video tape. His face was pink with excitement.

"Bingo!" he exclaimed. He laid the video on Castle's desk like a dog bringing a slipper to its master. "Guess who's starring on that, sir!"

"Amaze me," said Castle, hoping his silent guess was about to be proved correct.

"Mr Terence Holland!" The young officer was grinning from ear to ear. "They ran it through for me and there he was, paying in his five grand shortly after eleven thirty yesterday morning. No doubt about it at all."

"Great! Did the girl remember how the notes were done up?"

"She sure did. Elastic bands the colour of candy floss, she said. The guy gathered them all up and took them away . . . said they were for his kid."

"Nice to know he tells the truth now and again." Castle went over to a steel cupboard and locked the tape away. "Now, if only we could get Mr Chant to admit that he had a large quantity of money in that floor safe, fastened in bundles with candy pink elastic bands, we'd be well on our way to cooking Mr Holland's goose for him." As he spoke, he spotted a note under a paperweight on his desk, picked it up and read it. "That's good, it seems I have an appointment

166

with Chant this afternoon. And I've got something here that I think will make his day."

"What's that, sir?"

Castle slid the lacquered box from its envelope and carefully opened the lid. Hill gave an appreciative whistle. "That some of the stuff belonging to Mrs Chant, sir? Very pretty."

"Very valuable too, I'd guess. Once Chant has identified it, I'll have it checked for fingerprints. Other people will have handled it since Holland lifted it, but you never know – we might be lucky."

"You reckon Holland's our man, sir?"

"I'm sure of it."

Castle's spirits were further lifted by the appearance of DS Radcliffe, who entered the office waving a sheet of paper. "Terence Walter Holland's got form all right, Guv!" he exclaimed. "Get a load of that!"

"Walter!" Castle's normal sang-froid momentarily deserted him as he snatched the printout from Radcliffe's hand. "Walter *Baby*! Of course! So Sukey could be right – maybe Lorraine Chant did enjoy a bit of rough." He ran his eye down the list of convictions. "Armed robbery, manslaughter. On the face of it, this has got to be our man."

"With a string of previous going back to his schooldays," Radcliffe pointed out gleefully.

"Yes, but let's not get carried away." After the initial surge of excitement, Castle's analytical brain began examining the fresh evidence for snags. "None of these was for a violent offence. All right, there was the bank job, but it was the other guy who hit the old man with the sawn-off shotgun, not Holland. And Walter isn't such an uncommon name, so the presumed link with Mrs Chant could still be a coincidence. And all his previous offences were committed within a comparatively small area of London—"

"So maybe he decided it was time to set up shop somewhere else," Radcliffe interposed.

Castle pursed his lips. "It'd be unusual. Villains like Holland don't often stray from their own patch, where all their contacts are." Reading the disappointment on the sergeant's face, he said apologetically, "I'm sorry, Andy, I'm as certain as you are that he's our man, but you know what the Super's going to say – it's still only circumstantial. Now, if I could only get Arthur Chant to admit that he's missing a load of cash fastened with pink rubber bands . . ."

Chapter Seventeen

The highly successful empire of Chantertainment, comprising a string of lucrative amusement arcades throughout the Midlands, was administered from offices just off Westgate, almost literally in the shadow of the magnificent Gothic cathedral and a short walk from the central police station. Before leaving to keep his appointment with Arthur Chant, DI Castle put his head round the door of the SOCOs' office. Sergeant George Barnes, who ran the section, was in earnest discussion on the telephone. A couple of members of his team were busy at their desks, but there was no sign of Sukey. He had been hoping to catch a word with her to try and find out, under the pretext of telling her about the discovery of the necklace, whether she had spoken to Inspector Mahony at Headquarters. Disappointed, he left the building.

After yesterday's rain the sky had cleared, leaving behind nothing more menacing than a few scattered clouds floating like dollops of beaten egg white on a background of cobalt blue. Herring gulls from the nearby River Severn wheeled and screeched in the limpid air or regarded the human activity below them from lofty perches on roofs and chimney pots. Castle had allowed himself a quarter of an hour for a five minute walk and for once he moved at a relaxed pace, observing more closely than usual the ancient buildings lining the narrow alleys that criss-crossed the main thoroughfares of the city. He passed under a stone arch into College Green, where he loitered for a while observing the tourists milling around outside

Betty Rowlands

the cathedral. Some had their noses in maps and guide books, others stood in clusters listening to their guides before heading for the great west door to begin their pilgrimage. Castle reflected wryly that despite having been born in Gloucester he had not been inside the splendid medieval building since leaving school. The visitors probably went home with a more up-to-date knowledge of its history than his own.

Entering the offices of Chantertainment was like stepping into a different world. The furniture in the outer office, where a pretty young receptionist with a mane of natural blonde hair sat filing her nails and reading a teenage magazine, was modern and functional. In startling contrast, the inner sanctum, where Arthur Chant rose from behind an imposing mahogany desk to greet him, reminded the detective of a New Orleans room setting he remembered from a visit to the American Museum in Bath. Everything that was not made of dark, elaborately carved wood seemed to be crimson, crystal or gilt. All it needed to complete the decadent ambience was some seductive enchantress showing off her cleavage on a plush-covered couch. Chant's study at home, which until that moment Castle would have described as lavishly furnished, was austere by comparison.

There was a subtle difference about the man himself as well. At home, he was just another prosperous businessman with an expensively appointed house in an exclusive neighbourhood, a top-of-the-market car and, until her sudden and violent death, a young and beautiful wife on whom he showered every luxury. Castle guessed that at Priory View it had been Mrs Chant who occupied the throne with her husband the adoring slave. Here, the man was in his true element. From this room he wielded power.

After an exchange of polite greetings it was Chant who opened the conversation by asking, "Do I understand that you have made some progress with your investigation, Inspector?"

"I believe so, sir. We have recovered what we believe to be some pieces of your late wife's missing jewellery." From his pocket, Castle took a transparent envelope containing the necklace and earrings and passed it across the desk.

As Chant reached out and took it, Castle saw the muscles round his jaw tighten. He laid the envelope on the desk and sat staring down at it from beneath his heavy brows, his face inscrutable. It was several seconds before he drew a deep, juddering breath and whispered shakily, "Yes, they were my wife's."

"You are absolutely certain?"

"Of course. I had them made especially for her – the design is unique. Let me show you something."

Without taking his eyes from the jewellery he reached into a drawer in the desk, drew out a manila folder and handed Castle a beautifully executed drawing that showed every detail of the intricate workmanship. "I spent a day with one of the finest craftsmen in Birmingham while he created it in accordance with my own ideas," he said. His voice had steadied, but Castle felt a surge of pity at the misery in his expression. "It was made for her last birthday . . . but she didn't like it and I don't believe she ever took it out of its case." Sadly, Chant handed the envelope back to the detective. "I imagine you need this as evidence, Inspector. Where did you find it?"

"It was being worn by a lady in Cheltenham who said her husband had given it to her. Sadly, he died yesterday so we haven't yet been able to establish where he obtained it. Enquiries are proceeding and we expect in due course to recover more items."

"I see." Mechanically, Chant took the drawing from Castle and put it away. "Do I take it this is your only lead so far?"

"In our search for Mrs Chant's killer? On the contrary, I have every reason to hope that we shall soon be in a position to make an arrest."

"Oh?" Chant's head shot up and he appeared almost startled.

171

"I had no idea . . . do I know the man? It's not young Holland is it?" The possibility appeared to cause him considerable dismay. "I would never have believed—"

Castle leaned forward and put his elbows on the desk, fixing Chant squarely in the eye. "We know that our suspect has a criminal record, but the evidence against him in this case is far from complete," he said. "In fact, unless you, sir, can give me certain information, it may never be complete."

"I don't understand."

The detective sat back in his chair without taking his eyes from the other man's face. "You may remember, sir, that I asked you about the money you are in the habit of keeping in your floor safe at home. You assured me at the time that there was none there on the day your wife was killed."

Chant gave a slight nod. "That is correct," he said guardedly. He picked up a paper knife in the shape of a sword with a jewelled handle and began turning it between broad, spatulate fingers.

"I'm asking you to think again, sir."

"How many times do I have to tell you? That safe was empty. Why do you keep asking the same question?"

There was a touch of defiance in Chant's manner which convinced Castle that he was not telling the truth. He leaned forward again. "Because," he said, "yesterday morning our suspect paid five thousand pounds in cash into his building society account." From his wallet, he extracted two matching pink elastic bands and dangled them in front of Chant. "I have reason to believe that one of these was used to secure some of the notes. The other, I took from your desk at home when I came to your house the other day. As you can see, they appear identical."

"And you call that evidence?" In an instant, Chant's demeanour had changed from that of a grieving widower readily cooperating with the police to one of blustering resentment and anger. He threw down the knife, snatched

172

the bands from Castle's fingers and gave them a dismissive glance before tossing them aside. "What do you expect to prove from a couple of scraps of pink rubber?" he asked scornfully.

"The colour is so distinctive that we should have no difficulty in tracing the suppliers," Castle explained patiently. "With luck they'll be able to identify the batch number and give us a list of the shops they sold the bands to. Then we can start tracking down the people who bought them." He spoke with more confidence than he felt. Still, it was amazing what a combination of science and legwork could achieve nowadays. Aloud, he continued, "It'll be a long and wearisome process. It would make our task so much easier if you would—"

"For the last time, Inspector, I have nothing more to tell you," Chant interrupted. He rose to his feet and walked round his desk towards the door. "Now, if you'll excuse me, I have other calls on my time."

"Then I won't take up any more of it." Castle spoke politely, but he was careful not to appear in a hurry as, having replaced the bands in his wallet, he stowed it carefully in the inside pocket of his coat. "There's one more thing I'd like to say before I leave, sir."

"Well?"

Chant's attitude as he stood gripping the door handle with one powerful hand was belligerent, even intimidating, yet Castle was convinced that beneath it he was on the defensive. "If we can establish a link between this man and the stolen jewellery," he said, "it should give us sufficient evidence to charge him with theft, but not necessarily to be confident of securing a conviction for murder."

"So go out and get hold of some more evidence."

"That's exactly what I intend to do, sir." As if that was the end of the matter, Castle got up to leave. As Chant made to open the door, the detective put out a hand and leaned his weight against it, holding it shut. "I'd like to ask you a hypothetical question," he said.

Chant scowled and made a show of consulting his heavy gold watch. "Ten seconds," he said curtly.

Keeping his tone casual and his voice deliberately low to avoid being overheard by anyone in the outer office, Castle said, "What would your advice be to someone who claimed that withholding information from the Inland Revenue was worth the risk – if the stakes were high enough?"

Chant's face reddened and he thrust out his jaw. "What the hell are you insinuating?" he demanded.

"I'm insinuating nothing. As I said, it was a hypothetical question. And here's another one. If, as a result of insufficient evidence, your wife's killer were to go free, possibly to strike again, would you consider that possibility a risk worth taking?" Castle waited for a response, but none came. "Think about it, sir," he said softly.

He took his hand from the door and Chant wrenched it open, his expression was savage. "Kindly get out of my office this minute!" he ordered, in a voice so thick with emotion as to be unrecognisable.

"Good day, Mr Chant, and thank you for your time," replied Castle politely. "I'll keep you informed." As he strode towards the exit, Chant's door slammed behind him. The young receptionist, startled, looked up from her magazine and stared first in the direction of her employer's office and then at the policeman. Their eyes met in a fleeting glance of compassion at the muffled, but unmistakable, sound of a strong man weeping.

Back at the police station, Castle went straight to the SOCOs' office. His spirits lifted when he found Sukey there on her own. She looked less tired and more alert, but at the same time more relaxed, than he remembered from the previous evening. "How did it go this morning?" he asked.

"OK, I think," she said, "but guess what! Mr Bayliss was

found dead in his sauna yesterday evening . . . or perhaps you already know?" she added as her eye fell on the contents of the transparent envelope Castle laid on her desk.

"Yes, I know. I got that from the sorrowing widow this morning," he said. He had not been entirely convinced by Barbie Bayliss's show of grief and realised from the sharp look Sukey gave him that his tone must have betrayed his misgivings. "Maybe I'm being callous, but I noticed that when she started sniffling into a handkerchief there were no actual tears," he explained. "And I'm pretty sure you were right about the bruises."

"Was she on her own?"

"No, she was being comforted by a chap called Lovett from her husband's office. He was very protective, but I suppose there's nothing remarkable in that. By the way, when you gave your statement to Inspector Mahony, did he say if they'd checked on the intruder?"

"They sent someone round this morning – that was when they found out about Bayliss having died. Mrs Bayliss was quite adamant that nothing had been disturbed and she wanted the whole thing dropped."

Castle frowned and shook his head. "Mahony won't agree to that. He's more likely to apply for permission to have the house searched for drugs."

"You think she's deliberately shielding someone?"

"It looks like it. That fellow Lovett – he behaved perfectly properly and I certainly didn't notice anything suspicious in his manner to Mrs Bayliss, but you never know, do you?"

"It wouldn't be surprising in a way if Mrs Bayliss had found a lover. Even with all that luxury, life with Hugo can't have been a bed of roses."

"It could hardly account for such a violent attack on you. I'd love to know what was in that bag that it was so important you shouldn't see." Castle's brain began probing for possible explanations. Then he told himself it wasn't his case and it was

175

up to Mahony and his team to decide what action, if any, they should take. He switched his mind back to the job in hand.

"See what you can get off that in the way of prints," he said, indicating the necklace. "Here's the box Mrs Bayliss kept it in. You'd better take the prints off that as well, for comparison with any on the necklace. You're unlikely to find the victim's. Chant said his wife didn't like it and never wore it."

"She must have been hard to please," Sukey sighed. There was a wistful look on her face as her fingers caressed the finely-wrought piece through the protective film.

"He had it designed and made especially for her, but she turned her nose up at it."

"Poor chap – he must have been hurt."

"I felt sorry for him too, until I tackled him about the money he kept in the safe. He turned into a real hard case then. He knows the Revenue would tear him apart if they suspected there was anything dodgy about his accounting system. I suppose the way he sees it, nothing can bring his wife back, but if as a result of admitting the loss of all that money it came to light he's been filing false returns, he could end up in big trouble – a possible prison sentence, loss of his business, you name it."

"So he's prepared to let his wife's killer get away with it?" Sukey's mobile features registered disgust at such a callous attitude.

Castle shrugged. "That's your big tycoon for you," he said morosely, "and unless we're lucky enough to find Holland's prints on that little trinket, it's quite likely he *will* get away with it." He turned to go just as Sergeant Barnes came into the room. "Ah, just the man I want. I've turned up some more evidence in the Chant murder inquiry and I'd be obliged if you'd give it priority."

"Sure, Guv, no problem."

"Oh, and by the way." Castle turned back to Sukey.

"Holland's definitely got form, and guess what. He's 'Walter Baby'!"

She gave an impish grin that made him long to take her face between his hands and kiss her to death. "There, what did I tell you?" she said cheekily.

Back in the incident room, Castle found a message asking him to ring Inspector Mahony at Headquarters.

"I thought you'd be interested to know that there's to be a PM on Bayliss," Mahony told him when he got through.

"Does that mean the death is being treated as suspicious?"

"Not in the sense that you or I would use the word – not so far, anyway. There's some doubt about the precise cause, a suggestion the temperature in the sauna could have been abnormally high, possibly due to some malfunction."

"In which case the widow might be in a position to sue whoever installed it."

Mahony gave one of his dry chuckles. "That's the laugh. It was put in by Bayliss's own company, Bodywise Systems."

"The outfit that owns the health clubs?"

"The clubs are a fairly recent venture and so are the saunas. Their core business is swimming pools, ornamental fountains, stuff like that."

It struck Castle as ironic that a man whose business was primarily concerned with water should end his days in the dry heat of a sauna.

Chapter Eighteen

Later that afternoon, the Superintendent buttonholed DI Castle and demanded a progress report on the Lorraine Chant investigation. He was not over-impressed by the circumstantial evidence on which the case against Terry Holland rested so far, expressed doubts about the relevance of the pink elastic bands and was in no mood to authorise the allocation of precious man-hours for a check on every retail outlet that might have supplied them. He did, however, concede that only a limited quantity of that peculiarly lurid colour might have been imported and was prepared to allow a certain amount of desk work to be devoted to checking with distributors. His reaction on hearing about the cash paid into the Western Building Society by Terry Holland was marginally more encouraging, although he pointed out with, in Castle's opinion, unnecessary emphasis and repetition, that since no money had been reported stolen, the link with the case was tenuous, to say the least.

The Superintendent also – not surprisingly for a man noted for his mistrust of coincidences – warned his inspector against attaching too much significance to the suspect's previous record. In support of this caveat he spent some time on a prolix re-statement of the reservations Castle himself had earlier expressed to Sergeant Radcliffe. And finally, he returned to a possibility he had raised at the outset, namely that it was Arthur Chant who had killed his wife.

"I did consider that of course, sir, and I questioned him

very closely about his movements," Castle said patiently. "He admits returning home to collect a file he'd left behind, although as it happens we haven't found anyone who saw his car during the crucial period. He claims he and his wife had coffee together and we found two used mugs in the kitchen to bear that out. He got back to his office in plenty of time for his meeting and nobody noticed anything unusual about his manner. I agree it isn't possible to eliminate him altogether, but he made no attempt whatever to conceal the body and his shock and grief seemed perfectly genuine."

"Hmm . . . well, don't lose sight of him in your obsession with Holland."

"Of course not, sir." Castle tried not to show resentment at the word 'obsession'.

"All right," the Superintendent ended graciously. "If you're certain Holland's your man go after him by all means, but make sure you've got something concrete on him before you pull him in."

When Castle emerged from the interview his optimism, while not entirely dispelled, was considerably dented. As things stood the only hope of an imminent breakthrough lay with the gold necklet, and in his present frame of mind he would not have been surprised to learn that it bore no identifiable prints at all. The afternoon dragged past with no further developments of any significance and at six o'clock, resisting the temptation to check with George Barnes, he went in search of an early dinner. He deliberately chose a restaurant some distance from the police station to minimise the chance of bumping into any of his colleagues. Not that many of them ate out in the evening. The women cooked for themselves and their families, if any, while the majority of the men had wives who prepared their meals, and children who waited up in the hope that Dad would be home in time to hear about the goals they had scored or the good marks they had been awarded at school. Castle had never had kids, but he had once had a wife. He thought it might be

179

nice to have one again. That made him think of Sukey. He had a date with her in two days' time, but in his present state of mind Saturday seemed light years away.

While masticating his way through an over-cooked steak – he had ordered medium rare, but couldn't summon the energy to complain – he mentally chewed over the case. His thoughts switched to the victim herself: young, beautiful and, according to hearsay, with a voracious sexual appetite that her adoring but much older husband could not satisfy. It was reasonably certain that she had been on the point of leaving him; the fact that all her jewellery was missing but that the cases had been carefully replaced in the safe indicated that she had intended to postpone for as long as possible the moment when he realised she had no intention of returning.

What about the money? Castle was convinced to the marrow of his bones that it had come from the safe, and here he was presented with two possibilities: either, despite her husband's assertion to the contrary, the victim had known where it was and where he kept the key, or someone else had similar knowledge. Holland had installed the safe and could easily have obtained a spare key beforehand. In Castle's book it was a racing certainty that he was now in possession of its contents, some of which he had been carrying on the day he brought his van in for forensic examination; the remainder he had hung on to for a few days before paying it into his building society account. Where he had fenced the jewellery was anybody's guess, but sooner or later they'd track it down. And it was quite possible he had been stupid enough to keep some of it to give to his wife. A search of the Holland residence was indicated.

Despite Sukey's belief that Lorraine Chant might have enjoyed 'a bit of rough' and the fact that Holland's second name was Walter, Castle strongly doubted that he was the man she had been planning to leave home with. Instinct told him that if she had been going to keep an assignation, it would have been with someone with more style. House-to-house enquiries had revealed that a dark green Jaguar had occasionally been seen near The Hill, but appeals on the local radio and television stations for the driver to come forward had so far produced no result.

By the time the waiter brought his coffee, Castle's mind had moved on to his latest interview with Arthur Chant. That afternoon, the man had revealed the hard centre that lay beneath the pain. While never doubting the genuine nature of his grief, the detective had glimpsed a streak of ruthlessness, a determination to do whatever was necessary to protect his assets and his reputation. It could well have been Chant himself who had relocked the empty safe and restored the study to its original state before summoning help . . . something else that would never be known for certain unless he could be persuaded to own up to it. With a sigh, Castle paid his bill and made his way back to his office.

He reached it just as Sukey was coming out and his spirits immediately soared as if they had bounced off a trampoline. She was grinning broadly as she followed him back into the room, exclaimed "Tara!" and pointed to the envelope on his desk.

"What have you found?"

"Double whammy!" She stood beside him as he extracted the contents. "There you have a very nice thumb and forefinger. Terry Holland's. Right in the middle of the necklace where you've got a section of plain, undecorated gold. Might have been designed to make our job easy," she said smugly. "And what an obliging fence, not to give it a polish before flogging it!"

"It probably wasn't necessary, if Mrs Chant hadn't even bothered to try it on. You're absolutely sure the prints are his?" After all the frustration, it was almost too good to be true.

"Sixteen points, a perfect match," Sukey assured him. "There are other prints on the box and on the jewellery. Some of them are pretty smudgy, but as you can see, Holland's are good and sharp. Those are the only ones of his, by the way, there are none on the box itself."

"That figures. The original case was left in the safe, remember. The necklace is what matters." Castle rubbed his hands together in glee. "I must have left one or two prints myself when I took the box from Mrs Bayliss, although I made a point of touching it as little as possible . . . and then presumably Bayliss himself handled it . . . and his wife." He caught Sukey's eye and detected a hint of impatience. "Sorry, you hinted at something else?"

Her eyes sparkled in a way that almost made him forget they were on duty. "Wait till you hear this!" she said. "Most of the prints on the necklace were round the clasp and therefore incomplete, not easy to identify. Likewise on the earrings – but the box has a high gloss, ideal for lifting prints. Remember the ones we found on the underside of the loo seat at the Chants' place?" She straightened up and lifted both thumbs in a triumphant gesture as she delivered her *pièce de résistance*. "We found a match on the box!"

It took Castle a second or two to spot the connection. Then he snapped his fingers and said, "Bayliss! You're saying *Bayliss* could have been one of Lorraine Chant's fancy men!"

"It's a thought. D'you reckon the widow will cut up rough if we ask permission to take his prints?"

"That shouldn't be a problem. There's to be a PM. Will you take care of it?"

"Sure, but why the PM?"

Castle repeated what Dave Mahony had told him and Sukey suddenly burst out laughing. "I didn't think it was that funny," he said.

"It was *water*, not *Walter* that Mrs Hapwood overheard," she explained. "Don't you see . . . Hugo Bayliss was Lorraine Chant's *Water Baby*. It's more than likely his firm installed her swimming pool – maybe that's how they met."

Castle was not amused. "Thanks, you've just chipped away

a bit of my case," he informed her. "Not that it shakes my conviction that Holland's our man, especially after what you've turned up."

Sukey did not reply. He saw from her expression that she was busy with some thought that had just occurred to her and he waited for her to share it.

"Supposing it was Bayliss that Lorraine was planning to go off with?" she said after a few moments. "He was obviously pretty well-heeled, but maybe he didn't have enough to pay for her extravagant tastes. Or maybe she just couldn't bear the thought of leaving all that lovely money and jewellery behind? Supposing she did know about the safe and decided to empty it."

"Chant said quite positively that she didn't. It's not the sort of thing a man like him would be likely to confide to anyone, not even his wife."

"There's nothing to say she didn't find it when he wasn't around, though," Sukey pointed out. She went on to develop her theory. "Lorraine might have been busy filling a bag with the spoils when Holland got into the house and started hoovering up the goodies downstairs. She's so absorbed in what she's doing – or maybe she was in the bathroom with the taps running at the crucial time – that she never hears him."

"Or maybe, she hears something but thinks it's her lover come to help with the packing," Castle continued as Sukey paused for breath. "Then Holland comes charging in, she recognises him because he's been to the house before, doing odd jobs—"

"So he kills her and makes off with the loot," Sukey finished. Then she frowned and shook her head. "On second thoughts, I'm not so sure it was Bayliss she was planning to elope with."

"Why d'you say that?"

"Only just over a week ago, he started chatting me up, asking me to go to his place to take photographs. Would

183

he have bothered, if he was planning to go off with Lorraine Chant? And would he have repeated the offer so soon after his lover had been murdered?"

"Hard to tell without knowing the man, although he comes across to me as a pretty unpleasant, amoral sort of person. But that's something else he won't be telling us. Inconsiderate blighter, dying on us like that," Castle added, recalling Dave Mahony's wry comment. He put the exhibits back in the envelope and locked it away. He checked the time; it was a little after seven. "I'll see if I can catch the Super and bring him up to date. Then I'll get a warrant to search Holland's place and bring him in for questioning." He gave one of the official smiles with which he rewarded any of his team for a job well done. "Good work, Sukey."

"Thank you, sir," she replied formally. At the door, she hesitated. "There's one other thing that occurred to me."

"Oh?"

"Only a small point. That window, the one we think Holland used to enter the house."

"What about it?"

"It struck me as odd that it was left unfastened. Both Mrs Chant and her husband seem to have been very security conscious."

"Everyone gets careless at times. In any case, she'd probably have checked all round before leaving the house. Not that she'd have cared any more, as she wasn't planning to come back."

"Yes, I suppose that's it." Sukey went out of the room. A sensation of light and warmth seemed to go with her. But at least, he reflected, Saturday no longer felt so far away.

With Radcliffe and Hill for back-up, DI Castle knocked at the door of the house in Exeter Street. It was opened by Rita Holland; she took one look at them and exclaimed, "Don't you lot ever give up?" before scuttling along the passage shouting, "Tel, it's the coppers again!"

"Well, that saved us asking if he's in," muttered Radcliffe. "D'you think one of us should be round the back in case he does a runner, Guv?"

Terry Holland made a reply to the question unnecessary by emerging from the kitchen with a child's book in his hand. "What is it this time?" he demanded.

"Terence Walter Holland, I'm arresting you on suspicion of being involved in the murder of Mrs Lorraine Chant on Friday the 8th of June," Castle began, but before he could proceed with the formal caution there was a shriek of mingled rage and terror from Rita, who threw herself in front of Castle and pummelled her husband in the chest.

"You bloody fool, why didn't you listen to me?" she sobbed. "I told you not to have any more to do with Charlie Foss! We was all right till you caught up with him . . . I knew it'd all go wrong—"

"Shut up and go and look after Billy!" Holland pushed her aside and thrust the book into her hands. She clutched it to her chest like a shield and shrank away from him, her expression distraught. Behind her, the boy appeared in the doorway, his eyes round with alarm beneath the shock of brown hair that tumbled over his forehead. His mother pushed him back into the kitchen and closed the door behind her.

"This is rubbish . . . you've got it all wrong," Holland said angrily, shaking off the hand that Radcliffe had laid on his arm. His resistance collapsed when Hill came to the sergeant's assistance; between them they got the handcuffs on, but still he protested. "I told you, I don't know nothing about no murder, you've got the wrong man."

"You can tell us all about it at the station," said Castle. To Radcliffe he said, "Take him to the car and wait. I'll be a few minutes. And I want you," he turned to Hill, "to come back here and carry out a search, after I've had a word with Mrs Holland."

The scene that greeted Castle in the kitchen was one he had

185

encountered, with variations, many times before. It was at moments like this that he wished he had chosen a different job. Rita Holland was sitting in a chair with her arms round Billy, who was standing with his face hidden in her shoulder. Tears were pouring down her face as she silently stroked the boy's hair, her cheek resting against his temple, her expression one of utter defeat. She raised her eyes as Castle entered, then looked away as if the sight of him added to her misery. The kitchen was shabby, but spotlessly clean. A window hung with blue and white checked curtains gave onto a tiny but well-tended back garden where roses bloomed and birds fluttered round a feeding table. For the umpteenth time Castle found himself asking the question, *Don't they care about the effect on their families?* Sometimes, of course, the wives were in it up to their necks. He knew instinctively that it was not the case here.

He reached for a chair. "May I?" he said, and waited for her nod before sitting down. "I have to ask you a few questions, Mrs Holland. Do you think it might be better if Billy went out to play?"

"He wants to stay here with me," she replied dully as, without showing his face, the child tightened his grip round her neck.

"All right, I'll make it as easy for you as I can. First of all, I have to tell you that we have reason to believe there is stolen property in the house. I have a warrant to have it searched."

He half expected her to protest, but she merely shrugged. "Go ahead, you won't find nothing."

"And I'd like you to tell me about Charlie Foss."

"Who?"

"When I arrested your husband, you mentioned someone called Charlie Foss. Who is he?"

"He and Terry used to be mates, back in London," she said after a pause. Castle could see her mind working, asking herself how much she should say, how much he might already know.

186

"When did Terry last see him?"

"Don't know."

"But you think it might have been recently?"

"Why don't you ask him?"

"I will, when we get back to the station. At the moment, I'm asking you."

She squeezed her lips tightly together as if to prevent the wrong words coming out. "I can't tell you nothing," she mumbled.

"Can't, or won't?" Silence. "You don't like Charlie, do you? You didn't want Terry to have anything to do with him?" Still no reply. "Are you protecting Charlie . . . scared of him, perhaps?"

"Protect that weasel – you must be joking!" Contempt overcame her determination not to speak. Then, without warning, the tears began to fall again. "Sure, I'm scared," she admitted in a broken whisper. "But not the way you mean. I wanted Terry to stay away from him because I knew there'd be trouble. Charlie's evil. My dad used to say, if he fell off the QE2 he'd come up with a fish in both hands and he wouldn't give a toss if everyone else got drowned. I wanted Terry to promise to stay away from him, but—"

"But you think he took up with him again?" She nodded, still quietly weeping. "That suggests Charlie's living somewhere round here. Do you know where?" That time she shook her head. "Well, thank you Mrs Holland, you've been very helpful."

Castle got up and left the room. At the front door he met DC Hill. "Go ahead and search," he ordered. "She won't give you any trouble."

Chapter Nineteen

Terry couldn't believe it was really happening. Surely some creature out of a nightmare had grabbed hold of him and dragged him backwards into the past, rubbing his nose in its horror, forcing him to relive the events that had ended his freedom for so many soul-destroying years. The arrest, the caution, the drive to the nick in the police car, the barked order to turn out his pockets, the hands that searched for a concealed weapon, the walk along endless grey corridors . . . it all had a dreamlike quality that convinced him that at any minute he would wake up in his own bed with Rita beside him. It was only when they went through the ritual of reminding him that he was entitled to the advice of a solicitor that he at last faced up to the sickening reality. Maybe he should ask for a brief – but why the hell should he? He'd done his time, wiped the slate clean.

As for all this crap about a murder . . . he hadn't touched that woman, had only set eyes on her once when her husband had been there, hadn't been near the place since installing the safe and no one could prove he had. Didn't that fingerprint on his rear-view mirror, in a place where he himself never touched it, prove that someone else had been driving it? OK, so it was too smudged to identify, but the point was, it was *there* and he was ready to swear on his mother's grave that it wasn't his. Whoever had left it, the bleeder who'd nicked his van that day, was the one the coppers should be out looking for, not pulling in an honest citizen and upsetting his wife

188

and kid. He'd done his best to help them, but he'd think twice about cooperating with coppers from now on. He made this clear to them, defiantly and not particularly politely. They made it equally clear that they were not impressed.

It worried him that the DI with the face like an eagle had stayed behind to talk to Rita after they'd cuffed him and put him in the car. It had been stupid of her, blurting out Charlie Foss's name like that. He hoped she'd had the sense not to say any more. Not that there was much she could tell them about where Charlie was now or what he was calling himself. He'd kept her in the dark about everything except that Charlie had come across with some of the money.

The money. Well, that was safely stashed away and that young copper who'd stayed behind to search wouldn't find it, or anything else that could incriminate him. Anyway, it had nothing to do with the present bit of bother. He had every right to it. He'd earned it by all those weary years spent inside while Charlie had been using everything he and Frank had lifted from the bank job to feather his own nest. He'd made a bloody fortune . . . enough to run a Jag and buy a posh house with a swimming pool and a sauna and gold necklaces for Brenda. It was high time he settled his account with his old partners.

What had been surprising was the way he'd caved in after that episode by the pool. Terry had expected more resistance – more of the smarmy, 'Now look here, old son', sort of bullshit that he'd used in days gone by when the three of them had argued about who was taking the most risk and deserved the biggest cut. It was odd, too, the way the money had been handed over. Some bloke who wouldn't give a name phoning to tell him when and where to find it. At the time, he'd been so chuffed to get his hands on it that he hadn't given much thought to the whys and wherefores. But this was no time to bother his head with all that. There was this bloody stupid murder inquiry that he'd somehow got tangled up in.

He slumped down in his chair in the interview room, watched

189

listlessly as the tape was switched on, heard the time, his name and the names of the two policemen spoken into it. The eagle-faced DI Castle and grey-haired, bushy-eyebrowed Sergeant Radcliffe, whose ruddy face reminded him of the vicar in the church he used to attend as a kid. He was a big bloke, the vicar, who stood tall behind the brass lectern to read the lesson. The lectern had an eagle's head . . . and here they were again, the Vicar and the Eagle . . . this wouldn't do, he had to stay calm, answer their questions, get the whole thing sorted.

They began quietly. No hectoring, no bullying, just spelling out what they had against him, asking what he had to say about it. The gravel from Mr Chant's drive they'd picked out of his tyres. The thread from his overalls found under the window, the plaster dust from his van that had left prints of his trainers on the floor inside the house. The diamond earring that Mr Chant had said belonged to his murdered wife. All he said in reply, all he *could* say, was that he knew nothing about it, some other bugger had been using his van and wearing his gear. He kept on saying it, and each time the Eagle and the Vicar looked at one another and smiled, and he knew what they were thinking: *Pull the other one, Terry. Can't you think of something better than that threadbare old yarn?*

Then they started about the money from his overall pocket. Was it from Mr Chant's safe, the one he'd supplied and fitted? Had he ordered a spare key before installing it? It would be easy enough to find out, enquiries were already being made but it'd save a lot of time if he'd tell them now. They put their questions forwards, backwards and sideways. How had he got the money, if not from Mr Chant's safe? It was money that was owed to me, he kept insisting. Who owed it to you? That ain't none of your business.

They asked him about Charlie Foss. He knew they would, because of what Rita had said. He'd have given anything to know how much she'd told them. He explained that Charlie was just an old mate he ran into recently. Rita had never liked him, but they had a drink together for old times' sake. Where does he live, Terry? I dunno, do I? We met in a pub. What pub? Can't remember.

Then they sprang the first nasty surprise. They knew about the five grand. Where did he get it? Was it from Mr Chant's safe? I keep telling you, I don't know nothing about what was in the safe. I wasn't there, it must have been the bloke who nicked my van.

There was a short silence after that. For a moment, Terry had a wild hope that they'd given up, that they were ready to admit they were getting nowhere. They looked at one another and then back at him. Then the Eagle put a plastic envelope containing something shiny on the table in front of him. The gold necklace, the one in the picture, the one he'd been tricked into pretending he'd seen Mrs Chant wearing because the Eagle knew he'd recognised it and the last thing he wanted to do was put them onto Charlie. Not while the bleeder still owed him a packet. After that, OK, stuff him.

"This necklace belonged to Mrs Lorraine Chant," the Eagle explained. "But you already know that, don't you? We reckon it was stolen by whoever killed her." He leaned forward and fixed Terry with those unblinking, greenish eyes. "It's got your prints on it," he said softly. "How d'you explain that?"

Until now, Terry had felt more anger and resentment than anything else. Now, for the first time, fear crept in and chilled him like a breath of cold air. He stared in stupefaction at the necklace that Brenda Foss had been wearing that evening and knew he was cornered. He remembered admiring it, picturing something like it round Rita's neck. The scene by the pool came rushing back . . . the way he'd shown Charlie who was top dog . . . the surge of adrenalin as he dropped the slimy bastard in the water, soaking the fancy suit . . . the look on Brenda's face as she stood watching her husband spluttering and floundering at her feet. Then he had reached out and touched the necklace, held it for a moment between his thumb and forefinger. Such

191

an innocent thing to do, and it had landed him in this mess. It was all because of Charlie. Rita had been right, over and over again she'd warned him to have nothing more to do with Charlie, he should have listened to her. Bobbing on the surface of the dislocated jumble of thought that was swirling around in his brain was the conviction that it was Charlie's doing that he was here. Somehow, Charlie had stitched him up. Christ alone knew how, but he'd stitched him up good and proper. His head was aching, splitting – it was like having it crunched between the jaws of a monstrous nut-cracker. He let out a groan of mingled pain and despair.

The Eagle repeated his question. Terry covered his face with his hands. "I ain't saying no more," he muttered. "Not till I've talked to a brief."

DI Castle sat behind his desk and cursed his luck. Sergeant Radcliffe stood leaning against a filing cabinet while he sounded off, sympathising but saying nothing. He knew from experience that it was best not to comment for the moment, just listen until the storm subsided.

Castle got up and strode round the office. He took his keys from his pocket and began tossing them up in the air, closing his fist tightly round the bunch each time he caught it as if wishing he could get his fingers round Terry Holland's collar and shake the truth out of him. "We nearly had him, Andy," he muttered. "I swear he was on the point of cracking . . . now we've got to wait for a duty solicitor, who's unlikely to get here before," he stopped flinging the keys up and down to consult his watch, "ten o'clock at the earliest. Next thing, Holland will be claiming he's too tired to answer any more questions."

"Maybe that'd be no bad thing," Radcliffe suggested. "If you don't mind me saying so, Guv, you're looking pretty done in yourself. And besides, this fax has just come in. Some background information from the Yard about the robbery

Holland got sent down for." He handed Castle a sheet of paper. "Makes interesting reading."

Castle put the keys back in his pocket, slumped into his chair and shut his eyes. Radcliffe was right; he was feeling done in. He had been exposed to quite a bit of raw emotion during the day and it was beginning to tell. First there had been Mrs Bayliss's distress – how genuine was it, though? – at having to part with her husband's last gift while still traumatised by his sudden death. Then Arthur Chant's outburst – a mixture of anger and guilt over the suggestions about illicit profits or merely a cloak for his private anguish? And finally, Rita Holland's despair at her husband's arrest. That, at least, had been genuine.

With an effort, he opened his eyes and scanned the text of the message. In a moment, he was wide awake and reading aloud. "'Driver of the getaway car alleged by defendants to be one Charlie Foss, no record, present address unknown. Defendants unable to produce any evidence to support the allegation. All attempts to find the stolen money unsuccessful.' Well, well, well." Castle sat back in his chair and locked his hands behind his head. "So that's why Holland's wife got so upset when she found her old man had taken up with Charlie Foss again," he mused. "Scared of what he might do to get hold of his share of the loot."

"It explains why he didn't look too happy when you asked him about Foss," said Radcliffe.

"Exactly." Castle sat up and reached for his jacket. "Come on Andy, we've got a bit of time to spare. Let's go out for a pint."

The noise level in the saloon bar of the Bear Inn was low enough to make conversation possible without shouting yet high enough for the two men to speak normally without the risk of being overheard. Castle bought two pints of best bitter and carried them to a corner table. Radcliffe followed with two large bags of crisps.

"Any ideas, Guv?" the sergeant asked above the crackle of plastic as he ripped one of the bags open.

Castle dived into his crisps and began munching. It wasn't that long ago that he'd eaten, but already he was feeling peckish again. "According to that report," he said ruminatively, "although the police didn't succeed in tracing Foss, they spoke to people who knew him and were quite ready to believe him capable of running out on his mates and taking the money with him. If it's true, then he was clever enough to cover his tracks completely. *But*," Castle went on, with heavy emphasis on the word, "our Terry seems to have succeeded where the Met failed."

"It could have been luck, the way Holland explained it."

"You reckon? Two villains from London coming to Gloucestershire and meeting up again by chance?"

Radcliffe upended his crisp bag to catch the last few crumbs in the palm of one hand, emptied his tankard and held out his hand for Castle's. "Same again?"

"Thanks."

When he came back with the second round Radcliffe said, "This is all very interesting, but I don't see how it helps our case against Holland."

"Holland's wife said she reckons Foss is living somewhere on our patch and she knows they've been in touch, but she doesn't know how or where. Supposing Terry put the squeeze on Charlie to cough up his share. Charlie might have pleaded poverty – said the money was all gone. Supposing they plotted this heist together and Charlie is up to his old tricks, leaving his partner to do the dirty work and take the rap?"

"You could be right, Guv. From what that report says, a trick like that'd be right up his street."

"At least, if that theory's correct, Charlie didn't get away with all the loot this time. I think we'll have another go at Terry on the subject of his old mate when we restart the interview. If it dawns on him that Foss has dropped him in

194

the shit again, he might change his tune . . . and maybe then we can get to Foss before he does another runner." Castle checked the time by the clock above the bar. It was almost ten. "Drink up, Andy, we'd better be getting back."

The desk officer greeted them with the news that Terry Holland was closeted with his solicitor, who emerged shortly afterwards to inform them that his client categorically denied any involvement in either robbery or murder, but was too exhausted to answer further questions that night.

Chapter Twenty

It was almost eleven o'clock when Jim Castle returned to his flat in Tewkesbury Road. He had taken it, initially on a six-month lease, after returning to Gloucester following the collapse of his short-lived marriage. At the time, he told himself that it was a temporary expedient, that once he had settled down he would look out for a village property, a renovated cottage with a garden perhaps. Despite having been born in the city he had always had a yen to live in the country, something that his ex-wife had flatly refused even to consider. Two years after the divorce and his return to his roots, he had still taken no steps to fulfil his dream. Meeting Sukey again and finding that she too was free once more had held him back. It was like having a hand on his shoulder, a voice in his ear whispering, *Wait awhile, wait and see how things turn out. Maybe one day the two of you will go house-hunting together*.

Meanwhile, the flat was convenient. Jim parked the Mondeo in his allocated space, closing the door as quietly as he could because the retired civil servant in the flat above his was quick to complain if his slumber was disturbed. For the same reason, despite his weariness, he climbed the three flights of stairs instead of using the lift. He let himself in at his front door, bolted it, put his jacket and briefcase in the hall cupboard and went into the kitchen, pulling a face at the sight of the used breakfast crockery stacked in the sink. He wandered into the bedroom, kicked off his shoes and picked up the pyjama bottoms that he had thrown towards the bed that

196

morning before taking his shower. His aim had been bad and the garment lay where it had fallen in an oddly contorted heap, as if it had been worn by someone writhing in pain. He went back into the kitchen, made a pot of tea and took a mug into the living room, dragging off his tie and undoing the top button of his shirt with one hand as he drank.

He checked his answering machine for messages, but there were none. He told himself that it was illogical to expect to hear from Sukey when he had been speaking to her in the flesh so recently. Just the same, he was tempted to call her, had already tapped out the first part of her number without thinking about it before it occurred to him that she was quite likely in bed and possibly asleep. He hung up; it wasn't as if there was anything of real significance to tell her.

He felt depressed and discouraged. All the softly softly tactics had come to a grinding halt when Terry Holland, faced with the one solid, indisputable piece of evidence against him, had clammed up and demanded a brief. The dismayed expression that replaced the look of sullen obstinacy on the doughy features, the way his roughened hands balled into fists and the refusal to speak another word without first consulting a solicitor were not, Castle was convinced, the reactions of an innocent man. Nor, he judged, a particularly intelligent one either. It would be interesting to learn what line he would take after legal advice followed by a night's rest.

Castle went into the bathroom, brushed his teeth, thought about a shower but decided to wait until the morning. He got into bed and tried to read, but found it impossible to concentrate and threw the book aside. Yawning, he lay down and put out the light but, despite his weariness, his brain was still active. There was so much to think about, so much still to be done before the case was wrapped up. There was Charlie Foss to track down; it was possible that he held the key to the whole business. A vague bell rang at the back of his mind, a faint suggestion that somewhere among the tangle of contradictory evidence there was something he hadn't recognised as significant. He spent a long time trying unsuccessfully to pin it down before falling asleep.

In the darkness of his cell, Terry Holland wrestled with a dilemma. Again and again he went over his interview with the duty solicitor, a thin-faced individual whose sparse grey hair matched his rumpled suit. His manner, as Terry gave a somewhat garbled account of his predicament, had been like that of a doctor listening to a patient describing his symptoms as, with pursed lips and a succession of raised eyebrows and curt nods, he sat scribbling in his notebook. From time to time he had interrupted with a question, scrutinising his client over the tops of his half-glasses as if trying to judge his state of health.

His assessment of the situation, when he finally got around to giving it, brought little solace to the beleaguered Terry. Despite its circumstantial nature, the evidence of the van was pretty damning and could well be accepted by a jury. Didn't he have a better explanation than the one he had offered the police? As for the money, Charlie Foss, alias Hugo Bayliss, could hardly be expected to confirm Terry's account of how he had come by it, but in the unlikely event that he did, the five grand – being indirectly part of the proceeds of a crime – would almost certainly be forfeit. The alternative explanation for the sudden acquisition of so much cash, the one the police obviously believed, was even less in Terry's favour. If, after Lorraine Chant's murder, a substantial sum was found to be missing . . . well, the inference was obvious, wasn't it?

There remained the matter of the fingerprints on the necklace. The way in which they came to be there was, on the face of it, perfectly innocent, but it immediately gave rise to the question: what had brought Terry to The Laurels that afternoon? Would Mr and Mrs Bayliss confirm his story?

The net woven so ingeniously by his former partner in crime

was slowly, inexorably tightening around Terry Holland. It was one of life's ironies that, unknown to Terry, Charlie Foss was dead and would never know how successful his plan had been. As for his confused victim, tossing restlessly on the hard mattress, it seemed that he had only two choices: either to refuse to add to or alter his story, in the hope that the evidence of the necklace alone would be considered insufficient to bring a charge, or tell the truth about touching the necklace and kiss the money goodbye. With his record, the first alternative was decidedly dodgy. He could hardly bear to contemplate the second.

Rita Holland lay alone in her darkened bedroom. The brief period of rain had done little to relieve the stuffy atmosphere indoors, although she had opened the window as soon as it stopped and parted the curtains after putting out the light to admit as much as possible of the cool, still air. She stared up at the shadow of the window frame thrown on the ceiling by a street lamp outside the house and listened to the hum of traffic along Eastern Avenue. Sound and light. *Son et Lumière* . . . that was the name of the show she and Terry had taken Billy to see at some place by the river last August, only a couple of months or so after they had moved to Gloucester. Things had been tough then; they couldn't afford the price of a ticket to get into the enclosure, but there had been a mound a short distance away and they'd watched from there. Billy had been ecstatic at the music, the bright figures against the floodlit walls of the ancient building where the show was being staged and the fantastic coloured lights reflected in the water. The three of them had been so happy, happy, *happy*. And now it was over.

Rita's mind wandered through the intervening months up to the present time, reflecting on the way things had gradually improved. She had found a job, Billy had settled down at school and was doing well, and Terry had started getting recommendations which led to him picking up more and more work. Only a couple of weeks ago he'd talked about taking them down to Barry Island for a few days during the school holidays, said he'd met someone who would rent them a caravan cheap. She had at last come to believe he had kept his promise never to go back to the old ways or take up with the old crowd, to accept that this was the reason, the *only* reason, why he had insisted on coming to live in Gloucester. She knew different now.

There was no hope of sleep and she felt too exhausted and too drained to cry. She lay awake and open-eyed until the door opened softly and Billy crept into the room. She raised the thin covers and he slipped under them and nestled against her, the way he used to after a bad dream when he was a toddler, pillowing his head on her shoulder.

"Mum," he whispered in a voice thickened by tears, "when will Dad be home?"

"Soon, I hope," she whispered back, stroking his head.

It was not until she heard his soft, regular breathing and knew that he was asleep that her own tears began to fall.

Sukey went to bed reasonably satisfied with her day's work. It always gave her a buzz when her efforts yielded a piece of evidence that would support and strengthen the case against an offender. She had been hoping to hear from Jim before turning in, but was not unduly surprised when he did not call.

She was not looking forward to tomorrow. It would not be the first time she had taken prints from a corpse, but the contact with cold, dead flesh always gave her a shudder. Still, it had to be done. Her thoughts turned to her meeting with Hugo Bayliss at the Bodywise Club. Even though she had played it cool, refused to respond to the overtly sexual signals he had sent out, she could not help but recognise his charm and admire his superb physique. There had been a magnetism about him which, she had no doubt, he would have played on for all he was worth once the two of them were alone. Maybe it was just as well she had never been put to the test.

Quite certainly, there had been a darker side to the man. His bullying manner towards young Rick was probably typical of the way he treated all his employees, and the bruises on his wife's face pointed to a violent, possibly sadistic streak. Sukey wondered how much Mrs Bayliss had suffered at his hands and why, if he had regularly ill-treated her, she had stayed with him. Money probably had something to do with it. It was obvious from the house they lived in that there was plenty of that. Still, she couldn't help feeling sorry for the poor woman. She was such a little thing, no match for Hugo if things got physical. She would probably have a better life without him although, with the illogical, perverse nature of so many victims of domestic violence, it was quite likely she had still been in love with him. His death must have been a terrible shock and it couldn't have helped to know – or at any rate, suspect – that on the very day of his death he had planned an assignation with another woman.

Perhaps there was something Sukey could do to put the widow's mind at rest on that point at least. She had the prints of the shots she had taken of the house and garden. They might not be of any interest in themselves, but they would bear out her story. Tomorrow morning she would drive over to Cheltenham and call in at The Laurels.

Having made this resolution, Sukey fell asleep.

Chapter Twenty-One

When Sukey arrived at The Laurels on Friday morning she was surprised to find an assortment of vehicles, including several private cars, already on the drive. Among them was a large white van bearing on its side a streamlined figure of a woman in a multi-coloured swimming costume diving into a pool surrounded by palm trees. Alongside was the legend 'Bodywise Systems Ltd – Outdoor Water Installations and Fitness Equipment'.

Since there was no convenient space left for her to park, Sukey left the Astra in the street and walked towards the house. Halfway up the drive, she hesitated. Normally on such an errand she would have telephoned to make an appointment, but since she did not know the number it had not been possible. The other cars, a dark blue Ford Granada, a grey Cavalier and a bright red Metro, probably belonged to friends who had called to offer their condolences. It might be embarrassing for the widow if a strange woman were to appear on the doorstep, claiming that what might have seemed like an assignation had in fact been a strictly business arrangement, offering as proof nothing more than a few photographs. From some points of view, it might look like an attempt to extort money.

She was considering whether to abandon her mission when the wrought-iron gate leading to the garden swung open and a man emerged, got into the Cavalier and drove away. There was something about him that seemed familiar and it took her only a few seconds to remember when and where she had

202

seen him before . . . the previous morning at the County Police Headquarters in Cheltenham, talking to Inspector Mahony while she waited to give her statement. She remembered what Jim Castle had said about a possible malfunction of the sauna in which Hugo Bayliss had died. That would account for the presence of Bodywise Systems, who had probably sent one of their experts to examine it in the presence of a police officer. As if to confirm her theory, two men in overalls, one carrying a toolkit and the other an electric hand-lamp and a length of cable, appeared from the same direction as the detective. They stowed their gear in the back of the van, slammed the doors and climbed into the cab. Moments later they too drove off.

Deciding eventually that since she had taken the trouble to come this far she might as well carry out her intention, Sukey went up to the house and rang the bell. After a few seconds she heard shuffling footsteps and someone coughing; then the door was opened by a stout, red-faced woman with straggling white hair, leaning on a stick. A lighted cigarette dangled from her lips and she eyed Sukey up and down for a second or two, squinting through the smoke, before croaking, "Oo're you?"

"My name's Mrs Reynolds," said Sukey, trying not to show surprise at the contrast between the woman's slatternly appearance and that of the mistress of the house. "I'd like a word with Mrs Bayliss, if it's convenient."

The watery eyes narrowed with suspicion. "What about?" she demanded.

"I have something I'd like to give her," Sukey replied.

The woman held out a hand and said, "Give it 'ere, I'll see she gets it."

"If you don't mind, I'd rather give it to her myself. There's something I'd like to tell her." Sukey tried to keep her voice and manner pleasant, but she could feel her hackles rising in response to this hostile reception. "It'll only take a moment."

The woman took a drag on her cigarette before removing it from her mouth and calling over her shoulder, "Bren! Someone to see yer – a woman!" She turned back to Sukey. "Oodja say y'are?"

"Mrs Reynolds," Sukey replied and the name was repeated in a hoarse shout.

There was a pause before a female voice called back, "All right Auntie, show her in." The door was grudgingly opened and Sukey stepped into the hall.

It felt creepy, being back in the house where only two days ago she had had the most hair-raising experience of her life. Under the sleeves of her loose cotton jacket she felt gooseflesh breaking out on her arms at the sight of the staircase down which she had fled with the helmeted figure in murderous pursuit. The shapeless old woman hobbling ahead of her, scattering ash on the carpet, was leading the way to the sitting room through which she had made her panic-stricken dash for freedom. Her pulse rate quickened at the thought of what might have happened had she not had the presence of mind to swerve and grab at the man's ankle, catching him off balance and sending him flying helplessly into the pool. It could so easily have gone the other way; if she had been the one to land in the water it was unlikely that she would have come out alive. At this very moment her drowned body, like that of the man whose dubious invitation had brought her here, would be lying on a slab in the mortuary.

There were three people in the room. Mrs Bayliss was seated on a couch and lounging beside her was a man whom Sukey recognised from Jim Castle's description as Hugo's office manager, Steven Lovett. Almost deliberately, it seemed to her, he raised his right foot and placed it on his left thigh as she came through the door, as if to make it clear that he had no intention of doing her the courtesy of standing up.

In front of the patio window with his back to the room was a young man wearing joggers, trainers and a black sweatshirt on which the word 'Instructor' was printed in large blue letters. His momentary surprise when he turned round and saw Sukey changed to a slightly embarrassed grin as he greeted her by name.

"Hi, Rick, fancy seeing you here," she said, instantly feeling a lot more relaxed at finding someone she knew, someone sympathetic who would vouch for her if necessary.

"Me and the other instructors had a whip round for some flowers," he explained. "Just to say how sorry we are about . . . you know." Like many people, he seemed reluctant to mention death by name.

"Wasn't it sweet of them?" said the widow. She picked up a large bouquet of carnations and irises that lay on a low table and sniffed delicately with a finely chiselled nose. She was immaculately groomed and made-up, and with her back to the light the bruises hardly showed. She glanced from Rick to Sukey and back again. "You know this lady?"

"Sure, she's one of our members," he replied. "Been working out at the club regular for a long time."

"It was at the Bodywise Club that I got chatting to your husband," Sukey told Mrs Bayliss. "I was so sorry to hear about his death." The neatly styled head gave a barely perceptible bob of acknowledgement. "I think I explained the day he . . . the day I came round here," Sukey continued. "He had he asked me about my job, and when he learned I was a photographer he asked me if I'd come and do a series of shots of your house and garden."

There was a disbelieving cackle from behind her. "Oh yeah? 'Ow was 'e goin' to pay yer – in kind?"

"*Auntie Gwen!*" Mrs Bayliss shot her a reproachful glance.

"Well, you know what Charlie was like." The crone lit a fresh cigarette from the stub of the old one, which she crushed into an ashtray with nicotine-stained fingers. "Always lookin' for the chance to get 'is 'ands into another woman's knickers."

Sukey felt her colour rise. "I assure you, Mrs Bayliss,"

205

she said, "there was absolutely nothing improper about my arrangement with your husband."

"No, no, I'm sure there wasn't," said the widow, with a shake of the head at her offending relative. "Don't take any notice of Auntie Gwen, she don't . . . doesn't mean it." She turned back to Sukey. "I remember you, of course, you arrived just as I was leaving on Wednesday to go to London." She turned to Lovett. "I mentioned it, didn't I Steven, when you came round that evening . . . when we found . . ." She put a hand to her mouth and turned away, apparently overcome by emotion at the memory.

"You did indeed." Lovett spoke for the first time. Sukey was conscious that he was scrutinising her closely through wire-framed glasses. "How did you know Mr Bayliss was dead?" he asked. "There's been nothing in the papers."

For a moment, Sukey felt wrong-footed. It was true there had been no mention of the tragedy in Thursday's *Gazette* and it was too early for today's lunchtime edition. The last thing she wanted was to reveal her connection with the police. Thinking on her feet, she said, "I've got a friend in the ambulance service."

"I see." She had the feeling that Lovett was unconvinced. She remembered Jim Castle's suggestion that there might be something between him and Mrs Bayliss and thought it could well be true. He certainly gave the impression of being thoroughly at home and it struck her that it was slightly unusual for an office manager to spend so much time with the widow of his late employer, especially now she had her aunt for company. Not that the old harridan seemed a particularly agreeable companion, but there was no accounting for taste. She decided to get the business over with and leave as soon as possible.

"I'm aware that my visit on Wednesday morning took you by surprise," she began. "I was under the impression that you knew about it." There was another cackle from Auntie Gwen that turned into a fit of raucous coughing. Her niece hurried to her side and patted her between the shoulders until the spasm was over. When conversation was once more possible, Sukey pulled the packet of photographs from her pocket. "Perhaps I was taking a liberty," she went on, "but Mr Bayliss had given me what I took to be a genuine commission, and the gate to the garden was open so I went through and took the pictures anyway. I intended to give them to him at the club next time I saw him – he used to come in on a Monday sometimes when I was doing my workout. I thought you might like to have them."

After a moment's hesitation, Mrs Bayliss took the envelope and put it on the table. "Thank you," she said quietly. "I'm sorry if I seemed rude the other day. I was in a hurry and—"

"It doesn't matter. I'll go now." Sukey turned as she spoke, but found her way barred by Auntie Gwen.

"Not so fast, young woman!" she said aggressively. "Better check that envelope, Bren – see what's really in it. I know your sort," she went on, thrusting her face close to Sukey's and treating her to a whiff of tobacco-laden breath. "After money, that's why you're 'ere. My niece ain't goin' to part with none till we see what she's getting for it."

Sukey felt her temper rising. "I don't recall asking for money, but since your aunt sees fit to raise the subject, your husband did offer me a fee," she informed Mrs Bayliss. "It was my intention to charge him fifty pounds for the job, but in the circumstances I decided not to mention it."

"Believe that an' you'll believe anything," sneered Auntie Gwen.

Sukey turned on her heel and pushed past her. "I'll find my own way out," she said curtly to no one in particular. She had almost reached the front door when Mrs Bayliss caught up with her. She was holding a leather handbag which she was trying to open with one hand while clutching at Sukey's arm with the other. She appeared genuinely distressed; her large eyes were swimming in tears.

"Please, wait a moment," she said. "Don't mind Auntie Gwen, she's only looking out for me, always has done . . . and she never liked Charlie, you see."

"It's all right."

"No, it isn't. I was a bit off to you as well, but you see, I thought at first . . . I mean, I know he sometimes . . ."

"Let's just forget it, shall we?"

"No, you did a job and you should get paid for it. Fifty pounds, you said?"

While she was speaking, Mrs Bayliss had taken out a wad of money held together by an elastic band. She pulled out a single note and offered it to Sukey. "Here – you're sure that's enough?"

"There's no need to give me anything." Sukey felt acutely embarrassed. She had mentally written off the money, but it had seemed that no one really believed her. "That isn't why I came here, honestly."

"Take it, please!" Mrs Bayliss thrust the note into Sukey's pocket. "I'm not short, and a deal's a deal."

"Well, if you insist. Thank you. Would you like a receipt?"

"No, that's OK."

"Right, well, if you want extra copies of any of the pictures, let me know. I still have the negatives. The club has my address – you can get it from Rick."

She glanced across at the red Metro as she spoke. "Is that his car?"

"Yes, why d'you ask?"

"I don't remember seeing it in the club car park, that's all."

"I don't think he's had it long."

"That accounts for it." Sukey held out a hand. She thought how small and fragile the other woman's seemed as it rested

briefly in her own. "Goodbye, and thank you once again."
She went back to her own car and headed for home. In spite of
the odious Auntie Gwen and her unpleasant insinuations, she
thought the visit had passed off reasonably well. As a bonus,
she had fifty pounds towards Fergus's school trip.

She was halfway home before it occurred to her that the
elastic band holding Mrs Bayliss's wad of notes together was
of the same lurid colour as the one Jim Castle had filched from
Arthur Chant. And there was something else that struck her
as odd. The forename of the late Mr Bayliss, according to his
business card, was Hugo. So why had both his widow and her
aunt referred to him as Charlie?

Chapter Twenty-Two

At approximately the same time as Sukey arrived at The Laurels, DI Castle and DS Radcliffe emerged from another fruitless interview with Terry Holland. A night in a cell had done nothing to weaken the man's intransigence. He persisted with his claim that his van had been out of his possession all day on the Friday of the robbery and murder at the Chants' house, that he had never had occasion to pay a second visit there nor stolen any money from the safe. As to the source of the five thousand pounds, he stubbornly refused to add to his original assertion that it was 'money owed to him'. On the matter of his fingerprints on the necklace, he would say nothing at all.

"As things stand, all we can charge him with at present is handling stolen property," Castle said wearily. "I guess we'll have to bail him while we carry on with the enquiries. Yes, what is it?" he asked as DC Hill entered with a sheet of paper in his hand.

"I don't know if this will help us, Guv, but I've been speaking to the manager of a firm in London that imports toys and stationery. He remembers a line of novelties in bright fluorescent colours which included elastic bands with matching pencils and erasers. Says the stuff never caught on; the multiple stores weren't interested and the firm only shifted a small quantity – mostly to corner shops, newsagents and the like – and there were no repeat orders. He's just faxed me a list of outlets in the county where they did manage to sell a few. There's only a handful of them, and only one actually in Gloucester – here." Hill pointed to the last customer on the list, with an address in a street not far from the police station. "Mrs H. Patel, Cathedral News."

"Just round the corner from Arthur Chant's office," Castle observed. "I was planning to give him a bell in a minute. I think I'll make it a personal visit, after I've made some enquiries in the shop. Good work, Hill."

In addition to magazines, newspapers, cigarettes and confectionery, Cathedral News stocked an extraordinarily varied collection of snack foods, canned drinks, greetings cards, toys, games and novelties. The proprietor was a tiny, grey-haired Indian woman dressed in a colourful sari. When Castle entered and showed his warrant card she examined it closely, her bright dark eyes darting from the photograph to his face and back again. Then she gave a quick nod and said in a soft, lilting voice, "How may I help you, Inspector."

"I'd like to know if you have any of these in stock," he said, holding up the two elastic bands he had obtained from Arthur Chant's office and Terry Holland's living room.

She gave an instant nod of recognition. "I have indeed, Inspector. Too many. My husband bought them for the Christmas trade and most of them are still here." She bent down and took from a shelf under the glass-fronted counter a box containing half a dozen round objects the size of tennis balls in a variety of fluorescent colours, each made up of dozens of elastic bands. "Here, you see . . . we have sold only five out of a box of twelve, and only one of the pink ones. We thought people would buy them for their children's stockings but as you see, they were not popular." Beneath the sari, her shoulders lifted and fell and her smile came and went like sunshine amid passing clouds.

"I don't suppose you remember who bought the pink one?" said Castle.

The smile became radiant. "Yes Inspector, as it happens I do remember. It was only a short time ago – a lady who comes in quite often for newspapers and cigarettes bought it, to brighten up her desk, she said."

"Do you happen to know where she works?"

"I regret, no."

"Can you tell me what she looks like?"

"Indeed I can. She is quite young and pretty, with blonde hair, very long." Mrs Patel supplemented her words and her smile with flowing movements of her small delicate hands, setting off a musical jingling from the bangles at her wrists.

"Thank you very much, you've been most helpful," said Castle. "By the way, I'll take this." To Mrs Patel's almost palpable delight, he bought a ball of fluorescent pink elastic bands. With renewed thanks, he left the shop and headed for the offices of Chantertainment.

Arthur Chant's blonde receptionist was speaking on the telephone when Castle entered. If she recognised him from his previous visit, she showed no sign, merely giving his warrant card a perfunctory glance and waving him to a seat. When she put the phone down she turned to him with raised eyebrows and said, "If you want to see Mr Chant, he's out at the moment."

Castle got up and strolled over to her desk. "When will he be back?"

She glanced at her watch. "He said he wouldn't be long. Do you want to wait?"

"I'd like a word with you first, Miss . . .?"

"Watkins – Penny Watkins."

"Tell me, Penny, do you remember buying one of these?" Castle took the ball of elastic bands from the brown paper bag in which Mrs Patel had insisted in wrapping it and placed it on the palm of his hand.

Penny giggled. "Do I? It caught my eye when I went to Mrs Patel's for cigarettes one day. I thought it was a fun sort of colour; I used to leave it on my desk at first, but I got so many cheeky remarks from people coming into the office that Mr Chant told me to keep it out of sight." She screwed up her mouth and gave a knowing look that was almost a wink. "He can be a bit – you know – prissy," she confided.

Castle gave an understanding nod. "Have you still got it?" he asked.

"Sure." She dived into a drawer, fetched it out and plonked it on the desk. Castle could imagine what it might suggest to a certain type of mind. "Your ball's a lot bigger than mine," she said and giggled again.

"So it is," he replied with a straight face. "You must use a lot of elastic bands."

"Not me, him." She indicated the door of Chant's office with a flick of her blonde mane. "He asked for some to use at home, so I gave him a handful."

At that moment the outer door swung open and Chant himself entered. He appeared less than delighted to see his visitor. Penny hastily reached for the ball of elastic bands, but Castle was there before her. "I'd like to borrow this for a few minutes, if you don't mind," he said.

"Inspector, what are you doing here?" Chant demanded.

"I was having a word with Miss Watkins while waiting for you to come back, sir," Castle replied. "I'd be grateful if you could spare me a few minutes."

"He was shaken but not stirred into making an admission," was Castle's verdict on returning to the station. "I told him we'd made an arrest and would shortly be charging our suspect, but only with a comparatively minor offence. I want him to believe his wife's killer will get away with it unless he comes clean about the cash."

"It might still work," said Radcliffe. "Now you've as good as proved it came from his safe."

"I've proved it to my satisfaction and I made no bones

213

about it, but he's shrewd enough to know that the evidence we have at present is unlikely to be strong enough to convince a jury. I've left him to examine his conscience, so let's have a coffee and then we'll have another go at Holland. No, on second thoughts Andy, you and Hill have a go at him. Maybe a change of tactics will catch him off guard."

"Right, Guv. By the way, Sukey was trying to reach you earlier. Said it might be important and could you call her at home."

"OK, I'll do that first. See you in the canteen in a few minutes."

When Sukey told him about her visit to The Laurels to hand over the photographs, Castle felt only a passing interest, but he sat up when she mentioned the elastic band that secured the roll of money in Mrs Bayliss's handbag. "Maybe Chant and Bayliss had some sort of scam going," he speculated. "It could explain Chant's reluctance to admit to having all that cash in his safe. If that's the case it's probably outside the scope of this inquiry, but it's worth bearing in mind. And meanwhile, if our guess is correct, Bayliss has been screwing Lorraine Chant. I wonder if her husband knows about that."

"And I wonder if he's heard Bayliss is dead?" said Sukey thoughtfully. "Oh, one other thing." She told him about the anomaly concerning Bayliss's forename and immediately something clicked in his brain.

"That's it! I had a feeling there was some point I'd over-looked," he exclaimed. "I remember now, I heard Mrs Bayliss referring to 'her Charlie'. I'd forgotten the name on his business card was Hugo and it didn't register at the time." Castle's brain slipped into a higher gear as he remembered something else. "You didn't by any chance find out *her* first name as well, did you?"

"She had a ghastly old aunt there – Auntie Gwen, she called her – who addressed her as 'Bren'. I presume that's short for Brenda."

"And the office manager, Steven Lovett, called her 'Barbie', so it looks as if both the Baylisses adopted different names. Now, I wonder—" Castle broke off as his mind began considering various possibilities.

"It sounds as if you think it's important," said Sukey.

"It might be." He told her about Terry Holland's old associate, Charlie Foss, for whom Rita Holland had expressed an almost paranoid dislike and mistrust and who was believed to be living not far away. "This could put a whole new slant on the case, Sukey. Thanks for letting me know."

"I hope it turns out to be useful. I'm on duty at two o'clock and I'll be going straight to the morgue to get Bayliss's prints."

"Right. Ask Fingerprints to give them priority and let me have the result as soon as you get it."

"Will do."

"Incidentally, I understand the pathologist is still not happy about the cause of death. Maybe you'll pick up some details when you're at the morgue."

Castle put the phone down and headed for the canteen and his delayed cup of coffee, but he had barely reached the door before Reception rang to tell him that a Mr Arthur Chant was downstairs and wanted to speak to him on a matter of great urgency. He felt a surge of triumph. His persistence had paid off – the case was virtually in the bag. Chant was about to admit to having a large sum of undeclared cash in the house, cash that had been stolen on the day of his wife's murder. Armed with this new evidence, he would be in a position to charge Holland with the robbery and the killing. In a state of high optimism, he went downstairs.

It was immediately apparent that Chant was under considerable stress. His face was ashen and there were beads of sweat on his upper lip. When he entered the interview room he collapsed rather than sat down on the chair Castle indicated and began knotting and unknotting his hands in an apparent effort to

215

control their shaking. He seemed to be a crushed and beaten man. It was understandable; having lost his wife in the most tragic of circumstances, he now stood to lose a hefty slice of his fortune as well.

Castle sat down at the other side of the table and took out his notebook. "You want to make a statement, sir?" he prompted after several seconds of silence.

Chant drew a deep breath and said, "Inspector, am I right in believing that the man you are holding in connection with my wife's death is Terry Holland?"

"Our suspect's name has not been officially released," Castle replied.

"But can't you tell me unofficially?" The man's expression was abject, like a dog pleading not to be whipped.

Castle was intrigued. It was not the first time that Chant had shown concern about Holland and he seemed to be giving out strong signals that he would prefer the prisoner to be someone else. It would be interesting to find out why. Leaning across the table, he asked, "Does it make a difference?" There was no reply. He decided to take a shot at random. "Supposing it was another man – Hugo Bayliss, for example?" *Bullseye!* thought the detective on seeing the other man's body twitch as if he had been given an electric shock.

"What do you know about Bayliss?" Chant demanded harshly.

"We have reason to believe that you and he have had business dealings."

"Business dealings!" Chant's tone was bitter. "I gave him the contract to install the swimming pool and sauna that my wife wanted and ever since then, he and she . . ." His voice faltered and he seemed to be on the verge of tears, but with an effort he recovered. "Bayliss was her lover," he said miserably. "She was going to leave me for him."

"We suspected as much," Castle said quietly, "but the man we are holding is not Mr Bayliss. As a matter o

216

fact, Bayliss is dead . . . and there is some doubt about the circumstances."

"Dead?" First disbelief and then a flicker of savage pleasure passed over Chant's tortured features, followed by an odd blend of wariness and curiosity as he added sharply, "What sort of doubt? Are you saying he was murdered?"

"Nothing has been ruled out at this stage. For the moment, all I can tell you is that the cause of his death has not yet been established. Now sir, will you please come to the point and explain why you are here?"

Chant groaned and clutched at his temples with both hands. Every line of his body seemed to sag and shrivel in despair. For the second time, he was on the point of breaking down. "You're holding Holland . . . it must be Holland," he muttered. With his eyes fixed on the table as if he were talking to himself rather than Castle, he went on in a low voice, "If it was Bayliss, I'd let him rot in jail for the rest of his life and never say a word, but not a decent, hard-working chap like Holland . . . no, I can't let that happen."

Castle stared at him in bewilderment. "Mr Chant, what are you saying – what are you trying to tell me?"

With a sudden, determined movement, Chant straightened his shoulders, sat up and looked the detective full in the face. "Inspector, I wish to make a statement," he said, and the voice that had been threatening to fail became strong and resolute. "You must release Terry Holland at once. I am here to confess to killing my wife."

Chapter Twenty-Three

"I had a hunch all along that it could be Chant," said the Superintendent with a distinct trace of smugness. Castle felt his hackles rising, then told himself he had only himself to thank. He *had* shown a certain obsessiveness in his pursuit of Holland. Still, that individual wasn't out of the wood yet. He still had quite a few things to explain, even if Chant's confession turned out to be genuine. Meanwhile, the Superintendent continued to pontificate. "Nine times out of ten in these cases it's the husband . . . or the boyfriend or whatever. Didn't I say so, right at the outset?"

"You did indeed, sir, and for that very reason we went over Chant's original statement with a toothcomb," Castle replied. "Looking back, I'm amazed at how he kept it up. He had it all worked out and he never put a foot wrong – he must have a brain like a computer."

"So what's his story now?"

"He says the part about going home to fetch the file he'd left behind is true, but he didn't stay for an amicable cup of coffee with his wife. Something about her manner made him suspicious. He claims he had his doubts all along about the wedding she was supposed to be going to, thought it might be cover for a dirty weekend with Bayliss."

"He knew she was having an affair with Bayliss?"

"So he says. That part of the interview was pretty harrowing It seems she was something of a nympho and he . . . well, to pu it delicately, he admits sex has never been his strong point."

The Superintendent examined his fingernails and said, "That's enough to damage any man's self-esteem."

"Yes, sir. Well, the next part of his story will have to be checked on the ground, but he claims that when he left the house, ostensibly to go straight back to his office, what he actually did was back his car through a gate into a field adjoining his garden, out of sight of the house. The field belongs to a local farmer and one corner of it separates Chant's property from his neighbour's. No one reported seeing him there, but as both gardens are well screened by trees it sounds feasible."

The Superintendent grunted. "So what did he do – go back to the house?"

"Not straightaway . . . or so he says. He claims he just sat there, brooding, waiting for something to happen. He heard a vehicle go past – he was out of sight of the lane so he never actually saw it – and thought it went only a short distance, so he decided to investigate. He got out of the car and walked along the boundary hedge at the back of his house. Apparently there's a gap where some cattle once broke through."

"Something else to be verified. Never take a voluntary confession at its face value, Castle," interrupted the Superintendent, who was known to enjoy playing the rôle of devil's advocate.

"Quite so, sir."

"Well, go on."

"He slips through the hedge and makes his way up the garden towards the house, keeping under cover as far as possible." Without realising it, Castle continued his narrative in the present tense, seeing the events unfolding in his mind's eye like action on a screen. "Then he hears a vehicle start up and drive away in a hurry, but he can't see it from where he is so he forgets about not wanting to be seen and goes tearing round to the front of the house. There's no sign of the car, but the next moment his wife comes staggering out of the front door with a bruise on her face, screaming obscenities. When she sees her husband she goes into hysterics and retreats indoors with him after her. I think you can probably guess the rest, sir – it's all on the tape if you want to hear it for yourself."

The Superintendent declined the offer with a movement of one of his well-kept hands. "I'll hear it later. It seems pretty obvious. She thought she was going to elope with Bayliss, taking all the jewels and her husband's secret nest-egg, and Bayliss had planned to grab the lot and ditch her. I suppose the so-called break-in was a cover-up – they must have planned that together."

"So Chant alleges, but unfortunately there's no way we can confirm it."

"Why not?"

"Because Bayliss is dead as well. Cooked himself in his own sauna, apparently." Briefly, Castle outlined the circumstances. "Of course, if we'd known beforehand about the affair, Bayliss would have been the obvious suspect. That's what Chant was hoping for. He says the realisation that Terry Holland was under suspicion has been preying on his mind."

"And to let on that he knew his wife had been having it off with Bayliss would have made *him* an obvious suspect?" The Superintendent rubbed his hands together, then sat back in his chair and locked them behind his large, balding head. "Well, I know there was no evidence against him, but if you'd taken my warnings on board a little earlier, maybe you'd have found some . . . and saved quite a lot of police time."

"Point taken, sir."

With evident relish, the Superintendent resumed his own summary of events. "So when Chant got his hands on his wife, he grabbed her by the throat to shake the story out of her and ended up throttling her . . . without intending to, of course . . . horrified when he realised what he'd done and so on?"

"That's about the size of it, sir. One can feel a certain

sympathy for the man from that point of view, but the way he set about tidying things up, making coffee and putting his empty cup beside his wife's in the kitchen, re-locking the safes to make it appear they'd never been touched, denying that any money had been stolen to cover up the fact that he'd been withholding all that cash from the Revenue – all that confirms what I felt all along. I admit I found nothing to suggest he'd killed his wife, but I was convinced he was putting his business and financial interests above everything else from the word go."

"Hmm." The Superintendent began a re-examination of his fingernails. "Well, his confession in order to absolve Holland shows he's not a complete bastard," he commented. "Of course, none of this explains how some of his money got into Holland's possession."

"Radcliffe and Hill are questioning Holland now on that very point," said Castle. "In my mind, there's a strong possibility that he and Bayliss were in the robbery together."

"How d'you figure that out?"

"Another interesting detail that we've stumbled across is that Bayliss may in fact be one of his old partners in crime called Charlie Foss. At his trial, Holland claimed Foss was the third man in the bank robbery he and another man were sent down for." Without mentioning Sukey's part in the discovery, Castle explained how Barbie Bayliss had slipped up and referred to her husband as 'Charlie'.

"You reckon Holland and Bayliss – or Foss – were in the robbery together?" The Superintendent expressed his doubts with pursed lips and a ponderous shake of the head. "Who'd be daft enough to team up with a man who's already ratted on him?"

"Maybe Holland saw it as a way of recouping earlier losses. He's not over-bright, but he's smart enough to know Foss wouldn't want his image of a squeaky-clean businessman tarnished by any suggestion of a murky past which might attract media attention. Mrs Holland's convinced he's been in touch with Foss recently. She hates the man's guts."

"If that's the case, Bayliss – Foss, that is – was running true to form when he ditched the Chant woman and made off with her old man's money. He took a gamble, though . . . supposing Chant had called us in?"

"Not so much of a gamble really sir, if—" Just in time, Castle checked himself from saying 'if you think about it'. It was not the kind of remark that would have endeared him to the Superintendent. "Both Chant and his wife would have suffered public humiliation, but worse than that, he would have had to explain where all that money came from in the first place."

"Yes, I suppose you have a point there," the Superintendent allowed graciously.

"What I propose to do now is find out how Radcliffe and Hill are getting on with interviewing Holland. Then I'll go back to Marsdean with one of the SOCOs to see what evidence we can find to support Chant's story."

"Do that . . . and keep me posted."

"Of course, sir."

"Since you haven't referred to the search of Holland's house, I assume nothing was found."

"Er . . . no, sir," Castle admitted. "It's possible the money he paid into his building society represented his share of the job."

"We can't hold him on mere possibilities, Castle. If you've no hard evidence against him and he's made no significant admissions, you'll have to let him go for now."

"Let him go! But, sir—"

"Can't risk having him sue us for wrongful detention, can we? You can always bring him in again if the circumstances justify it." The Superintendent indicated that the discussion was at an end by reaching for a file and picking up his telephone. Inwardly seething, Castle withdrew.

He reached the interview room where Holland was being questioned just as Radcliffe and Hill were emerging. Behind them the prisoner, sullen-faced, was being escorted to his cell. Back in his own office, Castle asked, "How did it go?"

"Like a charm at first," Radcliffe told him. "Once he realised we knew that Hugo Bayliss was really his old mate Charlie Foss, he admitted going to see him. Just to renew an old acquaintance, of course. He said Foss's wife was wearing the necklace and that he must have left his prints on it when he admired it on her."

"So why didn't he say that before?"

"He muttered something about not wanting his wife to know. I suppose it was the best he could think up on the spur of the moment."

"And then what?"

"And then . . . nothing. He still refuses to say where the money came from."

"Hoping to go back for more," Castle surmised. "It's what he sees as his cut from the robbery, of course, so he's obviously trying to keep his options open."

"You mean the bank robbery, Guv?"

"Not necessarily. I'll explain in a minute," Castle added, seeing their puzzled expressions. "I take he now knows Foss is dead?"

"Of course. It appeared to shake him when we sprang that on him, but whether it was genuine shock or distress at seeing a nice little extortion racket going down the tube is anyone's guess. When we let on we knew the real nature of his earlier relationship with Foss he clammed up altogether. Won't say another word before he's talked to his brief again."

"I see. Well, we have to let him go for now – orders from the Super. Things have moved on in the last hour or so," Castle went on as the two officers stared at him in dismay. He unlocked his filing cabinet, took out the tape of his interview with Arthur Chant and put it on the desk. "This'll keep you

entertained while you're noshing your sandwiches. I'm off to
Marsdean now – see you later."

Sukey was on the point of leaving for work when her telephone
rang. To her surprise, Mrs Bayliss was on the line.
"Oh, Mrs Reynolds," she began. "I just want to thank you
again for bringing the pictures – it was so kind of you."
"Not at all. My pleasure."
"I wonder . . . I really would like more copies . . . to send
to friends, you know . . ."
"No problem. They're all numbered on the back. Just tell
me which ones you want and I'll get them done for you."
"I don't want to put you to all that trouble. If I could have
the negatives, I could see to it myself."
"That's not the way I work," Sukey said. One or two of the
shots had been so successful that she was thinking of entering
them in a competition and was not keen on the idea of letting
any of the negatives out of her possession. She reached for a
pencil and notepad. "Just give me the numbers – unless you'd
like the whole set."
There appeared to be some kind of discussion going on
at the other end of the line. Sukey heard the words, "Tell
'er you'll pay!" in what was unmistakably Auntie Gwen's
tobacco-roughened voice, followed by "Yes, all right," in a
whispered aside. Then Mrs Bayliss cleared her throat and said,
with a trace of self-consciousness mingled with anxiety, "Of
course, we're not asking you to *give* us the negatives, we're
prepared to pay for them. Would fifty pounds be enough?"
It was tempting. Had she been dealing with Mrs Bayliss
alone Sukey might have agreed, but the knowledge that she
was being pressured by that repulsive old woman made her
dig her toes in. "It's not a question of money," she said. "I've
been paid for the job and the negatives are my property."
"Yes, I understand that but . . . a hundred pounds then."
"I'm sorry."

There was the sound of an altercation in the background. Then Auntie Gwen came on the line. "Now look 'ere, those pictures are of my niece's 'ouse and you ain't got no right to keep them!" she said aggressively. "We don't 'ave to pay but we're offering good money, so don't be so bloody awkward!"

Who could resist such a charmingly worded request? Sukey thought to herself. Aloud, she said, "I haven't time to discuss this any further. I'm off to work now and I'm going to be late as it is. The negatives are not for sale." She put down the receiver, grabbed her jacket and camera bag and made for the front door, almost tripping over Fergus's cricket gear which he had left ready to pick up for that afternoon's practice.

Chapter Twenty-Four

Terry Holland, shoulders hunched and eyes fixed blankly on the floor of his cell, sat on the edge of the bed and cursed his luck. Everything, it seemed, was conspiring against him. It had started with those bleeding rubber bands. If they hadn't been such a pansy colour, no one would have noticed them. Then there was the necklace. How was he to know it was hot? You couldn't trust anyone nowadays. Even Rita had let him down by blurting out Charlie Foss's name in front of the filth. And what had he done? Nothing they knew about. Nothing they'd been able to charge him with. He'd gone to the house to stake a claim to what was rightfully his and it hadn't taken much persuasion to make Charlie see his point of view. You could hardly call that an assault – it was only a ducking after all. It wasn't as though he'd injured the rat, although no one deserved it better. In any case, nothing had been said about it and Charlie had left it a bit late to lodge a complaint, hadn't he?

That was another thing that got up Terry's nose. Charlie had really done the dirty on him by dying with the debt only partly settled. There must be more where the first lot came from. His brief had suggested it was money Charlie had nicked with the bands already on them. Maybe that was it, maybe he'd deliberately left them on the five grand in the hope that they could be traced and he'd be suspected. It was just the sort of snidey trick that would appeal to someone with Charlie's warped sense of humour.

Another odd thing was that although the coppers obviously believed the money had been taken from Chant's safe, they still hadn't charged him with nicking it. That, his brief told him, meant that Chant had never reported it stolen. He'd gone into some long-winded explanation about why anyone would let five grand go just like that, but it hadn't meant much to Terry. All he knew was that they could keep him banged up here for the rest of the day, maybe longer. And who could say what other nasty little surprises Charlie had cooked up for him? Not that the bastard would be there to see the results, not now he'd gone and cooked *himself* in his own sauna. Terry's depression lifted at that particular bit of rough justice, but only for a moment. Then his mind switched back to his own predicament. He thought of Billy and wondered what Rita had told him. He thought of Rita and wondered why she hadn't come to see him. He cursed his luck again.

All in all, it looked like being another lousy day. It therefore came as a pleasant surprise when they told him he could go. They wouldn't tell him anything of course, just gave him back his possessions and told him to piss off before they changed their minds.

"What about a ride home, then?" he grumbled.

The custody sergeant grinned and said, "The walk'll do you good after sitting on your backside all morning."

When Sukey reached the morgue she found Inspector Mahony talking to Doctor Yates, the pathologist, in the glassed-off partition that served him as an office. She hoped the conversation wouldn't go on for too long; she was not looking forward to the task ahead and wanted to be done with it and get out of the place as quickly as possible. She hated the cold bleakness, the bright lights, the echoing walls and above all the combination of disinfectant and blood overlaid with an indefinable something that 'all the perfumes of Arabia' could never quite disguise or eradicate – the all-pervading smell of death.

Mahony spotted her through the glass and with a word to the pathologist beckoned her inside. "Inspector Castle passed on your message about that elastic band and put me in the picture," he told her. "I've sent a team round to The Laurels with a warrant to give the place a going over and I'm about to join them to see how they're getting on. Well spotted, Mrs Reynolds."

"Thank you, Mr Mahony." It occurred to Sukey that if anything significant were to break as a result of her one and only excursion into moonlighting, it might perhaps count in her favour.

"You'll do what you can to hurry along the result of the blood test?" Mahony added, turning back to Doctor Yates.

"I know the lab is pretty choked with work at the moment, but I'll do my best," the pathologist promised.

"Fine. Let me know the minute you hear anything." Mahony was halfway to the main door when he swung round and came back. "I believe you told me you took some pictures of the Bayliss house and garden?" he said.

"That's right."

"Would there be any shots of the sauna?"

"Yes, at least a couple."

"I'd like to see them. Can you let me have them as soon as possible?"

"I only have the negatives, but I can easily get more prints done."

"Please do that and get them over to me as soon as you can."

"Of course, Mr Mahony. No problem."

"You're here to take Bayliss's fingerprints, I believe," said Doctor Yates when the inspector had finally left.

"That's right. Do I understand there's still some doubt about his death?"

"Ay, frankly, I'm a wee bit puzzled," the doctor replied. He had a deep, rumbling voice and despite a good quarter

228

of a century in the south of England he still retained traces of his Scottish burr." There's no doubt he was subjected to a much higher than normal temperature while he was in the sauna, but I'm told it has been examined and shows no sign of malfunction. I've sent blood samples away for testing . . . maybe they'll tell us something."

"I suppose that's why Inspector Mahony wants to see my pictures."

"I canna see what the *outside* will tell him, but you never know. Here, get into these before you start work."

Sukey put on the protective clothing that he handed her and waited while a trolley on which lay a corpse covered by a sheet was wheeled out of its cabinet. Yates checked the label attached to one of the big toes and said, "Ay, that's your laddie. Darren will look after you." He jerked his head at the gowned and masked attendant before wandering over to a work surface covered in pale grey laminate to examine something unpleasant-looking that lay in the dish of a weighing machine.

Sukey swallowed and turned away. She took her fingerprint kit from her case and waited while Darren extracted Hugo Bayliss's forearms from under the sheet and laid them across his chest like a grotesque caricature of a figure on a tombstone. Taking steady, regular breaths in an attempt to settle the queasiness in her stomach, she set about her task, fighting the revulsion she invariably experienced at contact, even through surgical gloves, with cold lifeless flesh. She finished with one hand, cleaned the ink off the dead man's fingers and reached for the other, then paused as something caught her eye.

"Excuse me Doctor Yates, could I have a word with you?" she called.

"Sure." He came over immediately. She was too excited by what she had noticed to be affected by the sight of the blood on his gloves and apron. "What is it?" he asked, peering at the hand she held up for his inspection.

"That scratch." She pointed to an inch-long mark on the back of the right wrist. "How old would you say it is?"

Yates made rumbling noises in his throat while he considered the question. "It's quite recent," he said after a moment or two. "Sustained just a few days before death, I'd say. Funnily enough, he's got a similar one on his backside which probably occurred about the same time. We thought it might have happened when he was pruning his roses. It's easily done – roses can be vicious things."

"Why would he be pruning his roses in the middle of June, I wonder?" said Sukey thoughtfully.

The pathologist shrugged. "There you have me. Why are you so interested?"

Sukey laid the hand back on Bayliss's chest and took out a fresh sheet of inked paper. "Someone got into the Chants' house and robbed it the day Mrs Chant was murdered," she explained. "The intruder entered through a ground-floor window with roses under it . . . strong roses with big sharp thorns growing up to the height of the sill. A thread from the overalls we believe he was wearing was found on one of the thorns. And we think he," she indicated the form beneath the sheet, "was the dead woman's lover and that she was planning to elope with him."

What was visible of Doctor Yates's features above the mask registered puzzlement. "Are you suggesting it was this laddie who did the breaking and entering?"

"It looks very like it."

"But if he was her lover, why did he have to climb in through a window? Wasn't there a garden door he could have used, if they didn't want him to be seen calling at the front?"

"I can't answer that one, I'm afraid," said Sukey, who had been asking herself the same questions. "All I know for sure is that prints we believe to be his were found in the bathroom – which is why I'm here, of course – and that the intruder didn't have to *literally* break in because the window had been left

230

unfastened. I thought at the time there was something fishy about that. It looks to me as if the supposed burglary was all part of the elopement plan."

"You should be in the CID, lassie," commented Doctor Yates. "I take it you want pictures of those scratches as well as the prints?"

"Please."

"Right. Darren!" The attendant came hurrying over. "Roll him over, will you. This lady wants a picture of his bum."

When Sukey had finished her work on the corpse of Hugo Bayliss she checked with the control room and was informed that Inspector Castle wanted her to meet him at the Chants' house in Marsdean. She sent a message back that she was on her way, but was making a short detour to pick up the negatives of the Bayliss property that Inspector Mahony had requested. She then headed for home.

There were fewer than a dozen houses in the little cul-de-sac where she lived and every one had a deserted appearance. Several of her neighbours were, she knew, on holiday; the absence of cars on the other drives indicated that people were either at work or otherwise away from home. It all looked very pleasant and peaceful in the warm afternoon sunshine. Birds fluttered to and fro in search of food for their ravenous broods, closely watched by a tabby cat sitting on an ornamental wall. June, Sukey thought, was the month when everything appeared at its best, with the flowering trees still retaining some of their springtime freshness and the gardens awash with multicoloured roses in their first flush of blooms.

She parked the van, went up the path and put her key in the front door. Fergus's cricket kit was still lying in the hall; evidently he had not yet called in to pick it up. Closing the door behind her, she dropped her handbag on the bottom stair and headed for the kitchen. Then she stopped short, her body tense and her pulse rate quickening as she noticed that both the kitchen and sitting room doors were open. She was absolutely certain that she had closed them before leaving the house. Her father had hammered into her from childhood that internal doors should always be kept closed at night and when the house was empty, to contain the fire that he seemed convinced would one day break out but had never actually done so. He had kept up the practice until the day he died and it was second nature to Sukey to do the same. Fergus had been less easy to indoctrinate. Had he been in to collect his kit, he would almost certainly have gone to the kitchen to raid the biscuit tin and ten to one would have left the door open.

With her heart leaping in her chest like a frog in a rain barrel, Sukey stood for several seconds, holding her breath and straining her ears. Taking the precaution of reopening the front door to be sure of an escape route if anyone came charging at her while making a getaway, she called, "Is anyone there?" No one answered and she called a second time. Then, assuming that whoever it was had grabbed what he wanted and left, she plucked up courage to push the sitting room door fully open.

It was a sight she had seen many times before in other people's homes – drawers pulled out, cupboards standing open, their contents scattered over the floor. Surprisingly, the television, video and hi-fi system were still there, her stock of CDs appeared undisturbed and the silver frames containing portraits of her parents and Fergus were in their normal places on the mantelpiece. She stood in the centre of the room for several seconds, considering. This was no ordinary, opportunist break-in. Whoever it was had been looking for something particular.

She heard a stealthy sound behind her. Whirling round, she confronted a masked figure with its right arm upraised, the hand grasping the largest of her own kitchen knives. The arm began its descent, the knife travelling in a swift, deadly arc towards her throat. Instinctively, she flung herself sideways and ducked, caught a glimpse of her assailant's legs, registered that he was wearing cut-off jeans that revealed the livid remains of a deep graze along the right shin-bone, and knew that this was the man who had attacked her in the house of Hugo Bayliss. Who he was, what he could be doing in her home or why she should be his intended victim she had no idea – might never know. The only thought in her mind in that moment of terror was that she was once more fighting for her life – and that this time the odds were against her.

She made a snatch at his right wrist with the object of forcing the knife from his hand and throwing him down, but he was ready for the move. His left hand shot out and locked round her throat, holding her at arm's length and forcing her backwards, pinning her against the far wall. She kicked out at his crotch, but he half-turned and took the impact on his thigh. In the forlorn hope that someone was within earshot she tried to scream, but the grip on her throat was tightening by the second and all she could utter was a faint, choking gasp. She clawed first at his fingers and then at his arm in an effort to relieve the pressure, but it continued, relentlessly, to increase. There was a drumming in her ears, her assailant's right hand was once more uplifted and the knife directed at her chest. She flung up an arm and managed to deflect the blow, but in an instant the weapon was raised for the third time. She parried again and felt a sharp pain in her shoulder. Her knees were buckling, the breath was being squeezed out of her body, she had no strength left to resist. She shut her eyes as the knife was poised for the kill.

It never reached its target. Instead there was a sharp sound like wood striking wood and the murderous grip round her throat relaxed. She heard a heavy thud as something crashed to the floor at her feet, and strange rasping noises that she was dimly aware came from her own mouth as she dragged life-giving air into her tortured lungs. From somewhere out in space a frantic voice was calling, "Mum! Mum! Are you all right?" She opened her eyes. Her bewildered gaze focused first on her assailant, sprawled face downward and motionless on the hearthrug, and then on Fergus, who was standing over him, white-faced, eyes dilated with fear, the handle of his cricket bat grasped between violently trembling hands.

For several seconds mother and son stared at one another above the recumbent form. Fergus spoke first. "I came by to collect my gear," he said shakily, as if some excuse for his presence was required.

Despite her ordeal, Sukey managed a smile. "You never put it to better use, my son." Her own hands were unsteady as she pulled out her radio and gave her call sign. "Urgently request assistance and an ambulance at number 6 Bramble Close," she said. "And please tell Inspector Castle I've been delayed."

Chapter Twenty-Five

"Oh Mum, d'you think he's dead?" asked Fergus in a thin, unsteady voice.

"Let's hope not." The same fearful thought was in Sukey's mind as she bent over the man who had been so determined to kill her – and who had so nearly succeeded.

"Do you know who he is?"

"No idea . . . except that this is the second time he's had a go at me."

"You . . . what?" His eyes were wide and fearful. "When? You never said . . ."

"Didn't want to scare you. I never dreamed he'd come and find me here."

"But why?"

"Wish I knew." She squatted down and grasped the unconscious man's wrist, searching for a pulse and finding it. It was on the slow side, but steady enough. "He's alive all right . . . probably only stunned."

"When they feel for a pulse on the telly, they go for the one under the jaw," Fergus remarked with a shaky attempt at humour.

"I'm sure you're right," said his mother drily, "I'd do the same, except that I can't be sure this one isn't shamming and getting ready to grab me if I give him half a chance." She straightened up and stepped back out of reach of the muscular arms. "As it happens, he's landed in the recovery position, so we'll wait for the paramedics to take care of him."

"Why don't we take his mask off, see if we recognise him?" As he spoke, Fergus took a step forward with one hand outstretched.

"Get away from him! What did I just say?" Sukey shouted.

"Sorry." He shot her an apologetic smile which changed to a look of consternation. "Mum, he's cut you . . . you're bleeding!"

Bemusedly, Sukey glanced down at the dark stain on her sleeve, aware for the first time of the warm stickiness trickling from the gash on her shoulder.

"So I am," she said, trying not to show the alarm she felt at the sight.

"I'll get a towel." Fergus dropped the cricket bat on the rug and started for the door.

"Come back here and pick that up, dummy! He might leap up and go for it, and while you're at it, get that thing out of his reach. No! Don't touch it, kick it!" Sukey's voice rose in exasperation as Fergus stooped to pick up the knife that had landed within a foot of the man's head.

Dumbly, the lad obeyed, sending the knife skimming across the carpet and picking up the bat with hands that shook more violently than ever. He was plainly in shock; his whole body was trembling and he seemed unable to take his eyes from the blood running from his mother's wound. "You'll bleed to death!" he said in an anguished, terrified voice. "Let me get something to bind it up with . . . please!"

"No! Stay there . . . I'll be all right . . . wait till someone comes." She put pressure on the arm with her other hand in an attempt to staunch the flow. She, too, was beginning to feel the effects of the life-and-death struggle, but until help arrived she had to keep a clear head and be strong for both of them. Acting in the heat of the moment, Fergus had unhesitatingly struck a man down to save his mother from a murderous attack. Now the reaction was setting in and he

236

might keel over at any moment. "Just keep an eye on him in case he tries any tricks," she ordered. "The police will be here any minute." *Please God*, she added silently. With one arm out of action and Fergus all but traumatised, she had no idea how they would cope with a second attack. Many times she had heard her police colleagues speak of apparently lifeless villains leaping to their feet and seizing anyone who happened to be within reach to use as a hostage or a human shield – or worse.

Her heart gave a lurch as the man on the floor gave a feeble groan and began to stir. She planted a foot between his shoulder blades and, injecting all the aggression and confidence that she could muster into her voice, said, "Lie still, Buster. You're nicked." At that moment, to her intense relief, came the sound of the first siren.

She had lost more blood than she realised. The minute the two police officers came rushing into the room, the floor heaved under her feet and the pictures on the walls began spinning in mad circles before vanishing in a grey mist. When she came round she was lying on the couch with Fergus leaning over her, bathing her forehead with a cold sponge while a girl with 'Paramedic' embroidered on her shirt bound up her left shoulder. "Hi, my name's Kelly," said the girl. "How are you feeling?"

"OK . . . I think." She tried to sit up and Kelly put a hand on her uninjured shoulder and pushed her back against the cushions.

"Stay there while I finish this dressing," she commanded. She had curly fair hair and a round, rosy face dusted with freckles, and she manipulated the bandages with deft, gentle hands. "There, that'll do for now," she said when she had finished. "Fergus, go and make your mother a cup of tea – good and strong, with plenty of sugar."

"You'd better have one too," Sukey told him, noticing with relief that his colour was back to normal.

237

"We'll get you down to casualty presently," Kelly informed her, "but there's a policewoman here would like a word with you first, if you feel up to it."

"Of course I feel up to it – I'm fine – but I can't waste time in casualty, I've got a job to do."

"It's only first aid I've given you. You ought to let a doctor see that gash – it's going to need stitching."

"It'll have to wait. Where's the police officer?"

"Here I am," said a cheerful voice that Sukey instantly recognised. "WPC Marshall, Gloucester Constabulary."

"Trudy!" Ignoring discouraging noises from Kelly, Sukey struggled into a sitting position to greet her colleague.

"Quite a change for you to be on the scene before us, isn't it?" said Trudy, sitting down beside her. "Do you feel like telling me what happened?"

"I came home to find the place in a mess and I realised someone had been in. Next thing I knew, there was this man in a mask going for me with a knife. That one." She pointed to where it lay, half hidden under the chair where Fergus had kicked it.

"Has anyone else touched it?" Sukey shook her head, relaxed now and able to smile at the memory of how she had yelled at Fergus. Trudy nodded approval. "Should have known better than to ask, shouldn't I? Then what?"

By the time Fergus appeared with the tea Sukey had ended her account and he was only too happy, now that he knew he was not a murderer and that his mother was not going to bleed to death, to add his version.

"And you say there's nothing missing?" said Trudy when she had finished scribbling in her notebook.

"None of the things you'd expect from a normal burglary . . . it's obvious he was looking for something else," Sukey said. "I can't think what," she added, frowning.

"And you've no idea who he is?"

"Only that he's the same man who attacked me once before."

Trudy's eyebrows shot up and she reopened her notebook. "Don't bother to write this down. DI Mahony in Cheltenham has my statement. I never saw the man's face – the first time he was wearing a crash helmet and today it was a mask. I didn't think to pull it off; once I'd made sure he was still alive I kept well out of his reach."

"Very wise," said Trudy. "Now, are you sure you won't follow Kelly's advice and go to casualty? I can take you . . . I have to give her a lift back anyway. Her ambulance has left with your attacker and my partner has gone with him."

"No thanks, I'll be fine. There's something I have to get for DI Mahony, that's what I came back for." Cautiously, Sukey got to her feet and was relieved to find that the room was no longer going round. With Fergus hovering anxiously at her elbow she made her way to the kitchen. She stopped in her tracks at the sight of the confusion. Every drawer had been pulled out and the contents spilled on the floor. "Oh, hell!" she exclaimed.

"Don't worry, Mum. I'll help you clear it up," said Fergus.

"It's not the mess I'm worried about," she said grimly. It took only a moment to confirm what was missing. She hurried back to the sitting room. "Trudy, will you please call your partner and tell him the prisoner is thought to be in possession of some photographic negatives urgently wanted at HQ," she said. "Say he's to get them off him right away, before he has a chance to destroy them."

"Roger." The policewoman whipped out her radio and gave her call sign. "Anything else?" she asked when she had delivered the message.

"Tell him I'm on my way to collect them." Sukey turned and grinned at Kelly. "What do you know – I'm going to casualty after all!"

When the front doorbell at The Laurels sounded, Auntie Gwen exclaimed, "My, Bren, that was quick work!"

Brenda Foss, happy to be rid once and for all of the name that Charlie had foisted on her, looked up from her copy of *Hello!* magazine and said, "Don't be daft, he can't be here yet. I told him not to go too soon."

"Wonder 'oo it can be, then? You expectin' anyone else?"

"No." Brenda yawned and settled herself more comfortably on the couch. "Why don't you go and see?"

Auntie Gwen heaved herself up from her chair and lumbered out of the room. She was back in no time, looking as if she had seen a ghost. "It's the Old Bill and they've got a bleedin' dawg wiv 'em!" she wheezed.

"What!" Brenda threw the magazine aside and sat bolt upright. Behind her aunt were what appeared to her alarmed gaze to be the entire Gloucestershire Constabulary, but turned out to be just four uniformed policemen, one leading a black and white spaniel. "What the hell d'you mean, busting in like this?" she demanded.

"Sergeant Fleming and Constables Cross, Peace and Starkey," said one of the officers, who appeared to be in charge. "We have a warrant to search the house."

"What for, for goodness' sake?" Brenda's heart was beating a drumroll in her chest and her stomach began coiling itself into knots. "If it's drugs you're after, you won't find none here."

As if he had not heard her, the sergeant said, "Right lads, you know what to do." The men melted away and he turned back to the two women. "Just relax, ladies. Why don't you sit down?" He made gestures towards the couch. "We won't be here any longer than necessary." Hesitantly, Brenda obeyed. "You as well, madam," he said to Auntie Gwen.

The old woman scowled. "I don't need the likes of you to tell me to sit down in me niece's 'ouse," she said resentfully. She sat down nevertheless, perching on the edge of her chair as if she suspected the cushion of concealing an explosive charge. She pulled out a crumpled pack of cigarettes, lit one and was immediately overcome by a prolonged fit of coughing which all but drowned the noise of tramping feet and banging doors that came from upstairs. "Bleedin' cheek!" she grumbled as soon as her power of speech returned.

After what seemed an age, during which it sounded to Brenda as if every piece of furniture in the house was being taken apart, one of the officers entered the room carrying a holdall. At the sight of it, her heart sank. She knew she should have found a safer hiding place for that stash as soon as she came across it, might have guessed that the money was hot. What with all the hoo-ha over Charlie's death, she'd put it off. Now it was too late.

"What have we got here, Cross?" Sergeant Fleming began poking among the wads of money. "Looks like you and your husband don't trust banks," he observed to Brenda.

"My *late* husband," she said, adopting a mournful expression and hoping against hope that reminding him of her recent widowhood might somehow count in her favour, "looked after all our financial and business affairs. I had nothing to do with any of it."

"So you've no idea where this lot came from?" Brenda shook her head. "How about this, then?" Like a child fishing for a present in a bran tub at a village fête, he rummaged at the bottom of the holdall and came up with a sparkling diamond bracelet. "Ever seen this before? No, of course not! He was saving it to put in your Christmas stocking. *Very* nice!"

Brenda's eyes popped. She insisted, this time with complete honesty, that she had absolutely no knowledge of the jewellery. She wondered what other treasures Charlie had hidden under the money and privately cursed herself even more furiously at not having investigated further. Just to have that incredible stash to dip into had been enough without expecting the contents of Aladdin's cave as well.

Auntie Gwen's chin had almost hit her ample chest. "Jesus Christ, where'd the bugger nick that from?" she exclaimed, forgetting discretion in her astonishment.

"Good question," said the sergeant genially, while Brenda shot her aunt a withering glance. That was one thing Charlie had been right about, she thought viciously, the old bag *has* got a big mouth. For the moment, she felt her devotion to her relative wearing a little thin.

Fleming turned to the officer who had given him the holdall. "Has the dog come up with anything, Cross?" he asked.

"Nothing so far, Sarge. He's just going to give the kitchen a going over."

"Right, well, let's leave the others to get on with it, shall we? You can come back to the station with me and this lady." He turned to Brenda. "I'm arresting you for being in possession of stolen property," he informed her. "You do not have to say anything, but . . ." The remainder of the caution was uttered in the teeth of a stream of abuse from Auntie Gwen and an outburst of hysterical weeping from Brenda Foss.

Ignoring Kelly's protests, Sukey leapt out of the patrol car in which Trudy had driven the two of them to the hospital, rushed through the swing doors leading to the casualty department and collided with a young nurse carrying an armful of manila folders.

"I'm so sorry!" Sukey fielded a couple of the folders as they slid from the top of the heap. "Can you help me, please?" Awkwardly on account of her injured shoulder, she fished her ID card from her pocket. "A patient – a young man with a head injury – was brought in a short time ago under police escort. Where will I find him?"

She stood fuming with impatience while the startled nurse pulled herself together, adjusted her spectacles, peered at the card and carefully compared the photograph with the original before saying, "Round the corner, last cubicle on the left."

A uniformed constable whom Sukey did not recognise was standing at the far end of the corridor. When she introduced herself he said, "I got your message, but I haven't been able to do anything about it. The doctor won't allow any questions until she's given the patient a thorough check-up." He looked curiously at her, taking in the bandage and her generally dishevelled appearance. "What's it all about?"

"The negatives are of some outdoor shots I took at a house in Cheltenham. DI Mahoney at Headquarters wants to see them in connection with a possible suspicious death inquiry. That's really all I know, except that our friend in there was very anxious to get hold of them before anyone else did. By the way, did you get his name?"

The officer consulted his notebook. "Palmer," he said. "Richard Palmer. Does it mean anything to you?"

"No." She put a hand to her forehead, trying to think. She was beginning to feel dizzy again; nothing made sense.

The officer caught her by her uninjured arm. "You need treatment yourself," he said anxiously.

Impatiently, she shook him off. "I'm OK. It's just reaction I guess. Ah, here's the doctor." A middle-aged woman in a white coat with a stethoscope round her neck emerged from the cubicle and looked questioningly from one to the other.

Sukey explained her mission. The doctor nodded, a look of enlightenment dawning on her face. She disappeared behind the curtains; there was the sound of a scuffle and the constable plunged in after her with Sukey at his heels. After a brief tussle, a crumpled, semi-transparent envelope was wrenched from the patient's unwilling hand.

"There was nothing in his pockets, but the nurse spotted him putting something in the waste bin when he was brought in," the doctor explained as she handed it to Sukey. "When I went to retrieve it, he jumped on me."

Sukey stood staring in amazement while the officer hand-cuffed and cautioned his sullen-faced prisoner. "You *do* know him, don't you?" he said.

Sukey nodded. "He's an instructor at the health club where I do fitness training," she said. "He's known there as Rick."

243

Chapter Twenty-Six

After handing the negatives to a police motorcyclist despatched by Inspector Mahony from Headquarters, Sukey finally submitted to having her wound stitched before being driven home by Trudy. There, she was handed over to Fergus along with a supply of painkillers, which made her too woozy to argue when he ordered her to go and lie down while he finished clearing up the muddle that Rick had left behind. At seven o'clock he roused her to announce that supper was ready and the two of them sat down in an unnaturally tidy kitchen to a meal of shepherd's pie from the freezer and a stir-fry of fresh vegetables that he had prepared himself.

"This is brilliant," she told him as he served the food. "You even remembered to warm the plates."

Fergus gave a self-conscious grin. "I got told off the other evening for giving Anita hot chicken pie on a cold plate."

"I see. You don't take any notice when I tell you something, but when the girlfriend—"

"OK, point taken. Eat that while it's hot."

Sukey picked up her fork. "Now that *is* your mother talking." Presently, she glanced at the clock and said, "I wonder how things are going at the station. I'd give anything to be a fly on the wall while Rick's being interviewed."

"You might learn something later on." Fergus helped himself to more vegetables before adding, "Jim phoned while you were asleep."

Sukey paused with a forkful of food halfway to her mouth. "Why didn't you wake me?" she demanded.

"Because he told me not to. He wanted to know how you were . . . he sounded really upset about you being hurt. He sends his love and says he'll try and get round later, if he can make it at a reasonable hour. If not, he'll phone again. Would you like some more pie?"

"No thanks, that was super."

"Right. Give me your plate. What would you like next?"

"How about bananas and ice cream? I'll get it."

He was on his feet like a shot. "No you won't. You'll stay right there."

"D'you boss Anita around like this?"

"Of course." He brought the bananas to the table and spooned out the ice cream. "And when you've finished that, you're going to sit on the couch with your feet up and watch the telly."

"If you say so."

She woke three hours later with Fergus gently shaking her sound shoulder. "Visitor," he announced.

"Jim!" She blinked at him through eyes bleared with sleep, then peered at the clock on the mantelpiece behind him. "Gracious! It's after eleven. You must be out on your feet. And you," she turned to Fergus, "should be in bed, young man."

"She must be OK, she's started bossing us around," Jim remarked to Fergus. The boy responded with a conspiratorial grin and Sukey felt a twinge of mingled pleasure and amusement at this display of male solidarity. "We've brought you some coffee," Jim went on, holding out a steaming mug. She took it from him with a grateful smile and he sat down beside her. "How are you feeling?"

"The shoulder's a bit sore, but otherwise I'm fine," she replied between sips. "What about you? Have you found out what I've done to Rick to make him have two attempts at killing me?"

He patted her free hand. "Don't feel offended, it was nothing personal." His tone was jocular, but his eyes were serious and she knew that the levity was a cloak for the concern he was feeling for her.

"Then what was it? And why did he want the negatives?"

"Because they prove that his father had been murdered."

"His father? I don't understand."

"Richard Palmer, the young man you know as Rick, is the illegitimate son of Charlie Foss."

Sukey felt her eyes bulging. "You're kidding!" was all she could think of on the spur of the moment.

"It's true. He's grown up hating Foss because of the way he ditched his mother the moment she told him she was pregnant and gave her no money at all to help her bring up her child. By all accounts the poor woman had a pretty thin time from then on, and not long ago she suffered a very painful death from cancer. Some extra comforts towards the end wouldn't have come amiss, but even then Charlie wouldn't cough up a brass farthing."

"What a nasty piece of work," Sukey commented.

"Too right. And from what's been coming out during the past few hours, it's clear his son isn't the only person who won't be shedding tears at the funeral. If you believe only half of what his wife and her aunt and his office manager have to say about him, Charlie Foss, alias Hugo Bayliss, was an out-and-out shit."

"Just asking to be topped," said Sukey drily. "So, what was the scheme?"

"Very simple. They waited for an opportunity, when Foss was about to take a sauna—"

"Just a minute. *They*? This isn't some *Murder on the Orient Express*-type scenario, is it?"

"No. Just Rick and Charlie Foss's wife, Brenda. The aunt knew nothing about the murder plot, but I suspect she'd quite happily have joined in if she'd been invited. Steven Lovett – who's in love with Brenda Foss, by the way – wasn't in the scheme either, but by all accounts he had no great opinion of his employer. He only carried on working for him because of Brenda. He's pretty devastated at what she's done, but as good as says that after the way Foss treated her, he got what he deserved."

"So what exactly did they do?"

"It started with something Brenda talked about to Rick from time to time . . . not, she maintains, with any serious intention of putting it into practice, more to relieve her feelings when Foss had given her a particularly hard time. She used to say things like, 'How can we fix it so Charlie keels over in the sauna, just like the consultant warned him might happen?' They often discussed possible ways and means, but never, she insists, really intending to do anything about it."

"What changed their minds?"

"It was last Monday, when Charlie beat her until she was almost unconscious, that she felt enough was enough, got on the blower to Rick and said, 'Let's do it.' He had some barbiturate tablets left over from an old prescription of his mother's and he gave them to Brenda. The idea was to find an opportunity to slip Foss a couple – not a lethal dose, just enough to make him drowsy – at a moment when he was preparing to take a sauna. Once he was in the cabin and beginning to drop off, Rick was to turn the heat up full blast and wedge the door shut from the outside. Because of his heart condition they were banking on death being fairly rapid and put down to natural causes. They struck lucky with the first, but there were some doubts about the cause."

"And all this happened on Wednesday morning?" Sukey put a hand over her mouth. "That means . . . oh, my God! He was in there cooking while I was wandering around admiring his garden."

Her stomach heaved at the realisation, but Jim was able to give at least partial reassurance. "There was no intention of leaving him there to cook," he said. "Brenda called Rick to say that her part of the job was done. His was to get round there straightaway, fix the sauna and put everything back to normal once he was sure Foss was dead, while she went off to London as arranged."

"And I turned up and started taking photos instead of doing what Brenda told me and going quietly away," said Sukey. It was beginning to make sense. "And one of the photos I gave them must have shown the sauna door with the wedge in place and the setting on high."

"Exactly. They were already a bit jumpy because a post-mortem had been ordered and they knew that if the police got hold of those negatives they'd be sunk. They had to destroy them – hence the break-in here. And for the second time, you turned up at the wrong moment."

Sukey finished her coffee in silence, digesting the information, mentally slotting the jigsaw together but finding one or two pieces missing.

"How come Foss gave Rick a job?" she asked after a few moments' thought.

"Obviously he had no idea who he was. When Rick finished his fitness and leisure course at the technical college, there just happened to be a vacancy at one of the Bodywise Clubs and Brenda suggested he went after it."

"I see." Sukey was silent again for a while, recalling the anger in the young man's eyes at the arrogant way 'Gary' had shouted at him. Then she thought of something else. "That first time Rick attacked me, when I went into the house and started poking around," she said, "there was an open holdall on the bed. What was in it?"

"The proceeds of the robbery at the Chants' house . . . tens of thousands of pounds plus a load of valuable jewellery."

"So that *was* Foss. I guessed as much when I saw the scratches."

"What scratches?"

She explained about her discovery in the mortuary, adding

"I suppose he stole Terry Holland's van to stitch him up for the robbery and the killing."

"Not the killing. That was Chant himself. He's made a full confession." Seeing Sukey's look of bewilderment, Jim explained. "Listen, Sook, it's time you got some rest. You too, Fergus, got to be in good shape for the match."

"You're right . . . I'm sure we're both pretty whacked." Sukey got up from the couch. Her shoulder was beginning to ache again; a second dose of painkillers might be a good idea. Then another point occurred to her.

"When I turned up at The Laurels on Wednesday morning, Brenda was all ready to leave, but she went back indoors for a few seconds before the taxi arrived. I suppose she was warning Rick to keep an eye open and make sure I didn't hang around. He must have slipped out into the garden himself at one point to see what I was up to and forgotten to close the patio door when he went back. I'd never have realised anything was up if he hadn't left it wide open."

"Ah, but it wasn't Rick who left it open, it was Terry Holland," said Jim.

"Holland? Whatever was he doing there?"

"Collecting the five grand he'd demanded from Foss a couple of nights previously. Brenda had only just learned how Charlie had swindled his partners in crime out of their share of the bank robbery that Holland and another bloke got sent down for. She knew her husband was a crook who'd always managed to stay ahead of the law and she's been quite happy to live on the proceeds of crime, but she has her own set of values. When she stumbled on the money Charlie had stolen from Chant's safe, she reckoned Holland was entitled to a share. She left five grand in an envelope tucked behind some cushions in the sitting room and got Rick to give him a call and tell him when and where to find it. What Rick never thought to do was tell him to close the patio door behind him, once he'd collected it. Then, of course, you noticed the door was open and started ferreting around, and we know what happened after that." A mischievous smile softened Jim's tired features.

"What's so funny? I nearly got throttled! I suppose it served me right for being nosy!" said Sukey, feigning indignation.

"I didn't say that."

"No, but you thought it." Momentarily forgetting her injury, she gave him a playful thump on the arm, then winced and put a hand to her shoulder.

"Is it hurting?" Fergus asked. "Shall I get you some more pills?"

"In a minute." She turned back to Jim. "I can understand Rick feeling murderous towards Foss after the callous way he treated his mother, but Brenda . . . is a jury going to accept that her life with him was really that intolerable?"

"Who can tell? Battered wives get more sympathy nowadays than they used to. She claims, and the aunt confirms, that Foss had bullied and abused her for years. He seems to have considered it his right, in return for providing her with every luxury. The beating he gave her when he thought she'd betrayed him to Holland was the final straw. On the other hand, the killing wasn't done on the spur of the moment and that will almost certainly count against both of them."

"And have they both admitted all this?"

"Brenda has. She started to crack once she was told that barbiturates had been found in her husband's blood. His consultant was quite positive they hadn't been prescribed for him, so the drug had to have been administered deliberately."

"And what about Rick?"

Jim gave a slightly cynical laugh. "He's trying to throw the blame for the whole scheme onto Brenda. Says she threatened that if he didn't do everything she told him, she'd tell he husband who he was and he'd lose his job on the spot. don't believe that for a moment and I doubt if any jury would either."

"He sounds a real chip off the old block," said Sukey i

surprise. "And I always thought he was such a pleasant young man."

"You'd have seen a very different side of him if you'd been there during the interview. Look, I really must go . . . we all need to catch up with some sleep.

"See you tomorrow afternoon," he called to Fergus as Sukey was showing him out. "Sleep well, you," he added in a low voice, dropping a kiss on her forehead.

She closed the front door behind him and went into the kitchen where Fergus was rinsing out the coffee mugs. There was a glow of pleasure on his face as he said, "Fancy Jim remembering about the match, with all this going on. D'you think he really will come and watch?"

"If he says he'll be there, he will," Sukey assured him with complete confidence. "He's that sort of person."

Epilogue

Brenda Gwendoline Foss and Richard Foss Palmer pleaded not guilty to the murder of Charles Frederick Foss, but were convicted and sentenced to life imprisonment.

Arthur Edwin Chant pleaded guilty to the manslaughter of Lorraine Chant and was sentenced to five years' imprisonment.

With the death of Charles Foss, the police file on the armed robbery which took place at the Willesden Branch of the Regional Bank in April 1990 has been officially closed.

The Regional Bank has instituted proceedings against the estate of Charles Frederick Foss for the recovery of the stolen money. The Inland Revenue has filed charges of submitting falsified tax returns against Arthur Edwin Chant. Both actions are being contested.